WELCOME TO THE WORLD OF

Shallow Cove™

DARK DIMENSIONS

SUBMERGED

THE MONSTER STALKER SERIES BOOK 2

JANUARY RAYNE

This edition is published by The INKfluence LLC

Graphic: Adobe Stock

Graphic Designer: Dallas Ann Designs

Chapter Art: FemKenri

***

Fang v__v bang on fangbangers

ALSO BY
JANUARY RAYNE

Shallow Cove™ Dimensions
The Eternally Series:
Book 1: Eternally Hers
Book 2: Eternally Damned
Book 3: Carnival of Creeps
Book 4: Eternally Cursed
Book 5: Eternally Rare
Book 6: Eternally Lost

Shallow Cove™ Dark Dimensions
The Monster Stalker Series:
Book 1: Honeysuckles
Book 2: Snapdragons
Book 3: Hollyhocks

AUTHOR'S NOTE

PLEASE READ THIS BEFORE ENTERING THIS WEIRD BOOK

Heads up: Everything in this book is fiction. If you find it hard to believe that any of this would happen in real life, you're right. **Nothing about this story is believable.** My imagination went wild.

Content Warnings: This book contains Domestic violence (NOT MMC), stalking, dark themes, nonconsent, S/A, somnophilia, forced pregnancy, birth control tampering, blood sharing, mutilation, period play, sleepwalking, and murder. Please refrain from reading if you are affected by these subjects. Mental health matters. You matter.

DEDICATION

To everyone who said that this series isn't realistic.

FREAKIN' DUH.

Now, let's fuck some gargoyle statues.

PROLOGUE

MICKEY

Six months ago

Stupid describes the girl living inside me.

The girl who listened to his every word, his promis-es, and his lies, hoping he'd be the man I fell in love with. Even that man was a lie. He fed me hopes and dreams to get me where he wanted me.

Now, I'm afraid to leave.

He's threatened to kill my siblings if I dared to try to escape again.

Escape. Not leave.

Because I have no free will. I have no freedom. No rights. I've been stripped bare of dignity and left a broken shell of a woman he has created.

I've lost the woman I used to be. I'm alienated.

Now, I'm just a stupid girl who daydreamed of finding love. The only piece of me left is the one that somehow manages to hope for more. I know that love doesn't exist. It's a construct, it's built and manipulated, a tactic used to make naïve women like me fall for men with bad intentions.

So I'm not sure what *more* means for me. Maybe more, in my new world, means independence.

God, I swear, when I met him, he was amazing. I never thought he was capable of evil. Every time he smiled, it was like I experienced what happiness was truly like. Little did I know the evil he was capable of... he played me so well. I fell for everything. The jokes, the laughs, the gentleman-like gestures, the 'I love you's,' and it was all a mask to cover the animal who lurked beneath his skin.

The beauty of lies is that you get everything you want.

Until you realize what you want can be taken away with two simple words.

Stupid Girl.

That's what he calls me now and I have to say, I don't disagree with him.

I am a stupid girl and I hate myself for falling for the first man who showed me any attention.

The door to the closet rips open, the sunlight spilling in and nearly blinding me since I've been sitting in the dark for so long, I've lost track of time. Tyler looks down on me, hulking as always, proving his dominance with his size. His hands clench into fists just as his jaw twitches with that rage he hid so well when I first met him.

His eyes hold no regret for what he has done to me.

I hold up my cuffed wrists to block the sun that's shining through the window.

He picks me up by my throat and yanks me close, the chain pulling tight against the wall. I'm kept like a dog. I'm not allowed to go too far. Tyler leans in and unlocks the clasp from the hook. The chain falls with slack, and he backs away, tugging it like a leash.

"Come on," he orders. "You fucking stink. Get in the shower."

Of course I smell, he's keeping me in a closet with no bucket, I can't bathe and he feeds me once a day, if I'm lucky. But I know better than to say anything in return.

I don't even know what my voice sounds like at this point, it's been so long since I've used it. That's something else he's taken from me too. Speaking means violence and my body already hurts. I'm his to do whatever he wants with. Until life finally pities me enough to let me die.

When we get into the restroom, he pulls the curtain back and anchors me in place using another hook. The metal of the lock scratches the steel of the chain as he tugs it to make sure it's secure. He has hooks all around the house to lock me down, ensuring I can't escape.

He peels my sweat-stained shirt off, then my shorts and panties, but no bra because he hates them. It's one more thing that gets in the way of what he wants to see.

"You are beautiful," he says, his eyes looking me up and down as if he is starved.

I stay quiet, not wanting to acknowledge him in any way.

He cranks the shower on, and cold water hits me in the back, stealing my breath.

"I said you're beautiful, Stupid Girl. If you want warm water, you'll be polite about my compliment." He tightens the chain and yanks me close. "What do you say when your boyfriend compliments you, Mickey?" He spits my name with hatred, the scent of aged smoke on his tongue from his last cigarette.

The smell makes my stomach curl in on itself.

"Thank you," I croak, my voice is hoarse from so many days of not speaking. I swallow, licking the cold water off my lips. "Thank you, Tyler," I say a little louder.

"Good." He tilts my head back, the cold water rushing down my body.

"The water?" My teeth begin to chatter, and goose-bumps rise on my skin.

He smirks. "I changed my mind. Your tits look good like this." He tweaks my hard nipple. "How long has it been, Mickey? I can't remember the last time I was inside you. I've forgotten how pretty you are." His hand slips down my stomach, then his fingers curl in my pubic hair before giving it a tug. "Not that I would touch you right now. You need to take better care of yourself. How about when you're done here, you get pretty for me? I'll get dinner delivered. We'll watch a movie. And then I'll fuck you into the couch like I used to. How's that sound?" He speaks gently, kissing my shoulder, cupping my breast, then takes my hand in his to force me to rub his erection.

I hate myself even more knowing this man was my first, the man I picked to sleep with for the first time, and he'll probably be my last.

"I remember how tight you are," he moans as he rocks his hips, his cock rubbing against my palm. "I miss it. Do you think I want it to be like this? I just want you to behave. We can have a good life if you will stop being stupid."

I turn my head away, squeezing my eyes shut and the sound of his zipper lowers. His cock smacks against my hand and the thin, short erection fits right in my palm.

It's smaller than my palm, but he says that's normal, that he's considered bigger than most men, and who am I to argue? I have never seen another, so I can't disprove what he's saying.

He forces my fingers around him and squeezes them tight to make a fist.

"Oh yeah, Mickey. Just like that. Watch. Watch what you do to me."

I can't.

I can't witness how he is violating me again.

He tugs my head back with my hair. "I said to fucking watch, Stupid Girl."

I tremble from the cold temperature of the water while I do as he says, sliding his cock in and out of the hole he made with my fist. The small blunt crown peeks out with every thrust. All I want to do is squeeze it until it hurts him so bad, he can never use it again.

"Oh fuck yes, Mickey. That's it. I'm going to come. You're going to make me come." He grunts, shooting white streams over my stomach.

I'm just glad it's over.

He won't be able to get it up again which means he won't chain me to the bed and fuck me. He hasn't done that in a while and I'm thankful. I'm hoping it's because he's out fucking other women. Those girls don't know that they are saving me from so much pain when they decide to have sex with him.

The last time he chained me to the bed, he kept the leash so tight my head bent back painfully. I was lying on my stomach while he used me. I only remember crying. Other than that, I felt absolutely nothing. My soul is nearly numb now. I expect the abuse and all I can do is power through it.

Then there are times when he ties me down just to whip me, another form of punishment. I have scars all over my back from the countless times I've angered him.

The water suddenly turns warm causing the quakes in my body to ease.

"Thank you," I whisper, my body melting from the warmth.

"I can be good to you. If only you let me."

The rise of rebellion is trapped in my throat. I want to lash out. I want to scream. I want to beat him until he stops breathing. I want revenge.

"I'll be better," I lie, knowing I'll never be the person he wants.

I'm such a stupid girl.

"I know," he states, sounding hopeful as I wash my hair. "I've already seen improvement. How about I get food from that Thai place you like so much?"

My stomach grumbles in approval. It's been ages since I've had Thai.

"That would be amazing. Thank you, Ty."

He grins when he hears the nickname I call him. "It's been so long since you've called me that. I've missed it." He snags my chin between his fingers.

Ty presses his lips to mine, the same lips I used to dream about kissing now live in my nightmares. I freeze, waiting for him to pull away.

When he does, I release a slow, careful breath so he doesn't hear it.

"You can call your siblings today too."

A smile comes over my face as my heart races at the thought of hearing their voices. "Really?"

"Really, but I have to be in the room."

I nod so hard I probably look like a bobblehead. "Of course. I wouldn't want you anywhere else," I lie, but it earns me more points when I see his chest puff out.

"That's what I like to hear. Let's get you washed, and we can have a good night."

The plain bar of soap smells better than usual as he rubs up and down my body. The old yellow tile that makes the shower stall isn't as dreadful either.

Ty sprays me clean, flips the shower off, and grabs a towel. He wraps the rough, cheap cotton around my body, unhooking me from the wall, only to anchor me to another one so I have enough room to step out of the shower. My reflection catches my eye, and the newfound excitement is sucked from my sails.

I'm thin— too thin. My cheeks are sunken, I have dark circles around my eyes, and I have scars all over my body. There's a T and a Y branded on my arm. I remember that one the most. He carved his name into my flesh with a knife until I passed out.

He's made sure no one else could ever love me, could ever want me, could ever stand to even look at me.

I'll die and he'll find some other poor girl to take my place.

Tyler brushes my long black hair, then braids it to get it out of the way. We fall silent for a few minutes as he dresses me. He tugs the panties up my body, then a simple white dress over my head. It's see-through, my nipples show, and he moans in approval.

"Look at you. You look stunning. Do you like this dress? I got it just for you."

I hate it.

"I love it. Thank you for getting it for me."

He unhooks me again, wraps an arm around my shoulders, and we stroll side by side to the living room. Every few feet there is a new hook, something to chain me to, and I realize I'm not a human to him. I'm a pet and this house is my kennel.

I stare at the pictures lining the wall, all the lies built from the beginning. It's all right there. A showcase of my stupidity. In the first picture, he has me in his arms in a wildflower field, both of us are smiling as if we have found the most important piece of life's puzzle. Then the last picture is of us, but a forced smile is on my face, and he is watching me with those calculating eyes to make sure I do nothing to cause suspicion.

My eye makeup was heavier that day to cover up the bruises. Those were the first of many black eyes and I'm still counting down to when the last will be.

The old, faded blue couch sits in the middle of the living room, the light of the TV flashing as a random show plays, causing the material of the sofa to seem darker in some spots. The coffee table is littered with beer cans and the ashtray is full.

"I'll take care of this if you'll allow me, Ty," I say, thinking of a way I can make a plan to get out of here.

He nods. "Do that. I'll order food, then when I'm done you can call your siblings. They've been fucking annoying dropping by and calling me to check in. They should know I take care of you. Get them off my back, Mickey." His voice changes to that deadly warning I wouldn't dare to challenge.

"I will. I'll tell them we have a date night. Is that okay?"

He nods, plopping down on the couch, and then pulling out his phone. "Fine. When you're in the kitchen, get me another beer."

I don't say anything and it's so hard not to, but I can't go back in that closet. I gather the empty bottles in my arms, then slowly walk to the kitchen, the chain dragging behind me. The distance between every room is calculated so I can't get too far.

The chain is heavy, the weight already exhausting me. I dump the cans in the trash, then lean against the wall to catch my breath.

"Mickey! Where's my beer? Food is ordered."

I lick my lips and press my hands against my eyes to stop myself from crying. Tears won't get me anywhere except back in the closet with a new bruise.

"Can I have a bottle of water, Ty?" I ask in my meek, quiet voice.

"Go ahead."

I race to the old white fridge and nearly rip the door off. The loud hum of the motor drowns out the TV. I take the moment of peace. Only a moment. It's all I can afford, then snag his beer and a water bottle before going to the living room.

He doesn't say thank you as he pops the cap off the glass bottle and chugs half of it down. He tugs the chain, forcing me to plop down next to him.

"Here." He hands me his phone. "Five minutes, Mickey. No more than that. Do you understand me?"

"Yes, I understand. Thank you for allowing me to call them."

"Yeah, well, I don't want the cops showing up at our door again. I mean it, Mickey. Fucking fix it or it won't end well for you."

I twist the cap off the water bottle to guzzle the cold liquid down. "I will, okay?"

I don't hear the attitude in my voice until it's too late. He backhands my cheek, the sting flourishing across my skin in a hot fever, and water I haven't swallowed flies out of my mouth.

"What did you say to me?"

I rub the warm spot, tears brimming my eyes. "I will fix it, Ty. I promise," I say low and calm, barely audible just how he likes. The weaker I sound, the better.

"Good. Now, I want to have a decent night with you. Call them and get it over with."

I type in Minnie's number because Milo will be with her. He always is. The last conversation we had was months ago and Milo told me that the code word for me is Snapdragons. All I have to do is say it and they will come get me.

But all I did was pretend I didn't hear him because Ty would kill them if they came here. I can't risk their safety. I won't.

Snapdragons.

My favorite flower, in part because when they die, they look like skulls. They are bright and beautiful but slowly shrivel to shells of themselves in the wrong conditions.

I relate to it so much.

I press the phone to my ear. It barely rings twice before Minnie's voice comes through.

"Mickey? Mickey, is that you?" She sounds excited and a bit breathless.

"Hey! It's so good to hear your voice. I miss you." Tears form in my eyes when I hear her sob. "Minnie," I whisper.

"Milo! It's Mickey," she shouts to my brother. "I'm putting you on speaker. How are you? What's going on? Is *he* there?" The distaste for Tyler is clear.

I side-eye Tyler to see if he heard Minnie, but his attention is on the TV. One hand is in his pants, grabbing his cock and the other holds his beer.

"We are great. We are about to have a date night. Thai food and a movie." I sound too excited for something so simple.

"Mickey, you can be honest with us," Milo whispers. "We can come get you. You don't have to be there."

"What do you have planned for the day?" I ask them, needing to change the subject before I break down and cry.

I'll be punished if I do that. He'll know what's going on. I won't put them at risk.

"We're going to figure out a way to get you out, Mickey. You deserve more than that monster. I can only imagine what he is doing to you, and I know it isn't good. Please, let us help."

"Two minutes," Tyler says, reminding me of the time I have left.

"Are you being timed?" Minnie sasses in astonished anger.

A knock on the door thankfully interrupts the growing tension. Tyler stands, the floor shaking from every heavy step. I curl a lip in disgust when he pulls his hand free from his crotch and then opens the door.

"Hey man, that will be forty bucks and eighty-seven cents," the delivery guy announces.

My heart hammers in my chest when a wild thought hits me. My eyes land on the beer bottle he left on the coffee table. The brown glass shines, tempting me to set myself free. This is it. This could be my only chance.

"Snapdragons," I whisper.

"Mickey? What? Say it again. I need to hear you say it again," Milo orders in desperation.

"Snapdragons. Snapdragons. Snapdragons!" I yell the codeword so loud, that it has Tyler turning to me and the delivery man getting a view of the crime my boyfriend has been hiding from everybody. I stand, grab the bottle, and smash it against the edge of the table.

"Woah. What the fuck is going on here? Lady, do you need help? What the hell man?" The delivery driver tries to push his way by Tyler but with one quick punch, my violent boyfriend knocks the innocent man out.

I'm quick, not wanting to waste any time while he has his back to me.

I run around the table, stepping through the glass, and I already feel the deep cuts. I don't care if I bleed if it means I get out.

Raising my arm, I slam the broken bottle into his side. Blood stains his shirt and he falls to his knees. Next, I smash the ragged bottle into the side of his neck, tears blurring my eyes as my intent becomes clear.

I have to kill him to be free.

I yank the bottle free and stab him again.

And again.

Then again.

Until he falls onto his back, coughing up blood, and bleeding out onto the floor. Red pulsates from the torn flesh on his throat, and he stares at me with wide, con-fused eyes.

"Stupid... Girl," he chokes, wrapping a hand around his

neck to apply pressure.

I rip the keys from his belt loop and get to work on all the locks that keep me trapped here. I keep the keys and without looking back, I run out the front door.

It's been ages since I've felt the evening air on my skin– since I've seen grass and felt it beneath me. I hiss with every step I take; the glass digging deeper into my feet.

"Snapdragons. Snapdragons. Snapdragons," I whisper to myself as I run.

The sound of tires squealing and a car coming around the corner makes me stop in my tracks.

They slam on the brakes in the middle of the road and jump out of the car.

"Milo," I weep, taking a step forward.

He sprints to me. "Mickey! Mickey. Oh my God, what has he done to you?" he chokes.

But as I take another step, I can't catch my weight and I fall forward, weak, hungry, and tired.

"I got you." My brother's arms are around me, keeping me safe from the ground. "I got you, Mickey. It's okay. You did good. I'm so proud of you."

The broken bottle is taken from my fist. "We need to get as far away from here as we can," Minnie says, opening the back door of the vehicle.

Milo picks me up and climbs in the back, allowing me to stretch out. My head is on his lap, and I stare up into his red, watery eyes.

"Snapdragons," I rasp, cupping his face.

He holds my hand with his. "Snapdragons, Mick. You did it. I'm so proud of you."

"Where do we go?" Minnie asks, pressing her foot on

the gas.

"Let's just go until we need gas. We need away from here and him."

"Snapdragons," I repeat, tired and broken, my eyes hooding with exhaustion.

"She needs a doctor."

"Let's find one when we are out of state," Milo states, combing his fingers through my hair. "You're okay now, Mick. No more snapdragons. You're safe."

I'll always need snapdragons.

It's the hope I've held onto for far too long and the determination I've needed to survive.

If only I had my own snapdragons, then I'd never have to be afraid again.

CHAPTER ONE

RHETT

Flashback to one year ago

They say money can't buy happiness, but fuck every-one who has ever said that. Those people have never been in unimaginable debt.

Like me.

I'm staring at one of many bills that has a big red stamp on the front that says, "Past Due." The amount owed keeps getting larger, the minimum payments keep increasing, and the money Royals' Garage makes is barely enough to keep the lights on and food on the table.

"Fuck." I wipe a hand over my mouth, picking up an-other bill that has too many zeroes for me to count before my eyes cross.

I'm not sure when times got so hard. Maybe it's always been like this. I've been in survival mode for so long, for so many years, I've forgotten what it is like to breathe without worry.

I've had to fire most of my crew because I couldn't afford to pay them. I hated to fire them because they were friends too. Now, it's just me and Fitz. My best friend. I think he knows that his time is limited here, but he has never once complained. He is always ready to work.

"How many more months do you think we got, Royals?"

I lift my head from the bills that have 'Rhett Royals' plastered on the front, and 'OVERDUE' stamped right next to it. Seeing how I went from having the dream to nearly nothing at all is embarrassing. Royals' Garage was my dream.

When I first opened the shop ten years ago, business boomed. Everyone brought their cars here, but then gas prices went up, people started losing their jobs, and they couldn't afford to bring their vehicles to Royals' Garage.

I stare at Fitz, the man who has been by my side since we were kids playing in mud puddles and learning how to ride bikes. He's wiping his hands on an oil-stained rag, leaning against the doorframe, his eyes locked on the overdue bills scattered across the desk.

Sighing, I lean back in my chair and lace my hands behind my head. "Maybe two more months? Even that is a stretch. I'm debating on just shutting the doors for good. This isn't fair to you. You need to be working at a place that's stable, Fitz."

"Why won't you take me up on my offer? I can be your partner. Let me invest. We can turn this place around. I believe in it, Royals."

A half, tired smirk crooks my mouth. "I know you do, Fitz. I'd love to do that one day, but this isn't the business to do it with. You'd be throwing your money away. There is too much debt to climb out of. I'm thinking a different town, a way to start over, maybe. I'm not sure how I'll be able to do it or if I can at all."

He steps into the office and throws the rag onto his right shoulder. "You can do it. This was a damn good business. The economy is hard right now. It will bounce back. We just have to hang on a little bit longer."

I stand, pushing out of the chair, and hold out my hand. "We have been hanging on brother. It's time to let it go."

He slaps my hand away and points a finger at my face. "No. Giving up is never an option. Moving on is, but giving up? No way in hell will I ever let you do that. We will figure out something." He looks at the clock and tosses the rag in the bin to get washed. "I have to head out. Meet me at Dilly's at nine?"

I shake my head. "Wish I could. I can't afford a drink, Fitz." My face flushes with shame, and I have to look away from Fitz's eyes.

"It's on me," he offers, his gaze softening with understanding.

I raise my brows, shaking my head. "You can't afford it either. Not with what I pay you."

"I have a savings account. Let me get you a beer, Royals. It's the least I can do for all the work you've done over the last year to keep this place afloat."

"Thank you. I promise I'll pay you back one day. I won't take this for granted."

"It's a beer, not a thousand-dollar loan. You don't have to pay me back." He looks at his wrist when his watch begins to beep. "Okay, I'm late. I have to go pick up my nephew from school and drop him at my sister's house. Nine, okay? You better be at Dilly's."

"I'll be there. Promise."

"Good. Now go home and shower. You reek of oil." He wrinkles his nose as he backs away.

I shove him out the door. "As if your kettle doesn't whistle," I mumble my sarcasm, slamming said door in his face.

He knocks on the glass for me to let him back in and I yank the blinds down, so I don't have to see him. It's all fun and games. If we didn't joke around, we would be too depressing to be around. Well, I would be. Fitz is always positive, but I let every problem weigh me down.

"Nine! Be there!" he shouts from the other side before the gravel scrapes and kicks from his footsteps as he walks away.

I run my fingers through my hair stressfully, my eyes straying back to the desk that holds all the reasons my life is falling apart. I know in my heart that my dream of having Royals Garage has shattered and there is nothing I can do. I have no savings. I have no retirement account. I have drained everything to keep this business alive– to keep me alive.

And it hasn't been enough.

I glance around the main lobby where customers used to sit and wait for their cars to be done, listening to the silence. There's a window that allows everyone to see out into the garage. Kids loved watching the cars being worked on. Every time a car would be lifted into the air by the hydraulics machine I have, they would press their faces against the glass and gasp in awe.

I couldn't wait to have my own kids. I wanted to show

my sons or daughters how to maintain or fix their cars. I wanted to teach them. I wanted this garage to be my legacy, but that's not something I have to worry about now.

In the decade of owning this shop, I never met the right woman. I never settled down. I never had kids. I'm pushing forty years old. Who would want to be with me now? A man who has no money, a failing business, and a lot of debt.

A heavy sigh escapes me and fills the room. "Yeah, I'm a real fucking winner," I grumble.

The longer I stare at the desk, the angrier I become. I am not this man. I am not a fucking loser. How is this my life?

In a fit of rage, a gut-wrenching roar filled with every damn emotion I've kept inside echoes all around me. I swipe all the bills from the desk. Papers fly everywhere, floating through the air like a feather before hitting the floor. I grab pictures hanging on the wall, pictures that show happiness and success, and I throw them on the floor.

The glass protecting the picture shatters, scattering across the floor. One by one, I rip everything from the walls, wrecking everything I've ever worked for.

Next is the lamp. I rip the cord from the wall and toss it across the room where it crashes into the window. The bulb breaks and the window cracks.

And I don't even care.

Sweat beads across the top of my forehead. The reality of my life crashes down on me and I stumble backward, my back thudding against the wall so hard, that another photo drops from its place, clattering to the floor.

I slide to the ground, running my fingers through

my hair until it is standing up on its ends. The back of my head bangs against the wall and my elbows sit on my knees while I stare into the empty lobby.

Empty.

That's a word I should be used to by now. Everything in my life is gone.

I bury my face in my hands and take a deep breath, my mind racing with ideas to salvage this business, but there's nothing.

The bell above the door jingles and without looking up, I grumble, "We're closed. There's another shop fifteen minutes from here. They will help you."

"I'm not here for service."

I sigh, rubbing my eyes as they begin to burn from exhaustion. "Listen, I know I owe money. I'll get it somehow, but coming here and harassing me isn't going to get you a dime when I don't even have a dollar. Please leave."

"I'm not here for money either."

I scoff, finally looking up to see a man with long thin brown hair. It's pulled back in a low, pathetic ponytail. His glasses make his eyes look bigger than normal because of the strong prescription.

Taking a deep breath to calm myself because the last thing I need to do is lose my temper and force myself to stand. No matter how low I feel, I won't ever have a man look down at me while he speaks.

"What can I do for you?" I ask, crossing my arms. "I'm closed so if you could make this quick, that would be great." That sounds rude, but I don't have it in me to care. Not today.

I'm done pretending everything will be okay.

"Of course, I understand." He pushes his glasses up

the bridge of his nose. "I'm from Shallow Cove Pharmaceuticals. I've been traveling the country searching for volunteers to try our new drug. I will admit, that I do my research and look for failing businesses because this is a paid drug trial. You'll get one hundred thousand dollars for participating. Granted, there are risks, including death if the drug and your body do not agree." He takes his middle finger and pushes his glasses up his nose again. "I know it is random. A too-good-to-be-true kind of deal. We do not want any volunteers from the street. We want to help people. We want to change lives. This drug could extend someone's life by decades. It can slow the aging process. I can't promise anything though. There is no guarantee you'd survive."

I scoff, my boots scuffing against the floor as I walk behind my desk. "You must think I'm stupid if you think I'm going to agree to that when I don't know you. I know more about my absent father who left my mom after I was born, so no offense, but you're the devil dressed up to portray a blessing. I know a scam when I hear one. I might have fallen on hard times, and I might be desperate." I reach under my desk and grab my gun, pointing it directly at his face, and pull the hammer back to cock it, the bullet sliding into place. "But there is one thing I will never be, and that's dumb. So get the fuck out of my shop before I bury you in it."

A smile takes over his face.

It isn't the nervous kind of smile.

It's the kind that sends shivers up the spine. The hair on the back of my neck stands up in warning. My instincts are telling me to run but my pride won't let anyone run me out of my shop.

Not yet, anyway.

"You'll be perfect, Mr. Royals. Just..." A giddy sigh escapes him as he looks me up and down, evaluating me. "Perfect."

"Listen, I don't know who the fuck you are–"

He straightens, his kind expression morphing into a statuesque slate, frozen, unnerving, and sinister. The man steps forward, pressing his forehead against the gun, a wicked gleam in his eye as he cocks his head.

"You don't have it in you, Mr. Royals."

I hold in a snarl, pressing the barrel harder against him, my finger idling on the trigger. "Try me and find out." I want to say his name, but I realize he never gave it.

And I don't care enough to ask.

"A man who has a failed business and is doing what he can to stay afloat shows just how cowardly you actually are. A successful person would do anything, lie, cheat, steal, and kill," his voice lowers an octave on the last word. "To save what they love."

I grind my teeth together, fighting the urge to pull the trigger for talking to me like that. I've done everything in my power to save the garage. I have loans that are unpaid. I took a second mortgage out on the house. I have so many credit cards that I've lost count. They are all maxed out.

I've sold my motorcycle, every possession I hold dear, my grandpa's truck, his watch, my mother's pearls, her engagement ring– anything and everything.

It still wasn't enough.

"A man like you doesn't have the fucking courage to kill a man, to watch the blood flow from his body, to hear him exhale his last breath, and to watch his pupils expand in death. If you did, do you really think I would be here? Hunting pathetic men who can't keep their lives together? I have stooped so low, but I have to do what is best for my study. It will change the world and you will be part of it."

"You're fucking insane. I'm not going anywhere with you."

He chuckles, then locks eyes with me. "That's where you are wrong." His gaze drifts over my shoulder, a slow nod tilting his chin, and the sense of someone behind me has me swinging around.

The man grabs my arm, slams it against the wall, and my finger pulls the trigger. Pieces of the ceiling fall down on us, dust getting into my eyes, and my attacker takes that slight moment of weakness.

A sharp pain enters my neck as a rush of something cold slips through my veins, my heart pumping it through my body. Whatever drug was in that syringe sends me to my knees quickly.

"I see you've met my bodyguard, Allen." The guy steps around the front desk and looks down at me as if I am beneath him in a way that is more than physical. He takes his glasses off and cleans the lenses on the hem of his shirt. "He's always been a little..." He hums loudly as he pretends to think. "Aggressive. You know, you should really be more careful when it comes to locking all your doors. Allen got in so easily. He didn't have to break anything, so unlike him."

"Fuck. You," I struggle to say. The words slur and my head begins to spin. The gun falls from my hand and Allen kicks it away. My only saving grace just slid across the floor.

"No." He grabs me by the roots of my hair and yanks

my head back. "Fuck you."

Spit lands on my face from the force of his words.

The lobby begins to spin. My eyes begin to hood. It's getting more difficult to keep my body upright.

"You should be thanking me. You should be worshiping me for what I'm about to give you. You'll be better than this," he hisses, then glances around my garage. "You'll be unstoppable. You'll be more than what the world is ready for. So, fucking. Thank. Me!" he roars until he is red in the face. He backhands me across the face next, causing me to fall onto my back.

"You'll see." He stands over me, his face a swirling blur as my eyes try to focus. "I am your savior, your last hope, and your dream. I am going to transform you, Rhett Royals and you will thank me."

The drug takes over. My body becomes heavier. The floor opens and swallows me whole, plunging me into darkness.

But there is one thought that holds strong.

I will kill myself before I ever mutter those words to him.

Or better yet, I'll kill him before he has the opportunity to beg for forgiveness.

Only then will I be thankful.

CHAPTER TWO

MICKEY

"Are you sure this is the place?" Milo stands in the living room with his hands on his hips, then spins in a slow circle to get a good look at the place. "I don't know. I'm not comfortable with you being here. Alone."

"I think it's perfect," I whisper, tugging at the ends of my long-sleeved shirt. It's a habit I've acquired to keep my scars covered.

Milo gently grabs my shoulders. I don't flinch when he touches me. I think he might be the only man I'll ever feel completely safe with again.

"This place is so rundown, Mick. It needs a lot of work. I mean, I saw the roof when we came in, it needs replac-ing. The porch needs to be fixed, most of the windows are broken, and the yard is overgrown. I'm going to either need a blow torch or a machete to get through that jungle."

His joke has me laughing, a sound that is few and far

between these days since so much weighs on my soul.

He grins at the success but doesn't say anything about it.

"That's what I like about it, Milo. It needs work." I rub my hands up my arms and cross them, then step over the hole in the floor to stand in front of the sliding glass door. "This place might be able to help me find myself again. I'll put in the work."

"There is a dead something in one of the bedrooms and it reeks." My sister, Minnie, shivers from head to toe as she comes out of the hallway, her face twisting in disgust. "No. Absolutely not, Mick. We have the apartment. It's close to the diner. It's safe. You're safe. I know Milo and I feel better knowing you are with us. You deserve more than this."

I shake my head and turn around, pressing my back against the glass. "I appreciate everything you have done for me in these past six months. You saved me from so much pain, and you've protected me every day since, but I need to do this on my own. I need my own space, my own..." I bite my lip as I search for the word and shake my head. "Freedom."

"You have freedom with us," she frowns. "We would never–"

"–I know," I'm quick to cut her off. "I'm lucky." My eyes begin to water at the thought of not living with them. "You two saved my life, but I'm ready to do this. This place isn't broken. It just needs love. I think this house will help me find myself again. I'll make it my own. It will give me a sense of purpose again. Plus, look at this view." I spin around again and unlock the door.

It slides without issue.

Whew. I really did not want to fight with it, so my siblings have another reason to hate this house.

I step out onto the deck, and yes, I hope I do not fall through the old wood that makes it. Every panel groans and creaks with my weight, something I have proudly gained back since being with my brother and sister.

The waves of constant havoc ease when I inhale the fresh cool air. I rest my elbows on the rail, sending a silent prayer to whatever deck god exists that it doesn't break and send me toppling over the edge.

At least it would be a quick death.

Death doesn't scare me.

It's the prolonged tortured road that leads to it that has me waking up in cold sweats at night.

"I'd live in a tent if it means I get to have this view."

Mountains are all around us, going as far as camouflaging themselves in the distance with fog. A large lake is settled below, the still water disturbed by insects landing and fish breaching the surface.

I'll never admit this out loud because it sounds insane, but there's something in the ominous black water that lures me in. Maybe it's a haunting death that waits for me, a trick to suck me under and never let me reach the surface again.

It's tempting. Life is hard. The nightmares are harder.

I'm damaged. My mind, my body, my heart, and my soul. The cracks are so deep, they can't be repaired, yet my will to live somehow finds a way to be stronger than all of it.

I'm safe here. I don't know how or why, but I feel it.

Long grass swishes together as the wind blows, grazing my cheeks and I close my eyes to enjoy the peace that settles over me.

"I can see you genuinely love it here." Milo stands next to me, mimicking my stance, and leans against the rails. "I only want you happy, Mick. That's all. It's all I've ever wanted. So if this place will make you happy, then we won't stop you."

Minnie sighs, flanking my other side, and presses her cheek against my shoulder. She loops her arm through mine, and we stand there in silence for a minute.

"I guess having all the creamer for the coffee will be nice."

I burst out laughing, knowing I do use way too much creamer in my coffee. There's been more than one occasion where she got mad at me for leaving an empty bottle in the fridge.

I did it on purpose. There was always another bottle behind the milk.

"I'll worry about you."

"Me too," Milo echoes Minnie's concern.

"I'll be okay. I've gotten stronger since..." Bile rises up my throat at the thought of Ty. "Since him. This is my chance to rebuild myself. I can't depend on you two forever."

"Yes, you can. You most definitely can. We don't mind. We are all we have. If it's just us three for the rest of our lives, I'd be fine with that. I don't need anyone else as long as I have my sisters."

I smile, staring at the lake. "I know, but I need this, and I need you two to understand. I need you with me on this."

"We support you." Minnie takes my hand and spins me around to meet her gaze. "We will always support you. If this is what you want, we want it too, and we will help you clean this place up." She holds up a finger. "But I am not touching that dead whatever in the bedroom. I draw the line there."

I chuckle and Milo groans.

"I suppose that will be a job for me."

Minnie and I turn to him with our best puppy dog eyes, then tackle him with a hug, and he wraps his arms around us. His chin rests on the top of my head and his hand rubs up and down my back.

"I have conditions with you being here," he says, causing me to pull away.

Conditions.

"Excuse me?" I become panicked. My breathing begins to speed up, my lungs struggle to expand, and my heart races.

My vision becomes blurry, and I stumble away from him, his face morphing into Tyler's.

"I won't– I won't–" I can't get the words out.

"Mick! No, no, it's okay. It's okay." Minnie wraps her arms around me, cupping the back of my head. "Not those kind of conditions. Never."

Milo wipes a tear from my cheek. I glance up at him, taking a deep breath in, and my cheeks heat with embarrassment. My brother would never put me in danger.

"I'm so sorry," I gasp, resting my head on Minnie's shoulder. I close my eyes, allowing shame to wash over me.

"I'm the one who is sorry. I shouldn't have worded it like that."

I shake my head, anger brewing in my chest at my own fear. "Don't. Don't tiptoe around me. Don't think about what you have to say. I know you wouldn't hurt me."

"I only meant that I want to install a security system, a damn good one. I want windows monitored, and finger-print scanners on every door– I want this place locked down. You obviously come and go as you please, Mickey, but when you are home, every single way into this house will be safeguarded. Please?" he asks desperately with a pinch of his brows, a wrinkle forming in between them.

I nod quickly in agreement. "That sounds good to me. How can we afford that?"

"We still have a chunk of life insurance money from Mom and Dad," Minnie admits. "We've invested some of it. We aren't rich or anything, but we can live a decent life. We didn't spend your chunk, so it's yours whenever you want it."

"You saved some for me? Even when…" I bury my face in my hands, sobbing, the guilt awakening from the home it's built inside my bones.

"We know you couldn't come to Mom and Dad's funeral. We don't hold that against you. We know you couldn't leave that house without risking your life. You were barely surviving, Mick. It isn't like you chose not to come because you went shopping instead. You were trapped." Milo takes my hand and tugs me to him, his palm cupping my face. "If you are looking to be forgiven, then fine, you're forgiven, but don't blame yourself. It isn't your fault. You would have been there if not for him."

I sniffle, glancing out onto the lake again, wanting nothing more than to strip bare and go for a swim. Maybe then the filth that lingers on my skin will wash away. I don't want to be this person anymore. I need to be differ-ent because this version of myself is slowly killing me.

Sometimes, I wonder if death would be easier because surviving is so hard.

"I think you're right, Mick. This place will be good for you. It needs healing and I think it will help you do the same." Minnie runs her fingers through my hair, smiling at me. "I'm still not touching that dead thing."

Another laugh bubbles free as I stand from my crouched position at the corner of the deck. I don't re-member backing myself into that corner or sitting, but I suppose that's the thing with trauma when it surfaces, it blacks everything out to leave you in a murky fog.

"So when do you sign the papers?"

I wipe the dirt from my jeans. "I already have. I did a few days ago right before buying my car. This place is mine. I've been cleaning out one of the spare rooms and it's livable. I'm having my bed brought over today."

"Today? Woah, wait a minute. Mick. This place is not ready for you to stay at. It's a gust of wind away from fall-ing apart. I need to check the foundation, the structure, the—"

"It's fine. I've had it checked." I tap my hand on his chest. "It's safe. It doesn't look it but looks can be deceiv-ing."

He points to the roof. "There is a hole in the roof, Mick. A hole." He moves his hand to point inside. "There is the bucket to catch whatever falls through said hole. How is that safe?"

I shrug my shoulders. "I don't know but it has to be safer than my previous home."

Minnie gasps.

Milo rolls his lips together.

And a giggle slips from me.

"Did you… did you just make a joke?" Milo questions, the corners of his lips fighting to grin due to the uncomfortable reality that this house is a million times better than my situation with Ty.

"I did." I hold my chin up high.

"Dark. And fucked up." He shakes his finger at me. "You know I can't laugh at that. That's wrong."

"Just trying to figure out my healing process."

Milo throws an arm around my neck, and we all walk back inside just as the alarm on his watch beeps.

"Damn. I have to head to the diner. I'll be back later tonight." He digs out his wallet and hands me a debit card with my name on it.

"What's this?"

"It's your account with your chunk of the money in it. We've been waiting to give it to you."

Minnie steps in to explain. "We didn't want you to feel rushed or pressured. We haven't been hiding it from you. We wanted you to focus on yourself first."

"And this looks like you're ready to move on. To do that, money will help," Milo adds. "You can make this house your home."

His watch beeps again and he sighs. "Okay, I have to go. I'm going to be late."

"Me too. Demi wants to talk to me."

I tuck the card in my back pocket. "Is everything okay? I mean, you aren't in trouble or anything, right?"

"No, I don't think so. She's been happy with our work. I think. Well, now I'm in my head about it." Her hand falls to her stomach, and she takes a deep breath in. "I'm nervous."

"Let's go before we do have something to worry

about." Milo ushers her to the door.

I step over the hole in the floor again to walk them to their car. When Milo opens the door, the handle falls off into his hand.

He holds the rusted gold piece of garbage in the air, lifting an eyebrow.

Wincing, I take it from him and toss it behind me. "I'll fix that today."

"You better or you aren't staying here tonight." He steps outside, his sneakers brushing against the cracked sidewalk, small scuffs sounding. Milo pushes the long arms of overgrown weeds from his path, reminding me to add lawn supplies to the list of things to get.

I might be over my head, but I can do this.

I *need* to do this.

"My God, what are you going to do with that atrocious thing?" Milo gapes at the gigantic statue in my yard.

I swear it wasn't there this morning, but maybe I wasn't looking.

It couldn't have been. I wouldn't have missed a gargoyle statue in the middle of my lawn. I have to lift my knees high to walk through the brush to get to the gargoyle. My eyes drift over the stone form. From the wide shoulders and chiseled abdomen to the large wings tucked behind his back.

I'm pulled to it.

The gargoyle is huge, hulking over my brother by a few feet. This thing has to be eight feet when it isn't crouched. Even in this position, it is taller than Milo, and definitely taller than me.

Another burst of wind blows. Long grass rustles again and tickles my legs. My hair grazes my cheeks and the clouds in the sky become darker, casting a shadow over us.

"I think it's beautiful," I whisper, not expecting anyone to hear me.

"If you say so," Minnie grumbles.

"You can't actually be thinking of keeping it here? It's... creepy," Milo tries to sound reasonable, but it falls on ears that are not listening. "It will scare everyone away."

"Good," I say fast and without doubt. "I don't want anyone here besides you two."

"Okay, well, if you change your mind, I'll get a sledge-hammer."

I spin around and stand protectively in front of my gargoyle.

Not *my* gargoyle, but *my* statue.

"You aren't allowed to touch it. I want it here. It's beautiful. Someone took the time to sculpt this. That must have taken so much time and energy. You can't destroy art, Milo. That's awful." I rein in my anger, my protection, and swallow it down.

Maybe it's because this statue is on my property. It's mine to care for now.

Milo clicks his tongue. "Okay, Mick. Whatever you want. We have to go. Be safe. Keep your phone on. And don't buy that security system, I'm going to, okay? We love you."

"Love you!" Minnie echoes, blowing me a kiss.

The old doors creak open. Milo and Minnie hop inside the vintage Bronco that has seen better days. Milo slaps the door in goodbye as he reverses down the driveway.

I'm alone.

I take a deep breath, the air a bit damp from the

storm brewing above.

Tracing the claws on the gargoyle, I then slide my hand up its thick forearms, my mouth suddenly becoming dry.

"I prefer to be alone," I say to the silent statue, knowing it can't talk back. "There's less worry that way, you know? I'm not afraid of my own company." I place my foot on one of its bulging thighs, my hand cupping its shoulder, and I pull myself up its body. "You really are giant. Where did you come from?" I trace its features, my finger dragging across his jaw.

Next, I travel over its teeth. Long fangs show through a snarl, its top lip curling as if it sees something it doesn't like.

"You're attractive in a way I shouldn't find you to be because I really dislike men. I never want to be with one again." My finger grazes over the strong bridge of his nose, then to his long pointed ears. "But you aren't a man, are you? You're just a statue. I don't have to worry about you torturing me or keeping me chained up. You'll protect me, right?"

Ty's voice whispers in the back of my mind, "*Stupid Girl. Talking to an inanimate object as if it cares about you. No one will care about you like I did. You'll do well to remember that.*"

I swallow hard, resting my forehead on the statue's chest. "You're warm." I lean away, flattening my hand in the middle of its chest. "So warm. Probably from the sun." I jump down, taking one last look at the stone beast.

I find peace in its presence because while I prefer to be alone, I am lonely.

And those are two completely different feelings.

CHAPTER THREE

RHETT

Night falls, and her touch haunts my flesh.

I want more of it.

Every caress she gives, every whisper she speaks, every curiosity that falls from her tongue, I want them for myself.

When she touched me, my body ached to burst free from the stone and capture her, whisking her away into the mountains. I knew she was important when I smelled her from the lake as I was swimming in my crocodile form.

Important how?

I'm not sure.

Every single monster that lives inside me roared from her scent. The gargoyle growled, the crocodile vibrated, the vampire craved her blood, the jellyfish tentacles around my cock charged with electricity, and the ghost wanted to possess her body.

This is who I am now, and the grace I had as a man, is

gone.

I do not care about anything other than having her as mine.

She wants a protector.

And I will do so much more than that.

Because I am not the gentleman I was raised to be, but the monster I am meant to be.

The beast I was created to be.

Flashback

I'm thrown into my room, naked and shivering. I'm covered in sweat. My teeth are chattering as my body tries to adjust to the changes happening inside me. Lifting my hand, I stare at the new adjustments made to me.

Every day that passes, I notice something new about myself, and the humanity inside me gets more distant. One moment I'm angry... soulless, and the next, my human nature bubbles inside my chest, reminding me it's fading away.

Right now, the man is at the surface, and I'm not sure how long that will last.

Bumpy, greenish-gray skin covers my hand, slowly fading up my arms. My nails are long and thick, pointed, and the color is an off-white. The rest of my skin is cracked and gray, reminding me of stone.

Lifting my fingers to my lips, I hiss when I rub over an elongated tooth.

A fang.

My head begins to pulse, the pressure mounting until a scream of pure agony rips through the concrete jail cell.

My body ignites, and every nerve ending is set ablaze. I flop to my back, my skin sticking to the cold, damp floor.

The ceiling blurs. The lights bend. The floor sinks. I lift my arms, reaching for something, anything, and notice I'm able to see through myself.

I gasp when the world rights itself. The pressure in my head eases and I'm able to catch my breath.

Until the pain rips through me again, paralyzing my lungs, and my entire body becomes invisible.

Again.

I hate it when this happens. It hurts like fucking hell. Like a bomb is going off inside my chest, over and over, the fuse being reignited just when I think the explosion is over. I squeeze my eyes closed, waiting for this episode to pass, and take a few deep breaths.

The more I calm, the more my solid figure forms.

I lift my arms to check, breathing a sigh of relief when I see my human-ish form. The stone-like crocodile skin is much more welcome than being able to see through myself.

Groaning, I roll to my side, spitting blood on the floor. I must have bit my tongue with my new fangs. My entire body feels like it's been hit by a fucking truck. I manage to stand, limping for only a moment before the gash the guard left on my thigh heals. The skin stitches itself back together, the dripping blood recoils into my body, and I'm left with no scar.

As if the torture didn't really happen.

Exhaustion hits so hard, that I stumble backward until the back of my knees hit the cot nestled in the corner of the room. A growl builds in my chest, my new beasts angry at being imprisoned.

I want out.

Cracking my neck, I lean back on my hands and tilt my chin to my chest.

I'm able to see everything. The new me.

My chest has crocodile skin fading to cracked stone on my stomach, down to my thighs, and the rest of my legs.

It's what is between my legs that bothers me more than anything else.

Hundreds of long skinny tentacles surround my cock. They sting too. The scientist, the one with the glasses, tests them every chance he can get. He relishes in how my body has changed, especially my cock.

He's fascinated.

The shaft has completely changed. It's bigger, wider, and on the sides are what look like folded ribbons. In jellyfish terms, my shaft is the oral arm, and the head is the umbrella.

And let's not forget my fucking tail.

According to Glasses, it's because of the gargoyle DNA.

A laugh bubbles free, a hysterical manic bellow that has me holding my hand to my stomach as reality hits me for the thousandth time being trapped here.

The door swings open to my cage and the extra eyelids I have, courtesy of the crocodile DNA, flicker.

"Your eyes reflect the light just like a crocodile does."

A hiss vibrates the tip of my tongue as I stare at the guard who decided to come into my cell. He takes out his taser, pressing the buttons to show the electrical charge zapping between the silver prongs.

"But you see, Patient Zero, you are what the scientists call a failed experiment. They don't like that you can shift into multiple forms. They want a test subject who has abilities without shifting. You're able to do both and that's too much. You'll be a variable they can't control eventually."

I stand from the cot, straightening to my new height, and tower over the guard. My tail whips from behind my back, curling around my leg.

He looks me up and down, biting his lip, and begins to undo his pants. "Why don't you be a good freak and come get on your knees before I kill you? Might as well make that pretty mouth useful before dumping you where no one will be able to find your pathetic body."

I roll my head over my shoulders, inhaling the putrid scent of his sweat. For someone who spews threats, he reeks of fear. Cocking my head, the extra eyelid slides over my irises again.

"Maybe this will help get you in the mood." He tucks the taser into his pocket, reaching into the other to pull out a recorder.

He chuckles before his thumb slams down the red button.

Thunder plays immediately, clashing with the loud hiss of rain.

I swallow, fighting the urge filling my cock.

"Oh, that sounds nice, doesn't it? I bet you're dying to mate, aren't you? I can help you with that."

The vibration of need begins to become too much, and my cock hardens until precome drips from the slit, falling onto the floor.

I've learned thunderstorms– rain for the most part–

are an aphrodisiac to saltwater crocodiles and can trigger a mating response.

In my case, I become blinded with lust, and nothing else matters except mating.

"I'll hate to kill you. I think you're perfect and unique. There won't be another like you. I need a taste, Patient Zero. You know you want to." He places the recorder on the floor, the thunderstorm sounding from the device becoming louder with every passing moment.

My claws elongate and I curl them into my palms, reminding the little bit of humanity that is left inside me that this isn't what I want.

None of this is what I want.

"Get on the bed."

"No," I grit out. "I'm stronger than the last time you walked in here. Try it and see what happens." My teeth flash and the urge to rip his throat out is a savory taste on my tongue.

But I want to play with my food first.

He pulls out the tranquilizer gun from his holster that is slung low on his hips. His pants are undone, his shirt half tucked in and half pulled out of the waistband. The guard, Franklin, aims the gun at me, licking the sweat from his top lip.

His teeth are a disgusting shade of yellow and I have no doubt that peanut shells are in his pockets.

"I said get on the fucking bed, Royals. I'm going to fuck the last remaining shred of what makes a man out of you. You are nothing, do you hear me? Useless. Worthless. No one wants you. You have no place in this world. I'll make your last time having sex worthy. I'll let you have one last orgasm. At least you'll have that."

I take a step forward, my cock still hard from the thunderstorm in the room, and I want nothing more than to seek relief.

He pulls the trigger, and the dart pierces the air. My chest shifts, my instincts calling upon my gargoyle, and from my ribcage to my shoulders turns to stone. The dart hits, clinking pathetically against my chest.

It falls to the floor, rolling to my feet. I bend down, pinching the small syringe between my hands, and hold it up. The needle is slightly bent from hitting my chest and by the look on Franklin's face, he wasn't expecting that.

My advanced hearing picks up on his rapid heartbeat and the sound of his nervous swallow. I inhale his fear again, feeding portions of the primal beasts. His blood begins to flow faster, the scent of the iron-laced drink has my tongue going dry.

I'm thirsty.

I blur until I'm standing directly in front of him, so close, I can see every pore, every bead of sweat. My vision focuses on the small droplets of salty water on his forehead, slowly dripping down his face.

"I bet you thought that would work," I grumble, my claw sliding under his chin.

Adding pressure, I force him to look up at me and pierce the skin with the point of my nail. Blood runs down my claw, yet it isn't enough to stop me from meeting his gaze.

"I think you forget who is in charge here now. It certainly isn't you."

He lifts his radio, his hand trembling. Static announces itself when he presses the button and he opens his mouth to speak, but my tail wraps around his throat. I snatch the radio from him, crushing it into pieces without any effort.

I'm beginning to like this new me.

"You'll die for this."

"Don't make promises you can't keep, Franklin." My tongue flattens against his cheek, and I lick the sweat from his cheekbones. Keeping my tail around his throat, I drag my nose across his thin beard and whisper, "It's not nice."

He stiffens in my hold, the only parts moving are his wide eyes, darting back and forth. My brows crease with wonder when his arms stop moving and his knees bend.

Unraveling my tail, I let him go, and Franklin crumbles to the floor.

"You can't move, can you?" I ask him, but all he does is let out a groan.

What could have caused this? I'm learning so much about myself, my body, my abilities, and everything I can do. While it's disturbing, I have to get used to the new me or life will be so much harder.

And I am so sick of living a hard life.

I snap my fingers when the idea strikes. I flip him onto his back, his entire body dead weight.

"Look who is worthless now," I singsong, my voice deepening. "You're supposed to kill me, right?"

His eyes dart up and down in a yes motion.

"I could do that to you right now." My entire body vibrates with the need to mate from that damn recorder, but I don't have it in me to turn it off.

The desire feels too fucking good.

"I'll leave you alive because the thought of you living with the fear in the back of your head of what someone

like me can do to you, maybe, just maybe, you'll be smart-
er with how you treat us going forward."

I straddle his waist, my tail gravitating to his throat
again so his eyes lock with mine. "I'm going to take care of
a problem you've created."

The tip of my tail spreads his mouth open while my
hand drifts to my cock. I give into the vibrations, allowing
the need to wash over me. I don't look away from him as I
stroke, faster, and harder.

"Isn't this what you wanted? You wanted to make sure
I got off, right?" I spit in his face, enjoying the fact that he
can't wipe it off. "They didn't warn you that I'd be at my
strongest when they sent you in here, did they?" I bend
down, gripping him by the roots of his hair, and lick the
shell of his ear, my saliva soaking into his skin. "Don't you
think that's a little questionable, Franklin?"

A small squeak leaves his throat.

I straighten, letting him see all of me, and his eyes fall
to my cock.

What I scent is more than fear. It's terror.

And it only makes me harder, adding to the wicked
lustful frenzy that is in my veins.

"Fuck." I roll my head over my shoulders, sucking my
bottom lip into my mouth. "Feels so good. It's been so
long." I close my eyes, my fangs stinging my bottom lip.

A need pulls at the back of my mind, a flash of an
image dancing at the forefront of my thoughts. I toss my
head back, my long blonde hair skimming the middle of
my back when I see a clear picture.

A woman.

She's beautiful.

Dark hair, black as my newly appointed soul, with

eyes so blue, they are nearly clear. They pierce me, the unknown woman sending my need to mate into a frenzy. I fuck my fist harder imagining her. Her pink lips are delicate. The bottom is bigger than the top, puffy as if she has a habit of nibbling it between her teeth.

Her eyes are red-rimmed and even with the brief image, her pain feeds the new sadistic parts of me.

Mate.

Mine.

Beloved.

Fated.

Synonyms of the same word slam through my mind all at once. Whoever this is, she's important, and I have to find her.

I open my eyes to see Franklin and his face morphs into hers, my mind playing tricks on me. I know it isn't her, I know, but the thought of being so close to what belongs to me, has come jetting from my cock.

His muted attempt at a scream ruins my orgasmic moment with my mate. I groan when another rope of pleasure falls onto his lips. Tears stream down his face and that's when I notice the electricity firing in my come.

Bright blue bolts of light fire within the bioluminescent spend.

I glance down, noticing a hue of neon blue glowing from my cock and tentacles. Another wave of vibrations builds in my chest for my mate. Only she isn't here. It's just the tape recorder.

With a snarl, I bend down, wrapping my hand around his throat. "You'll do best to tell them you killed me and got rid of the body. If I find out you didn't, I'll come back here, and I'll make sure you'll never be able to move again.

Am I clear?"

His eyes do the upward and downward motion again.

I use his head to push myself up onto my feet, the back of his skull banging against the ground which knocks him out. He looks like a mess.

Roaring, I step on the recorder, ending the constant loop of rain that is driving my desire crazy.

When the sound ends, I'm able to take a deep breath, the vibrations slowing to a stop.

Stepping onto his chest, he gasps for air the more pressure I apply. "I hope my come burns your fucking throat any time you begin to speak." I stroll to the wall, the gray concrete walls tempting me to test fate.

There's no way I can get through it, but I have to try. It's the only way out of this prison. If I go through the door, there might be a chance I won't make it out at all. I don't have a grip on my abilities yet. Every day there is a new one, every day I find out something new about my-self, and every moment, my humanity gets further away.

I don't mind.

My humanity is what got me here, but it isn't what is going to get me out.

I focus, wondering which beast I need to bring to the surface. The strongest, the one that can take the weight of each block that makes my cell.

There's that nagging in my head, the pressure. It builds to the point my eyes water, only this time, I let go.

I stop fighting it.

I accept.

A bass drop sounds as my body turns from solid to invisible. My ghost.

Stretching out my arm, I test to see if this will work.

My fingers vanish first, and a slight tingle rolls up my arm. I laugh in disbelief, wiggling my fingers to make sure I'm not seeing things.

Alarms blare. Loud wails in sync with red blinking lights let me know that playtime is over.

"I hope the next time I see you Franklin, it's in Hell, where I can torture you and be rewarded for it." Holding my breath, I leap through the wall, the tingling sensation crawling all over my body, like an itch I can't scratch.

Cool air hits my face, and the night sky is a welcome relief because I haven't seen the sun in months.

And then I fall.

Wings spread from my back, but I keep my invisibility, not wanting to alert anyone. My focus is on finding the woman who entered my mind somehow, heading in the direction completely opposite of where my old home is.

I'm not that man anymore.

I'm a monster and my beasts– I– want someone who couldn't be further away from home.

CHAPTER FOUR

MICKEY

"Don't lie to yourself, Stupid Girl. You love it when I force you down and fuck you. You've missed the only cock you've ever had, haven't you? You're so fucking tight. I'm so glad this pussy is mine to do whatever I want with."

I lie face down on the bed, my cheek pressed against the pillow, staring at the barred window. Tears flow effortlessly down my face as I silently cry, warm wet drops dampening the pillow. My legs are spread, each ankle tied and latched to the bedframe. My arms are behind my back, my wrists crossed and cuffed.

In and out, he takes me. With every stroke, I die a little more inside, becoming numb. Another piece of my soul is ruined, stained, and tainted with how he treats me. The bars on the windows blur from the tears welling in my eyes, the indefinite reminder that this is truly my jail.

He is my warden. I am his prisoner. And my sentence is death.

I gasp awake in the bare bones of my room; the sheets drenched in sweat from my nightmare. I place a hand over my heart, the beat fast with fear.

"I'm not there anymore," I whisper to myself. "I'm not there. He's dead. You're safe." It's something I tell myself every night when I wake up. "You're okay." I take a deep breath in, then slowly let it out.

I do that repeatedly until my heart slows and the sweat stops drenching my skin. I pull my legs to my chest and wrap my arms around them, pressing my left cheek against my knees as I look out the window.

It needs to be cleaned. It's a bit murky with grime that's built up over years of neglect, but I can still see the sky. The stars are out, twinkling without knowledge that the light inside me has been extinguished.

Perhaps, the stars have it, reminding me every night how I used to be.

The moon is nearly full, shining so bright, that its glow engulfs half my room. I shut my eyes, a small, tired smile curling my lips.

I can see the night sky now. There are no bars keeping me prisoner. There is nothing keeping me locked in this house. There are no hooks on the walls. There are no chains locked on my body.

I'm free.

And this home is my independence.

"You're okay," I tell myself again, my eyes burning from the truth— from the relief of my new reality.

A vibration coming from outside has me sitting up and opening the window. It takes some effort with all the paint that's been slathered on the frame in the past, but I manage. The refreshing night air hits my face and I inhale, smelling the wetness in the air from the lake.

Crickets chirp in harmony, an orchestra just for me as they rub their wings together. Fireflies flash and dance as if the music of their surroundings is affecting them. A frog croaks in the distance every few seconds, adding an odd bass to the earth's music that is soothing my broken, damaged soul.

This is where I will heal. I already feel the warm balm of the beauty this house holds bandaging every wound sliced into my spirit.

I cross my arms on the windowsill and lie my head down, staring out at my new view.

The lake ripples as a soft gust of wind blows, the grass swaying in a reminder that it is too long. I love how it sounds as the blades brush together, a soft hush of almost silence.

The vibration sounds again, sinking into my marrow and lassoing around my heart tempting me to go outside.

Who am I to say no? Maybe a midnight swim will be exactly what I need.

I roll out of bed, snagging the blanket, and the few clean towels I have folded on the chair. Slipping on my bright green slides, I flip on the bedroom light, then the hallway, and the living room, showing just how bare my new home is.

I'm mindful of the hole in the floor. It has to be one of the first things I fix because it's only a matter of time before I forget it's there and break my leg.

Or worse, my neck.

Taking a deep breath, I stare at the light switch next to the back door, then stare outside the glass. There's a small part of me wondering, will Ty be standing there when I turn on the light?

Defeating the ghost of him is my main goal. It is what I need so he doesn't keep haunting me. He still traumatizes me every day, my mind replaying all his wicked deeds on a loop.

I can't let the dead win. Not when there is so much of me that wants to live.

As fast as I can, I flip the light on. The dim yellow glow flickers, prevailing against the eerie cloak of the night, but nothing is as terrifying as Ty, who is not standing in the middle of my deck.

Opening the door, a burst of energy rushes through me and I run, jumping down the steps.

Once I hit the ground, I can't be contained. The vibrations coming from the lake add fuel to my desire to feel freedom. My long black hair falls from its loose, messy bun, swaying behind my back. The closer I get, the louder the vibrations are.

There's an old wooden bench that needs replacing on the small shore and I set my belongings there, sliding off my shoes. The dirt rubs between my toes and small rocks poke at the underbelly of my feet.

The frequency of the reverberations has my heart filling with hope. There's also desire, a need, something I don't understand. I have to get into the water. Whatever this is, it's beckoning me.

I slip off my shirt, and then my pajama bottoms, placing them neatly on the bench.

Hearing a rustle to my left, on instinct I cover my breasts, turning to see who it is.

"Hello?" My voice cracks with the niggling fear in the back of my head that causes goosebumps to arise over my body.

Or maybe that's just the breeze.

I scan the trees, the shadows the branches cast, and then the glass surface of the water.

Something is out here.

And it's watching me.

"It's all in your head, Mickey. No one is here. It's just you," I say to myself, repeating the phrases my therapist told me.

He is gone. It's just you. You are in control.

"I'm in control," I whisper to no one but myself.

Stronger and louder vibrations rippling the water have me taking my first step. The shock of the cool water makes me gasp as I step in. The moment I feel the silky touch of the lake reach my ankles, the storm inside me calms.

I'm safe.

I walk further, my feet slipping through the heavy wet sand at the bottom until it's too deep. Holding my breath, I duck my head under the surface, soaking myself in the vibrations that brought me here.

Popping up to take a breath, I flip onto my back and float, spreading my arms out while I stare up at the sky. This might be my new favorite pastime. I close my eyes and allow myself to relax. The water envelopes me in a hug as if someone is wrapping their arms around me, keeping me safe from drowning myself.

I could.

I could dip under the surface and sink to the bottom, struggling to hold my last breath until I have no choice but to inhale lake water. I could let it fill my lungs. I could let the last signs of me be bubbles containing my very last breath. They would reach the surface and pop, allowing the wind to carry the air away.

I could die right here and find peace. The option brings me relief. It's an option I shouldn't think about, but I'd be lying if I said I didn't think about death more than once a day.

But I won't succumb to the negative when I have a fresh start in life. I have a lot of hurdles to overcome, and I want to jump every single one of them in hopes I make it to the finish line of normalcy.

Those vibrations tickle my back as if I'm right against the cause of them. Water slips across my breasts, my nipples beading from the cool temperature, but it's my clit that begins to pulse with desire that makes panic grip me tightly.

I don't want to feel desire. I never want to have sex with anyone again.

Yet the embrace of peace or whatever is holding me has me slipping my hand down my body, my fingers grazing over the sensitive bud.

My eyes close, allowing my trust in being alone to dare to bring me pleasure.

Somehow, I'm still floating as I circle my clit.

I gasp in a wave of arousal I haven't felt in so long, it's as if it is the first time. The vibrations become stronger, and I swear I smell a sweet musk fill the air, drenching me from head to toe as if it is bathing me.

"Oh my God," I whine, the fear of orgasming mixed with need clash together.

I fight with my nightmares at the forefront of my mind.

"You are never allowed to touch yourself. You will not

come again unless you behave. I control you now. I decide when you feel pleasure and release."

I never had pleasure with Ty. I never had release. He only cared about himself.

Grinding my teeth together, I push his voice to the back of my head, exiling his voice to the depths of all I hate.

Circling my clit faster, my lips part, and my eyes snap open to see the stars twinkling again.

I don't feel like myself. It's as if I'm possessed and someone else is making me do this.

"Ah, fuck. Oh, fuck," I whine, tilting my chin down to see myself.

There's no one else here.

It's just me.

It's me who is increasing the pace in fast, small circles.

The vibrations sink into my chest and add sensations to my clit as if I have a toy pressed against me.

"Come for me, mate. Let me see how beautiful you look when I'm wrapped around you," a voice whispers softly into my ear.

I'm not sure if it's a whisper, it blends with the sound of the water, the wind, and the reverberations that are speaking to me already. The voice is soft, deep, and eager. I want to listen to it; I want to fall over the edge.

I want to be able to trust myself again.

"You'll have so much more from me soon, My Timid Little Bloom. More than you'll ever know."

My shout echoes through the empty space of the lake. The stars above aren't the only ones I see, and desire, real unhinged arousal rolls through me like a tidal wave.

"Such a good girl trusting your instincts. You'll do best to remember them," the unknown voice growls, an invisible hand stroking the soft skin between my breasts. "And you'll tell me who did this to you. You'll tell me who harmed my mate."

I close my eyes, relishing in the fever dream my fucked-up mind created to bring me peace.

"Every single scar on you, I'll put on him. I'll hunt him. I'll kill him for you. You are mine. You'll tell me. Promise me," he demands, but the tone doesn't scare me.

It fulfills me.

"I promise," I reply in a post-orgasmic rasp, my eyes hooding with relaxation.

"You deserve to exist at the highest volume. I will make that happen."

The passing conversation doesn't feel real. It probably isn't. It's another scenario I'm making up so I'm comfortable. The invisible hold on my body disappears, reminding myself I am alone. There's no one else.

It's just me and my fucked-up mind. If this is me completely losing it, then I don't care. Peace is hard enough to come by and if this is how I need to gain it, then I will.

I flip over onto my stomach, keeping my head above the water as I take my time swimming to shore with long breaststrokes. I cut through the water, a haze in my mind that leaves me in a permanent state of wonder.

The feeling of someone watching me is still there. I ignore it, knowing it's paranoia. Alarm bells aren't ringing in my head, so that has to mean something. If this is my new life, I could really get used to it.

I deserve peace instead of losing pieces of what makes me, me.

My feet hit the ground when I'm shallow enough and I walk to the shore, my long hair sticking down my back. I squeeze the water out of it and turn around to face the lake, curious about what magic wonders it holds for me to feel so new.

I grab the towel from the bench and wrap it around my torso, tucking in the edges just above my right breast.

Magic might not exist, but something close to it does here.

I head toward my house, open the door, and pause.

I glance down, brows furrowing when I notice I'm in a towel. I'm naked. I'm wet from head to toe. I had to have gone swimming.

"Damn it," I curse, hanging my head as a headache begins to form.

I must have been sleepwalking again which hasn't happened in a few months. I turn my head to my shoulder, darting my eyes over the questionable peace, and wonder what happened while I was out there.

No memory of the last thirty minutes exists.

CHAPTER FIVE

RHETT

She has no idea it was me holding her in the water, my arms wrapped around her tight while she floated on her back. She has no idea it was me who guided her hand between her legs, needing her to feel the pleasure she ignites in me.

The ability to be invisible truly has its perks. My mate is so beautiful, but scarred, physically and mentally. I sense so much, I can taste her fear even when she's still and relaxed.

Don't get me wrong, it tastes delicious.

I couldn't wait any longer to call her to me. Now that I've finally found her after flying around for months, living off the land like a beast. My abilities were hard to understand and learn. I flew west for weeks thinking I was following her scent, when really, I got further away. I made myself land in the middle of nowhere for months to learn my new self.

My beasts were becoming impatient while I learned them, educating myself on following different scents. Time ticked by– weeks and then months passed in frustration until finally, I had perfected controlling my beasts and took off again.

I landed in the lake outside of her house, shifting into my crocodile form, and watched her.

Now that I'm here, I can't control myself. I thought I'd watch her for a while, learn her habits, but no, fuck that stupid human-like idea.

She's mine. She needs to be claimed. She needs to understand that I'll protect her in life, in death, and everything in between. Fear? I'll consume it for her to sate my violence, so she never has to experience the bitterness. Nightmares? I'll invade them and give her dreams that make her scream my name. Weakness? I'll show her how strong she is while she has me on my back.

She'll see in time that I'm the best thing for her.

I'll convince her that there isn't one single part of me that is human. Why choose a man when she can have a beast? The scars she has all over her body that I saw when I was underwater, vibrating, staring up at her back, only a man would harm such perfection.

But me?

I'll scar the man who put them on her and then I'll give her one.

Just the one.

My bite, claiming her as mine.

The thought has my cock hardening in my crocodile form, the jellyfish shaft glowing under the water.

I can't wait any longer. I need something more.

There are only a few hours of darkness left before

sunrise. Once the sun touches me, I'll turn to stone, charging my body for what comes at night. My only hope is that it is cloudy. If it is, I can walk amongst the humans, catching curious glances, but then I'll be able to keep an eye on my mate.

Maybe even speak to her.

Until then, there's something I need that only she can give me.

She tempted me by the lakeside, under the stars, where her body was a hunting ground, and I was starved for her taste.

I'll be damned if anything stops me from getting it.

My tail slices through the murky water, propelling me to the shore. I shift into my humanoid form where I stand on two legs and have two arms, but that is where the similarities end. My stone skin replaces my crocodile scales in certain areas of my body. The one thing that has actually stayed true to form is my blonde hair. It's long, past my shoulders and a few pieces glow the same neon blue as my cock.

I glance down at the water, my reflection staring back at me.

My pupils are slits, and my irises are a mossy green. My fangs seem to stay unsheathed. My ears are pointed, the skin cracked like stone that creates the most of me.

The sound of the shower turning on in the house has me spinning around and staring at the back door. Without a second thought, without thinking how wrong it is, I growl, stomping forward.

Her grass needs cutting, the deck needs to be replaced, and there's a hole in the roof. I don't like that my mate— whatever that means— is living in such an unsafe house. I know she plans on renovating, but she won't be doing it alone.

I blur up the steps and call upon the phantom living secretly in my blood, turning invisible so I can easily enter her house without disturbing the locks. Not that it would be difficult to break into this place. One firm tug and I could rip the door from its place.

The tingling sensation travels through my body as I slip through the glass door. I stop just inside, glancing around my new home for the first time. The walls are filthy. There are holes in the floor and a giant one in the roof that allows the moonlight in.

A memory has my hands twitching to begin work, to fix everything, to make this house our home.

I can do that for her, but first, I need to claim her, bind her to me for all eternity, and breed her.

We will have our kids here. All the children she wants. I'll teach them how to swim, how to shift, and how to be in this form. We will be a family.

Fuck.

I inhale her scent, my tentacles around my cock stretching and swaying to touch her. My blood burns for hers, and the ache in my fangs is nearly painful from the need to be fed by her.

Taking a step forward, I follow her scent trail, my nostrils flaring as I get closer to her door. My arms turn out toward the wall and my claws lengthen, scratching five deep grooves in my wake.

My brows pinch together when the decrepit scent of death swarms my chest. I look to the left, staring at a shut door with a crack down the middle. Curiosity beguiles me but I stop myself from entering, sliding my gaze down the hall to the bathroom door.

The hiss of the shower is still spraying and a small hum from my mate has a purr trilling in my chest.

I love her voice.

And instead of turning the doorknob to the spare room, I put the rancid scent of something decaying behind me. Her magical voice is a rope, and it wraps around me, pulling me effortlessly.

Stopping just before I step through the wood, I notice it is new unlike everything else in the house. This door is wide and instead of having a square top, it arches. My heart pounds as my body sinks into the barrier and I come out on the other side.

The air is hot, seeping into my lungs with every inhale and exhale. Steam is a dense fog. I can't see her in the shower through the cloud formation, but I do scent her shampoo and it has me reaching for my cock.

I drift forward, needing a closer look at my mate.

The shower stall is old. The door slides and is made of frosted thick plastic instead of glass, it's trimmed with more plastic dipped in gold paint. The inside of this bathroom is old, but it's clean and in working condition.

For now, that's all that matters.

The stall is big enough for both of us and I stand with my back against the wall, watching the water drip down her body. Her body is perfection, a bit too thin, which I will fix. I'll have to hunt for her and bring her fresh kills. She needs meat.

With my new view, I lean forward, narrowing my eyes as they drag down her body. I want to be able to focus on her tits, how they are the perfect handful. I want to be able to flick my tongue out to tug her cherry-colored nipple into my mouth to see if it's as sweet as it looks. I want to focus on her pretty pussy. I want to fall to my knees and bury my face in the thick, yet trimmed, hair she keeps there.

But it's the brand on her arm that has me growling, promising violence and murder.

Ty, it states in puffy, pink skin.

"Hello?" she yelps, wiping the water and soap from her face.

Mickey, the name her brother called her while insulting my gargoyle form outside, slides the stall door open.

I might kill him for that.

I haven't decided.

Mickey.

I really love that name. I've never met anyone who had it.

"Hello? Is someone there?"

I roll my lips together, keeping them pressed tight so another growl doesn't slip free. My chest feels like it will burst if I don't roar to let the entire town know I'm with my mate.

"No one is there," Mickey whispers to herself, her shoulders falling in relief, and she slides the door shut again.

My Timid Little Bloom.

Someone is here, but you do not need to be afraid of me.

You only need to fear how much I'm going to love you.

"You're safe. He isn't here. He isn't here." Her breathing changes, her eyes welling with tears. "He isn't here," she chants, the putrid scent of fear beating down my desire.

I swallow my anger, hating to see her so afraid of a man who clearly abused her, and harmed her in ways I would never do.

She presses the palms of her hands against her eyes. "You're safe. You are okay. He isn't here. He is gone. He can't hurt you anymore."

Every sentence sounds rehearsed. Like they have been said a million times.

He won't ever touch her again but everywhere she goes, I'm going to be by her side.

My mate begins to sob, the tears washing away with the water, but I know they are there. I smell the salt and all I want to do is lick them away before they fall so I can take her pain away, bathing my insides with her agony so she no longer has to feel.

Unable to stop myself, I press my hand against her chest, right where her heart beats hard and fast. She's still in panic mode.

I'll be her ghost and bring her comfort she can't see.

I rub my thumb back and forth over the scars on her chest, hoping she can feel my need to protect her, to love her, letting her know that monster will never touch her again. The scars litter her body. Some are singular, others crisscross as if he decided to play ticktacktoe.

They travel down her stomach, her legs, and even the tops of her feet.

My beasts demand vengeance.

She gasps, her breathing finally slows, and her heart rate calms. Her electric blue eyes are wide in wonderment, one last single tear breaks free from her lower lash line. Her onyx velvet hair is drenched down her shoulders and her cheeks are red from the hot water. I'm seeing her in her barest, most vulnerable moment.

And I've never seen a woman more stunning.

She tries to rest her hand on mine. Instead, her palm slips through my form, a small part of our bodies becoming one.

I lick my lips, staring at where we touch. My cock throbs to life, the tentacles dying to touch her skin.

The feel of Mickey is pure electricity and bolts dance down my shaft. If I ever had any question as to why I was created to be this monster, my answer is standing right in front of me.

"What is this?" she asks, staring at me as if she can see me.

She can't and there's a small part of me that dies because what if this is all I will ever be? What if I'll always only ever be her ghost?

A small smile tugs on the right side of her face while her fingers wiggle against mine. Maybe deep down she can feel me. She can sense that something– that I– am here.

Mickey's hand falls so she can turn around, wetting the front of her body. I hold in another snarl when I see her back. Whoever did this treated her like a fucking animal. I'm so angry for her. The need to hunt possesses me, to kill something, someone.

Him, for starters.

I let a small, quiet growl slip out on accident, and Mickey pauses, gathering her hair over her shoulder to turn her head. Her lashes are wet and long, nearly reaching the bottom of her eyebrows.

"You are losing your mind, Mickey," she mutters to herself, snagging the face wash from the built-in shelf.

If I make her lose her mind enough, having her be with me will be much simpler.

I lean back against the wall, sliding my hand down my stomach as my attention locks on to the round, plump ass she has. It's free of scars and a sick twisted urge inside me wants to change that.

Tightening my fist and imagining it's her pussy, I stroke myself. I bite my tongue to hold in a groan as I watch the water sensually drip down her body. I can see the smallest peek of her pussy from the back. I imagine myself sinking into her right now, pressing her against the wall, smashing her face against it, and slamming into her while biting the curve of her neck.

I use my other hand and wrap it around the base while the other works the top half. In tandem, I twist and tighten, fucking myself harder. With every move she makes it causes the water to slip differently down her body, and I picture that those rivers are my tongue licking every crevice.

The ribbon-like sides on my shaft are extra sensitive with every glide of my fingers bringing me closer to orgasm.

I drop my phantom form, remaining quiet on the other side of the large stall as I watch her. Staying invisible takes so much energy.

She has no idea I'm right here, I'm behind her, and I'm hers for the taking if she'd just look. Mickey remains clueless.

My gaze locks on her neck, my enhanced vision zeroing in on her pulse. A silent hiss has me flashing my fangs and my cock begins to glow that familiar neon blue it becomes when I'm about to come. Just as I'm about to launch myself at her, I call onto my ghost and shift in time for her to turn around, giving me a view of those tits.

One day, they will be full of milk, and I'll feed myself, tasting the sweet food that she gives our children.

I can't hold back– I can't– Fuck– I'm going to come.

Her eyes are still shut, and I risk snagging her body wash. I have to release my cock to unscrew the top as silently as I can, but once I have enough space, I wrap my palm around myself again, fucking my hand at a blurring rate, my vampire needing this orgasm more than blood.

Aiming my jellyfish tip into the container, I watch the vein in my cock glow blue as my orgasm inches to my slit. I sink my fangs into my arm, holding in the urge to shout Mickey's name as I pour my electrified come into her body wash.

So many thick streams settle within the greenish body wash, that I lose count. I sag against the wall in dis-appointment, wishing every drop could have gone inside her, bringing me one step closer to getting her pregnant.

I screw the top on and give it a good shake before setting it back on the shelf.

At least now she'll be bathing in me again.

Between the lake and this body wash, she'll reek of me.

Mickey reaches for her loofah, then presses down on the handle, small bolts are still firing in the soap from my orgasm. I watch intently, holding my breath to see if she's really about to wash her body when a drip down my arm catches my attention.

The skin is healed from my bite but the blood is still there, waiting to drip to the floor. I wipe it with my finger and dare to get closer to my mate. The soap suds across her chest and a sweet melon scent carries to my nose but it's my musk that lies just underneath. I grin knowing my plan is working.

Needing more because still what has happened is not enough, I wipe the simple drop of blood on her bottom lip and she flinches, licking her lips.

"What the hell?" She reaches for her mouth. "Maybe I bit my lip."

Yes, perhaps you did, My Timid Little Bloom.

I seep through the stall until I'm on the other side, missing the sight of her body already, and write a note in the condensation on the mirror for her to see. Touching solid material uses more energy than I'm used to, but I'll do it for her.

"I'm yours, and you, are mine. Forever, Mickey."

CHAPTER SIX

MICKEY

I stop and look over my shoulder when the sensation of someone watching me has my hair standing on end. It's almost like static electricity, an energy, something I can't quite put my finger on.

"You okay?" Caden asks, leaning against the side of the building on his smoke break.

The wind stirs and clouds form above, promising rain. It's wild how fast it rains here. One moment, it's sunny, the next, a wicked storm has me seeking shelter.

"I'm fine." I take another glance around the parking lot to see if there is anything out of the ordinary.

There are only vehicles parked between the lines and the smell of Caden's cigarette. The wind rustles the leaves on the low-hanging branches. Suddenly I feel pressure on my chest again just like I did when I was in the shower a few nights ago.

And I calm instantly.

"Are you sure? You look like you've seen a ghost. You can take the day off. I know you have a lot going on with the new house. We can manage this shift," he offers, flicking the cigarette on the ground before toeing the ember out.

I shake my head. "No, I need to keep busy. I'm becoming restless, and I'm starting to sleepwalk again. I think it's just the stress of not being with Milo and Minnie, you know? I'm taking on a big project. I'll be fine. I just need more of a schedule."

He narrows his gaze, debating if he believes me or not. "Sleepwalking? That must be rough."

I give him a grim smile. "Yeah, it didn't happen until..." I look down at my feet. "Doesn't matter. I need to be out of the house anyway. They are replacing the floors and getting started on the roof."

"I can't wait to see it done. It's a great piece of property. I hated seeing it go to waste."

"Did you ever know anyone who lived there?"

He opens the diner door for me, the bell jingling. "No. I'm afraid that was before my time. It's worth the love it's getting." He eyes my long-sleeved shirt and pants. "Aren't you hot?"

I'm burning up, but I will never show my scars. "No, I'm fine. It's a bit cold in the diner." I step inside and see Demi behind the hostess stand.

She grins wide and happy, genuinely glad to see me, unlike her husband, Creed. He is standing behind her protectively, growling for no other reason than to growl. He means well. I like him for her. He is a bit odd with the tattooed skin, golden eyes, and fangs, but everyone has their preferences, right? There's no judgment.

But I think there's more to him than that. I think he's a beast, not that I'd ever admit that out loud or people would think I'm mental. I'm envious of Demi. I'd rather have a beast than a man any day of the week.

"Hey girl. How are you?" Demi greets, rubbing her pregnant belly.

Storm, their son, is currently crawling all over Creed's torso and Creed isn't flinching. He's scanning the diner as if he is waiting for someone to say something about his son.

"Good. Tired." I awkwardly tuck my hair behind my ear, not really knowing what else to say. I can't remember how to be with people. I've been my own company for so long and it's an adjustment. I'm not sure if I'll ever be normal. "How about you? How are you feeling?"

She groans, tapping her stomach. "If these babies would stop using me as a punching bag, I'd feel a lot bet-ter."

Creed grins.

I think.

It's very... toothy.

"My children are strong. This is good."

Demi squints her eyes at him, her cheeks turning red with frustration. "Oh? Is it good? How about I punch you over and over in the stomach and see how you like it? Maybe then you won't be so happy." She snags Storm from his shoulder, pops him on her hip, and waddles through the dining room to her office.

"What did I do?" Creed questions, his long black claw digging into the podium. "Makes no sense."

"I swear, sometimes I think you're clueless," Jake, the sheriff of this town, says from a nearby booth.

"Sometimes I think you'd be better off dead, but here I am, not allowed to kill you," Creed sneers.

Not wanting to get in the way of two men in a pissing match, I hurry by them.

I'm not quick enough though.

Creed snags me by my wrist, his hold gentle so he doesn't hurt me, but it's enough to stop me in my tracks. I freeze. Panic grips my sight, a reaper all in itself wanting to destroy me.

"You smell weird," he blurts so loud, that everyone in the diner turns to look at me.

My face heats with embarrassment and I think about the days with Ty where I went weeks without a bath. Now, I bathe twice a day. It's impossible for me to smell bad, not between the showers, the deodorant, and the perfume.

Oh my God, what if it's the long sleeves and I'm sweating more than I think?

"Creed," Caden grumbles in a low warning. "Remember how we talked about being rude? That's rude."

"I'm not trying to be rude," he huffs. "Something is off about your scent is all. Usually, it's a bit bitter with panic and fear but now it's something else."

"Again. Rude," Caden tells him.

"You can't scent panic and fear," I say warily. "But I have been swimming in the lake behind my house, maybe that's it."

"You smell fine, Mickey. Don't let that idiot tell you otherwise." Jake tosses a few dollars on the table before standing up.

"This idiot will—" Creed is silenced by Storm smashing into his leg, wrapping his arms and legs around him like a monkey before climbing up his body. "—You better be glad my kid is here, Jake. I've had it with you."

Jake snorts, pulling his pants up by his utility belt. "I've heard that before. Demi is my friend. You hurt me, you hurt her."

"She needs better friends."

"You two bickering gives me a headache." Caden rubs his temples, a bolt of lightning crashing directly outside the diner.

I jump, startled by the loud crash.

Creed finally lets go of me, tilting his head, and his nostrils flare. He's about to ask another question when another strike of lightning flashes and screeches.

Caden's eyes glow a bright blue in the quick glow the lightning brings but just as quick as the color is there, it's gone in the next instance.

I'm losing my mind. I'm hearing voices, feeling touches, and now I'm seeing things.

That familiar touch in the middle of my chest blankets me in peace, calming me almost instantly. I don't know what it is, or why, or again, if it is all in my head.

I'm a mess inside and out, a wreckage in the middle of the sea waiting to sink to the bottom of the ocean. I'm barely treading water and everyone else around me is swimming to shore.

"You okay, Mickey?" The safe sound of my brother's voice has me nodding.

"Yeah," I croak. "Sorry. I got lost in thought. I'm fine, everyone. And Creed, I'm sorry my scent isn't to your liking."

Storm tugs on Creed's hair and the man doesn't mind one bit as he shrugs his shoulder. "I don't like how anyone smells. Only Demi."

"You're so fucking weird," the sheriff mumbles.

His radio crackles and a female voice begins to speak. "All units. All units respond. There's been a robbery—"

Jake turns his radio off so we can't hear the rest. "That's my cue. I have to go."

"Finally," Creed says clearly. "Hope to see you never."

Jake smiles, resting his hand on his gun as he heads out the door. The bell jingles and the hard pellets of rain become louder.

Crap.

If it's raining, the roof won't get done today. Hopefully, they at least put a tarp over it.

I'm left with a million thoughts running through my mind about the house, wondering if this is something I can truly do. This renovation on the house is a test. I want to prove to myself I can put in hard work and give something that's been neglected for so long, a new look.

Sighing, I tie the apron around my waist, double knotting it in the back so the ties don't come undone. Milo is behind the bar, pouring beer and making milkshakes. He's a professional at charming customers so Demi promoted him to bar manager.

Minnie does more administrative work.

Me? I wait tables and I'm just trying to figure out what the hell to do with my life. I have no idea what I'm good at or what I like to do. I'm taking it one day at a time in hopes something will spark my interest.

Honestly, the only thing I can think about is going shopping for the house. I want to dive deep into the renovations.

"Stupid Girl, you'll mess that up too."

"No, I won't," I whisper through tight teeth to Ty's voice in my head.

"No, you won't, what?"

I scream, holding my hand to my chest as I twirl around so fast, I lose my footing and begin to fall. An arm wraps around my waist, saving me from breaking my neck.

"Oh my gosh, thank you. That was a close call."

"What was?" Creed asks from the hostess stand, Storm biting onto his shoulder with his mini teeth and still, the man doesn't flinch.

"This nice person caught me from falling." I point somewhere behind me.

Creed leans back where he stands, and Storm mimics him. His son stands on his shoulders, grabs his hair as reins, and leans. Two Creeds.

The world isn't ready.

"There's no one there, Mickey. Are you sure?"

"I nearly just busted my face. Yes, I'm sure." I turn around to speak to the person who saved me, but Creed is right.

No one is there.

I spin around, looking all over the diner. There are a few couples on the far side having a late lunch but other than that, the diner is empty.

"I swear, Creed. Someone was here. I felt his arm." I touch where the man touched, my waist still warm from where we connected.

I want to feel that again. I want to feel that momentary spark. There was a quietness that took over in that split second, the same silence that enveloped me when I felt the pressure against the middle of my chest.

"Well whatever it was, it's gone. I would be able to smell anything, man or not, and nothing is there, Mickey." Creed takes out a beanie from his pocket, tugging it over his head. "No more hair tugging for you. That shit hurts, Storm." He picks up his son by the back of his shirt and carries him just like that to the office where Demi is, leaving me alone standing in the middle of the diner.

Someone was there. I'm not losing my mind. I felt him. I felt... something.

"You good?" Caden asks, walking out of the kitchen with a tray covered in freshly cooked food.

"Yeah. Fine. I think I need a cup of coffee." I run into the kitchen, away from the diner, away from people, and lean against one of the counters.

I grip it with my hands, inhaling and exhaling for a few minutes before there is a tap on my shoulder.

My hand flies to my chest and my scream is caught in my throat when I see it's Holt. "I've been scared one too many times today, Holt." I chuckle, sighing in relief when it's him.

He's a big bear of a man, but his body doesn't match his soul. He's sweet and gentle, a bit shy, and very quiet. The man does not speak.

Holt holds a coffee mug in his right hand, making the cup look miniature in his wide palm. He holds it out to me, lifting his left hand. His fingers sign two, then one.

Two creams, one sugar.

I smile at him, knowing he must have overheard what I said to Caden. I reach for the mug, the steam instantly drifting through my nose as I inhale. The delicate porcelain warms my palms, and the first sip brings me back down to earth.

"Thank you, Holt. I really appreciate you bringing me this. Is there anything I can help you with in here? I don't think I'm needed out there right now. We are slow, especially with this storm rolling through."

He nods, spins around, and gestures for me to follow him. I do gladly. There aren't many men I trust in the world and even saying I trust is a stretch, but I've never felt unsafe with Holt. My instincts don't scream at me to run away from him.

I can't be afraid forever. Living in fear won't bring me any closer to healing, it will only keep me in the dark for longer, and the loneliness it brings is cold.

He stops at the station where he usually chops all the vegetables.

I grin. "Oh, really? You never did like chopping."

He shrugs, then points to the ingredients he is putting together to make loaves of fresh bread. I love his bread. He makes French toast with it, finishing it with powdered sugar and the bread is so fluffy.

My mouth waters. I'll need to put in a request for a big plate of French toast soon.

"Okay, you have a deal, only if I'm allowed to have one more cup of coffee."

He shakes his head, mouthing the word water.

I roll my eyes. "I had a glass this morning."

He tosses the rag over his shoulder and crosses his arms, lifting a bushy brow.

"Okay—" I drawl out, beginning to chop carrots "—I had half a glass. It still counts, Holt."

He shakes his head, leaving me to my chopping so he can make the bread. Being in the kitchen and away from the noise of the main dining room is nice. Soon I'm not sure how much time I've spent chopping, as time has flown by, and I crack my neck.

My coffee is cold.

The lights above flicker as thunder rolls. The knife clatters to the counter. A tremble works its way through my body and a memory of Ty chaining me outside in the middle of a storm with my hands tied behind my back and duct tape over my mouth slams into me.

An electric current slips down my arms in a caress as if the energy is taking its time to feel me.

A shaky breath escapes me, my eyes half-hooded from the touch. The hairs on my arms stand up. I watch the hairs move from something gliding down until it interlocks between my fingers.

My throat is dry. My heart is pounding. There's a warmth spreading from my stomach to my clit, a feeling I haven't had in a very long time. I swallow, licking my lips, remaining quiet so Holt doesn't hear me.

"You're okay, My Timid Little Bloom. I'll always be with you. You don't need to ever fear anything again. You only need to be afraid of how much I want you." A masculine, rough voice whispers into my ear.

I check to see if Holt can hear the voice too, but he is kneading the dough without a care in the world.

"You're doing a good job trying to better yourself. I'm proud of you, mate."

My hand reaches for the knife on its own accord. The tip of the knife digs into the cutting board and I twirl the blade– well, I don't– this being, this energy does. I should be so fucking afraid right now, but all I feel is protected.

"There's a scar I want to get rid of– a brand–" he whispers into the lost cause of my mind *"–I don't like another*

man's claim on you when you belong to me."

My tongue is tied. There's so much I want to say.

"I don't belong to anyone." I keep my voice so quiet, hardly I can hear it. I'm paranoid and glance over at Holt again.

I begin to chop celery, not of my own doing, and a dark villainous chuckle slides down my spine

"*That is where you are wrong, Mickey. You are mine. In all my forms.*"

"How do you know my name?" Tears form in my eyes, and I don't know if it's from fear or excitement. One breaks free and something wet slides over my cheek.

"*You taste so fucking good.*"

If this is the new warden in my mind, then I suppose losing all sense has never felt so good.

CHAPTER SEVEN

RHETT

The thought of possessing her body gives me too many ideas and not enough time to act on them.

I can't seem to get close enough. I want to touch her with my own hands, not as a ghost, but as me. And I want to watch her ache for my touch.

This storm isn't helping me control my needs. The vibrations in the atmosphere from the thunder are sending my need to mate into overdrive. The heavy rain is like an aphrodisiac drug causing my blood to heat and my cock to stir.

I'm lucky she has to go into the dining room to help take orders when a rush comes in. I want to follow her, to protect her, to be by her side with every person she confronts, but I also don't want to be too much of a distraction. Not at her place of work.

I know how important a job is. That much I haven't forgotten. Not that I can ever have a normal job again. It's why I robbed a few banks to stash money away for Mickey. It's currently buried under her house in my burrow.

Being part ghost really has its advantages. Granted, I'm a criminal now instead of a man who follows the rules.

Then again, I'm not a man anymore, so those rules don't apply to me.

The lights flicker again from the storm outside and the wind whistles by the building. I grip the counter, my cock becoming so hard it hurts. The vibrations are loud in my chest and impossible to hide.

Holt darts his eyes around the room, trying to figure out where it is coming from, and I rush out of the kitchen. I'm not sure how much longer I'll be able to keep this form. Or how long I'll be able to keep myself away from Mickey like I have been.

I've seen her scars and I want to take them away only to add my own.

The clock is ticking and the urge to mate gets stronger with every passing second. She'll be lucky to make it another two days without being filled with my come.

Leaning against the wall, I cross my arms, scenting Mickey before anyone else. She has her hair up in a ponytail, with a few wild pieces hanging around her face from rushing all over the dining room. Her cheeks are flushed, and she smiles at the couple sitting in the red booth. Mickey gets out her pen and notepad to take their order.

I lick my tongue across my teeth, wanting to kill the couple smiling at my mate. Her smiles belong to me. Everything she does belongs to me.

Unwilling to be away from her for too long, I drift through the air until I'm by her side. Already, the scent of her calms me, the closeness of her body against mine soothes the fire blazing in my chest.

Not the flames burning with lust, but the ones searing with rage.

"I'll be right back with your drinks, okay?" she tells the couple in the booth.

I let her walk a few feet away before I lean over the table and snarl, "You better leave her the best fucking tip of your life. All the cash in your wallet or so help me, you won't make it to your fucking car after your meal because I'll be picking my teeth with your bones."

"What the fuck was that?" The man shouts, scooting to the corner of the booth.

I want to call him a pussy, but I wouldn't dare insult something I love to eat.

The woman has lost all the color in her face as her eyes fill with tears.

Aw, did my threat scare them?

Good.

I shove away from the table, making my way to Mickey's side again.

"Your food will be ready in a minute," she reassures the man sitting alone.

She's so sweet and good at her job.

This is why she needs me. Sweet won't pay the bills.

I watch her ponytail sway as she walks away toward the kitchen. When I'm safe, I wrap my hand around the man's throat and squeeze it, yanking him closer to me. He gasps, slamming his hands on the table. Silverware clinks and his drink sloshes over the rim of the glass.

"You'll eat everything on your plate. You won't blame the waitress if something is wrong with it. And you'll pay my mate triple your bill as a tip. If you don't, I'll follow you home and wear your skin as a suit." I shove him across the booth until his side slams against the wall.

He coughs, as he rubs his neck. I sniff the air and scoff when I smell he has pissed his pants.

Coward.

My attention is stolen when another one of her customers on the other side of the diner gets up and tosses a few bucks on the table.

Oh, fuck no.

Is this how she's been making a living? A few dollars here and there? That ends fucking today.

A tingle swims up my spine as my body passes through a few tables before I'm standing in front of him.

"She deserves more," I bark at him.

His black, wild, unkept eyebrows dance in wonderment, curious if he heard what he thought he did.

"Maybe this will help." I swipe the fork from the table and stab his hand, then cover his mouth with my free hand to hold in his scream. "I said to give her more or I'll stab every inch of you with this fork and take you to the bottom of the lake to let my fish friends feed off you."

His body trembles. His good hand reaches for the wallet in his back pocket. I snag it from him and clink my teeth together when I part the folds.

There's a few hundred dollars sitting there, and he gave my mate a few bucks? He better be glad I can't kill him in the diner.

I snag all the money from his wallet and drop it on the table.

"Are we clear?"

Sweat drips from his temple as he lets out a high-pitched– yet agreeable– hum. I jerk the fork out of his hand and then wipe the blood on a napkin.

"Apply pressure and the bleeding will stop. Unless you fuck up again," I warn, my tone lethal.

He runs out of the diner, holding his hand to his chest, mumbling something about, "This place is crazy."

And it will get crazier if people don't tip my mate more.

The bell jingles above the door and everything about the man who enters has my senses on alert. He is wearing a leather jacket that he shakes the rain from, and his hair is styled and parted with too much gel. His calculating eyes roam the room to look for an ideal seat.

"You can sit wherever, and your server will be right with you," Caden says with a smile, bringing drinks to his table.

"Thanks. Is Mickey working today?"

"She is. Her section is over there if you're wanting her."

The man gives a sly smile with a slow nod. "Thanks. I'll do that."

I don't take my eyes off him. The closer he gets to me, the more I want to kill him. I don't like that he's asking for Mickey. Not *my* Mickey. If I could, I'd rip his head off in the middle of the diner and make it a blood bath.

His boots scuff across the floor, and the chains on his pants clink together with every step. When he sits down, he places his elbows on the counter and laces his hands together. Not wanting Mickey to meet this guy, I blur over, wanting to mystify him to tell him to leave, but Mickey beats me to the punch.

"Hi, welcome to Demi's Diner. Is there anything I can get to drink for you?" she asks, tugging the sleeve of her shirt to cover her wrist.

If she only knew how beautiful her marred skin was. It proves she's a survivor and when I get the chance, I'm going to kiss, lick, and bite every scar on her body.

Then, I'm going to fuck her tight cunt to show her just how much her body turns me on.

He tosses a twenty on the table and rubs his fingers over his lips. "No, no. Actually, I heard you were working here, and I wanted to come say hi. I don't know if you remember me from high school, but I'm Stephen Rowe."

Mickey's smile fades and she takes the smallest step back. "I'm sorry, no. I don't recognize that name."

"Are you sure? I sat a few seats behind you in English. It's been years. I'd love to be able to catch up sometime. Do you have a break coming up?"

"Um." Mickey becomes flustered. Her fear is putrid. "No, I just started my shift."

Good girl, for lying.

"How did you know I worked here? No one knows," her voice trembles.

"I heard people in town talking about the diner. Your name came up because they said you were a great waitress. I didn't mean to scare you." He places his hand on his chest. "I'm sorry about that. I'll go."

"No, you don't have to. You can order."

He shakes his head and pushes himself up to stand. "Don't worry about it. We can catch up another time, Mickey. It was good seeing you. You look great," he compliments. "Here is my card. Call me when it is a good time."

Mickey takes it because she has no choice. She doesn't say yes or no but gives him a tight closed smile before tucking it into the pocket of her apron.

"See you around, Mickey."

I growl, following him outside. I stop before I get wet, but he runs to a beat-up red truck before reversing out of the parking spot. The tires squeal against the wet pavement as he speeds away, the red taillights blurring in the heavy sheets of rain.

Snarling, I seep through the entryway, not allowing the bell above to alert anyone. Mickey is still standing near the table, staring at the spot where the man was sitting.

"*Do you want me to kill him?*" I ask her, dragging my knuckles down her arm. I nuzzle her cheek, bringing my lips to her ear. "*Because I will. I'll kill him for upsetting you.*"

"No," she whispers. "He isn't worth it, but there's something about him. I know him from somewhere. I think. I don't like how he made me feel," she says.

"*Good. Listen to that. Your instincts are never wrong.*" I think I'll kill him anyway.

"Mickey?" Her brother rushes to her side. "Mick, what's wrong? Talk to me."

"I want that security system installed as soon as possible, Milo." Her eyes water and she tilts her head back, staring at the bright lights to stop herself from crying.

I press my hand against the middle of her chest, and she relaxes, shoulders dropping, lungs opening to inhale fully.

"I don't want to be afraid anymore," she admits, snagging the twenty from the table to tuck it in her apron. "I'm done."

The lights flicker again from the storm, the patrons

murmuring with concern. Thunder rolls and my eyes roll to the back of my head, my nostrils flaring.

"Get your tips and go to our apartment. Don't go back to your house. It isn't safe yet," Milo pleads. "I'll call someone to get new doors, windows, and security installed as soon as I can, but please—"

"—I won't be forced out of my house. I won't run scared. I'm tired of being afraid."

"Then I'm coming over," Milo says, yanking the towel from Mickey's hand so she can't clean anymore.

I don't want him to come over.

"Milo, you don't have to. There's nowhere for you to sleep anyway. Really, I'll be fine."

He sighs, throwing his hands on his hips. "Fine, but you'll call me with the code word if anything is wrong?"

"You'll be protected, Mickey. I won't let anything happen to you," I whisper, standing directly behind her in hopes she can feel me.

"You know I will."

Milo hugs her tight. "And what's the code word?"

She releases a wobbly breath. "Snapdragons."

"Good. Now, go home. Your shift is about over anyway. Call me when you get there."

She nods without saying anything, snagging her tips from her other tables.

And when she's ready, I follow her home, keeping my promise that nothing will happen to her as long as I'm here.

By the time we get to the cottage-style house, the

storm has strengthened and has gotten worse. The sky is marbles of clouds ranging from black, deep purple, and shades of gray. As lightning strikes, it veins through the thickening domes. A hellish view to match the sinister cravings I have for her.

She parks her car in the driveway, gripping the wheel until her knuckles turn white. We are in silence. The radio isn't on. The rain bullets against the windshield. The wipers make a small squeak with every motion.

"What happened to the gargoyle statue?" She sniffles.

"*He came to life,*" I reply knowingly, licking my fang with smug satisfaction.

"Statues can't come to life. I'm going insane." She drops her forehead against the wheel, tears dripping off her jaw and onto her pants.

A waste.

"Hearing voices can't be good. I need to see someone. I'm fucked up."

"*We're all fucked up, Mickey.*"

She hits the side of her head, wanting the voice— me— to stop.

"No, not like this. People don't have conversations with themselves like this. I have to see someone. I have to get on medication. This isn't right."

I debate on revealing myself, but I'm not sure she's ready.

Haunting her mind, body, and soul is the only option. I need her to be consumed by me, by the thought of me, so she knows that seeking help is no longer needed. She'll turn to me, the voice in the back of her head.

She'll depend on me.

And when she sees me for the first time, she'll be relieved the monster isn't her, but me.

She climbs out of the car and dashes to the door, the rain already soaking her from head to toe in the few seconds she is in the downpour. I decide to give her some space— a break from the voice driving her to the brink of madness.

An insanity that's only meant for me.

I watch my mate get inside the house and hear the door lock. Only then do I get out and blur to the back of the house, shifting into my crocodile form.

Slipping under the foundation, I crawl through my burrow, following the trail that leads to her bedroom. The dirt under my webbed feet is soft. My three-hundred-and-sixty-degree vision allows me to see everything in the damp undercarriage of the house.

A spider crawls on the ground next to me, hurrying to the web it created while I was gone today. A snake slithers in front of me, and I open my wide jaws, hissing at it to get the hell out of my way. There used to be a family of skunks that lived under here, but I got hungry.

A choice I regret because they tasted just as badly as they smelled.

My belly slides across the ground with every step I take, my long tail swishing back and forth. I hear her footsteps above me in her bedroom, but I can't see her because she replaced her floorboards.

All the holes I made are gone.

That's fine.

I flip onto my back and shift into my humanoid form, using the burrow as extra space to lie down and lengthen my claws. I wait until her feet sound on the opposite end of the house before I punch my claw through, sawing a small circle.

Peeping through the hole, I partially shift my eye into my crocodile so I can see more of the surroundings in her room. Mickey comes back and begins to undress, shucking off the wet clothes until she's in nothing but her bra and panties.

"Hmm," I growl, reaching for my cock. "Such a pretty sight. Take more off for me, come on, My Timid Little Bloom. Let me see you." I squeeze my cock, the thunderstorm outside bringing me new energy.

She pulls her tips out of her apron and tosses them on the bed. The moment of having more than usual makes her pause.

"What in the… no way." She kneels on the bed and begins to count every dollar. "Four hundred and fifty bucks? How is that possible?"

"I have more under here for us, Mickey. You never have to worry about money again," I whisper so she can't hear. "Your life will no longer be difficult."

She jumps off the bed and dances, squealing with happiness, the biggest smile I've ever seen her wear.

Somehow, that turns me on more– her happiness. I stroke myself faster, needing a quick release to take the edge off. The jellyfish head of my sack slaps against my hand with every stroke.

Mickey tucks the money under her mattress since she has nowhere else to put it. Then, she snaps her bra off, revealing her palm-sized tits. She wiggles out of her panties and tosses them my way. They are so close; I can smell that sweet pussy.

My mouth waters.

Thunder shakes the entire house, feeding my stamina,

and I nearly want to weep with the need building in my fucking bones. My marrow begins to buzz, my mind begins to haze, and I groan, my orgasm painting my stomach.

I don't know how much longer I can force myself away from her. I don't want to add to her scars, I only want to heal the ones she has so they are forgotten, and then I want to mark her.

Shifting into my crocodile after the empty, non-satisfying orgasm, I follow the trail I've made for myself and crawl out from under the house. The grass is still long and it's able to hide my form as I slip into the lake.

I spin around, watching the home for anything out of the ordinary. I'm not sure how much time has passed, but the rain stops, the clouds open to reveal the galaxy above, and Mickey walks down the steps.

Her hair is in a bun, and she has a long gray cardigan wrapped tightly around her waist. I stay exactly where I'm at as she stops on the shore, her toes wiggling in the water.

She looks relieved to be home.

I propel my tail through the water, needing to get a little closer because she smells like her body wash, and in the best way I can, I smirk in my crocodile form.

Mickey screams when she sees me, falling backward on her ass. She scurries away, locking eyes with me.

"Holy shit, that's a crocodile. Oh my God. Don't eat me."

I shake my head, sloshing water everywhere.

She nervously gets to her knees, then stands, taking another step back. "I'm not trying to force you out of your home or anything. I promise. Great, I'm talking to a reptile that can't talk back. It's official. I've lost my mind."

I swim to shore, opening my jaws before closing them again. I do my best to look non-threatening. That's hard to do in this form.

"I've never seen a crocodile up close before. You're pretty big."

I open my jaws again and slam them shut, before vibrating naturally.

"That's the sound I heard the other night. I don't re-member much after that, but I've heard this before. That's you?"

I try to nod but it just looks like I'm swinging my head up and down.

"It's crazy, but I think you might understand me." She falls to her knees and reaches for my snout. She's slow, tentative, and unsure. "Can I pet you? No, right? You'll eat my hand."

I crawl up the shore to be closer and my nose bumps her palm. She grins and her hand runs over my head, down my neck, then back up again. My eyes close as she pets me. Vibrations become louder from my chest, and she slides closer, unable to stop herself from being pulled to me.

"You're softer than I thought a crocodile would be. You're beautiful too."

I purr a little louder at the compliment.

"I doubt all are like you, right? Wouldn't most drag me in the water?"

I want to snag her by the leg and take her to my depths, bind us in the water that allows me to live.

"You'll protect me right?"

Oh, you have no idea, My Timid Little Bloom.

No idea

CHAPTER EIGHT

MICKEY

"I want to open the kitchen up," I tell Milo, using the sledgehammer as a cane to lean against it. I'm not too sure if I can even pick it up, but I sure do look like I mean business with it by my side. "I'm thinking we knock down this wall." I show him with my hands, waving them in front of the wall in hopes that it paints him a picture of what I want.

The roofers above look down from the hole in my damn roof. "You're going to need to check that the wall isn't—"

"—Isn't load bearing." I roll my eyes when men try to explain something to me. I'm so sick of them. "I know."

The one peeking his head through the hole grins, and he takes off his hat. "Well then, a lady who knows a way to my heart. You want to maybe go out sometime?"

He isn't a bad-looking guy but every part of my body revolts at the thought of going out with him.

"I appreciate the offer, but no thank you, respectfully. I just don't want to date anyone." I grip Milo's arm, hoping this guy doesn't get angry from my rejection. My hand tightens around the handle of the sledgehammer, preparing myself to swing it if necessary.

"No problem. I understand. I had to try, right? I can check to make sure you don't need that wall if you like. No pressure," he adds.

"Thank you, but I'll figure it out." There's a small amount of defiance growing. I could take his help, but I don't want to. I'd rather pour myself into books and online searches. Maybe it's pride, but I want to prove I don't need his help.

I can do this.

Any man be damned.

"Sure, no problem. I respect a strong woman. I like it. You sure you don't want to go out to dinner?" he jokes, giving me a wink. "I'm kidding. If you need anything just holler at us up here. We'll be another day or so, maybe. I think we will need to replace some structural beams."

"I figured," I sigh tiredly, imagining the money vanishing from my comfortable bank account thanks to my parents wanting to take care of us after they died. "Do what you have to do. I want this house to be my forever home."

"You got it."

"Okay, let's check to see which way the joists run," I instruct Milo.

He lifts his brows, "Joists? Someone has been doing their homework."

"The house won't renovate itself." I shrug. "It's best I know what to do."

"I'm proud of you." Milo glances out the kitchen window, scowling. "I thought you got rid of that ugly statue."

"It's back?" I sprint to the front door and rip it open, grinning when a menacing gargoyle is snarling, reaching toward me with one hand as if he was trying to snatch me off the ground.

I wish.

Stepping over power tools, my strides are long and determined. I stand in front of the statue, press my hand into its palm, and skim my fingers down his arm, across his chest, and hold my hand there– because I swear– there is a small, slow beat.

All the wishing in the world wouldn't make this statue real.

"I can't believe you like that thing, but whatever makes you happy."

"I feel safer knowing it's here. I don't know why. Whoever took him before, I'm glad they brought him back." I turn around, pressing my back against its chest, cover my eyes to block the sun, and shout to the workers. "Hey! I just wanted to say to please be careful. This statue is important!"

"You got it!"

"No problem, lady!"

"Will do."

All the roofers sound off without a care in the world. The longer I stay outside, the warmth of the sun bearing down on my shoulders, the more I want to stay right here– in the embrace of a creature that can't hurt me.

I'm surrounded by men and I'm doing everything I can to remain calm.

"Come on, this wall isn't going to tear itself down," Milo shouts from inside the house.

I force myself away from the statue, a piece of my soul being carved out and left behind for reasons I don't understand. Am I so broken, so fucked up, that the only thing I could want in this world is a statue made of stone?

"While you were making googly eyes at the statue, I made sure to check that this wall—" Milo pats it, and a piece of grime flops onto the floor "—Isn't load bearing." He grabs the handle of the sledgehammer leaning against the wall and hands it to me. "Ready to obliterate it?" He knocks on the wall with his index and middle knuckles.

I reach for it only to freeze when I feel a rush of warmth between my legs, wetting my panties.

Oh, no.

I'm early.

"I need to use the restroom. I'll be back. Don't get started without me." I point at him, slowly backing away.

"You okay?"

I nod, not wanting to give away personal information. Milo is used to it, but I don't want anyone to overhear I'm on my period.

"I'll rip out the cabinets then while I wait."

"I'll just be a few minutes." I spin on my heels and charge down the hallway, flinging the spare bedroom door open to grab a new pair of panties. Tucking them in my back pocket so no one can see, I dash to the only working bathroom in the house and lock the door.

Rustling through the cabinets under the sink, I grab a tampon from out of the box and groan at the thought of renovating the house over the next week. It's going to be exhausting. Starting tomorrow, I'm going to want to bury myself in the cloud of my comforter, watch reruns of my favorite shows, and eat junk food.

Maybe even cry a little for no reason other than because I fucking feel like it.

"Damn it," I curse when I see the red covering the middle part of my panties. Usually, I would wash them, but I don't have a washer and dryer hooked up yet, so I have to take all my laundry to the laundry mat or my siblings' apartment.

I roll them up and stuff them in the garbage before sliding in a tampon and slipping on a fresh pair of underwear to get on with my day.

"This shit is so overrated, I swear," I grumble, already annoyed that I'm bleeding and it's only day one.

When I'm done, I wash my hands, dry them, and head toward Milo. I hear him ripping the cabinets apart followed by the splintering of wood and a few curses.

I stop in the middle of the hallway noticing deep grooves carved in the walls. I bend down, tracing the five scratch marks. "What could have done this?" I whisper curiously, placing each of my fingers on a mark, and then dragging them down each line.

With every small divot I graze, the tips of my fingers tingle. Sparks travel up my veins, spreading through my arms. My chin nearly hits my shoulder to study the other wall. I stand in the middle of the hall, stretch out my arms, and follow the scratches with my fingers while I walk.

They stop at the very end where the hallway opens to the living room.

I brainstorm what could have caused this. Was it recent? I don't remember those marks being there. The gargoyle statue staring at me through the glass panel on the front door could have done it— if something like that could come to life.

I scratch the side of my head and sigh at the ridiculous thought. I can't say that out loud, or else my brother will think I have lost my mind, and he would not let me live alone.

The inside of the house darkens, and the bowling of thunder clashes, yanking me out of my wandering thoughts. There is work that needs to be done! How can it be raining, again?

"Oh, no, no, no!" I run to the back door and slide it open, watching as black clouds burden my day. Rain doesn't mist or sprinkle but pours. "Damn it. I've never seen a town get so much rain before. At this rate, the roof will never get done," I complain to no one, wanting just a small pity party for myself.

I stare at the lake, entranced as the water becomes bothered by the immense force of rain falling into it. Small waves form from every drop, never-ending ripples as far as the eye can see.

"That's okay," Milo says. "We can still work inside. The roof is covered with a tarp so now you don't need to keep a bucket in your living room where that hole is."

"Best to keep it there. You never know," I mutter, a cramp working its way across my stomach.

"You okay?"

I nod, a wave of exhaustion hitting me, but I won't let it win before I demolish that wall. "Let's get to work."

He scoffs, chugging a bottle of water. "I've been working, you slacker."

I shove him out of the way, leaving the door open so I can feel the breeze. The sound of the thunderstorm doesn't scare me as much when Milo is here. Ty loved to take advantage of the storms.

The lightning and the wails of the wind would cover my screams.

I don't want to be afraid anymore. Fear won't allow my life to grow. The shadows are a cold place to be when you're forced into them, now, I don't know how to escape.

I'm in survival mode and the last thing I want to do is die without realizing I didn't need to hide myself away in the dark when my villain is dead.

I let out a shaky breath, I slowly wrap my fingers around the sledgehammer and grip it tight. My jaw clenches imagining Ty at the other end of this weapon. Flashes of me beating him with swing after swing fills my heart with too much satisfaction.

"Looks like one of the roofers took your statue. Ugly beast is gone."

Milo's words take the wind from my sails and the satisfaction of killing Ty for a second time is gone.

"*I'm right here*," a deep voice whispers from the inside of my mind. "*No one will ever take me away from you.*"

I try to pick up the sledgehammer, but I drop it, the floor shaking under my feet when it hits the ground.

Milo tosses the water bottle on the ground and dashes to me, trying to take the sledgehammer from me. "Are you insane? I didn't expect you to do this by yourself. I was going to help you swing it. You aren't–"

"–I'm not what?" I narrow my eyes at him, my grip even tighter around the handle.

"You aren't physically strong enough yet. I know you will be. But you're still recovering."

I slap his hand away, slighted at how he could hit me so low. "Excuse me?"

"That's not what I meant. I don't want you to hurt yourself. Mickey, you're still gaining weight. You're still healing. You're going to throw all that away? For what? For a wall?"

"It isn't just a wall!" I scream at him. "This house isn't just a house. This is my chance to start over. It isn't about renovating, it's...it's..." My eyes fill with tears and my breaths are ragged. "It's about me. This is my beginning. This is *my* renovation."

"You're renovating yourself," Milo says softly, his eyes crinkling at the sides with understanding and compassion.

"That wall will come down because I want it to."

"I can help you. Let me give you my strength, My Timid Little Bloom. Let me give you the power to annihilate anything and anyone you want."

The welcoming, soul-soothing voice has been missed today. I've been wondering where he has been.

"I can do it, Milo. I'm stronger than you think I am. Okay?" I tell the unknown stranger living inside my head. "I'm ready. I can do this."

"Good girl letting me inside you."

I want to know what his name is and what he wants with me, but I can't have a conversation with a ghost if my brother is around.

A warm, electrified cloak engulfs me from head to toe. A surge builds. My thoughts are blank, my tongue feels as though it is being licked from the inside, and arousal pools between my legs.

"Oh, I knew you'd feel good. Fuck, the things I want you to force yourself to do. Surrender yourself to me, Mickey."

My hand wraps around the sledgehammer again, but

there's something else, a hue around my fingers that I can barely see. A faint sheer hand plays in my vision.

And if I'm seeing what I think I am, the hand has long white claws and bumpy greenish-black skin that reminds me of a crocodile. The scales fade to gray where the color cracks in certain places.

Now, I'm hallucinating.

As the fingers wrap around mine, the strength of my grip is tighter.

"*Ready to demolish your pain with me?*" The phantom in my villainous mind asks, a proposal too sweet to say no to.

I'm falling in love with the safety and comfort a voice brings. I'd rather spend the rest of my life loving what I can't see, than experiencing the pain of what happens when I can.

The sharp inhale freezes midway to my lungs. The left arm of this delusion engulfs me, and the bicep bulges, nearly curling around my neck while reaching for the sledgehammer. I've never felt so infinitesimal before. This gentle giant curls his monsteresque fingers around mine until we are holding the weapon of destruction with all four hands.

I want to turn around and look up to see how tall my hallucination is, but if I do, my brother will know something is going on. I can't give him any reason to think that I can't live on my own.

I'm curious to know the face of my invader. If he has one. Would my mind think of someone new or would Ty's face be there to haunt me?

"*Trust me.*" The illusion of lips brushes my ear. "*I forgot to say, you smell fucking delicious today. You just wait until you're asleep. You just wait until I can have my way with you.*"

I'm still not able to imagine what my dreams will consist of. A strong buzz similar to a lightbulb humming is all that I hear in my mind. It's relaxing and I lean into it, hoping this visitant can take the weight off my bones.

They have been broken.

They have been bruised.

They have healed.

But they will never be as strong as they once were.

"*They will be even stronger,*" he growls, helping me swing the sledgehammer through the air.

He can hear me?

"*Everything you see. Everything you feel. It is mine.*"

"Yeah, there you go, Mick!" Milo cheers me on with a big smile on his face. I haven't seen him look so proud of me in such a long time.

"*I'll kill the man that made your inside webs, forcing your pain to stick and tangle.*"

Swing.

"*He's dead. I killed him,*" I reply in my head, talking to myself.

Swing.

"*Then I will dig up his bones and turn them to dust.*"

Swing.

"*I will desecrate his grave so he can no longer rest in peace.*"

Swing.

"*I will find his soul in Hell and ask the Devil himself to let me tear it to pieces.*"

Swing.

"*I will make his afterlife a curse.*"

Swing.

Tears form in my eyes, and I scream at the top of my lungs, letting out all the anger that has consumed me, the guilt, the regret, and the sadness.

"*I will make him beg for his spirit to be nonexistent.*"

Swing.

I sob, nearly dropping the sledgehammer, but the figment of my imagination is there to lift it, helping me squeeze it tighter. He isn't allowing me to let go.

"*I vow to be his death, his destruction, and his damnation. In this life and after.*"

Swing.

"*I vow to inherit all your good and make him insufferable.*"

Swing.

"*I vow to love you when you hate yourself.*"

"*I vow to protect you when the light of day and the dark of night become your enemy.*"

"*I will succumb to you.*"

And then he is gone, leaving me to gasp for air through a cascade of tears, a hurricane he created with his words. The sledgehammer falls from my grasp, and it slams against the new floors.

My knees buckle, but Milo is there, and he catches me. His arms wrap around my back and instead of holding me up on my feet, he takes us down to our knees.

"I got you. You did good, Mick. You did good." His hand cups the back of my head, and his other arm wraps around my waist to hold me against his chest.

I sob harder than I ever have, the loud, gut-wrenching wails that prove just how damaged someone's soul is. I struggle to breathe.

"I hate him," I cry, curling my fingers into Milo's shirt. "I hate him so much." The words are broken and drawn out with every wail.

Sweat drenches my body from bringing down the wall. My palms hurt from holding onto the handle. The release of agony from the depths of my bones is what is most debilitating.

"I know. I hate him too. I hate him so much."

I squeeze my eyes shut, allowing the tears to wet his shirt. "Snapdragons," I croak through my tears.

"No. None of that. Not anymore." Milo leans away and wipes my cheeks. "I will always be there when you say the codeword, but not now. Look what you did." He turns my chin to where the wall used to be. "You did that. You tore it down. Your pain is in ruins and your do-over starts now. Do you hear me, Mickey? There is nothing you can't do. Don't let him ever stop you from doing anything, even crying, even screaming. You let it out, but you let your laughter and happiness be the loudest so that son of a bitch can hear you from Hell."

Maybe what I saw wrap around me earlier was my own version of snapdragons. Instead of something beautiful, I conjured up a being that reminded me of what the snapdragon flower looks like once it's died.

A beast, waiting until the beauty dies to be shown.

CHAPTER NINE

RHETT

Staying in ghost form for long periods of time, especially when I'm sharing my energy with a solid human body, is hard. I feel the moment my charge to keep the form is gone from helping her swing the sledgehammer into the wall. The sun helps me charge all my forms when I'm turned to stone, but with all the rain recently, I haven't been able to soak in the heat.

It's how I find myself on the shore of the lake in my humanoid form, unable to call upon my ghost. I dive into the water and shift into my crocodile to get away from Mickey's pain-filled wails.

They are tearing me apart inside. I hurt for her, but I am also furious for her. If the man who harmed her wasn't dead, I would kill him so slowly, he'd plead for me to take his life quickly.

I want to know his name. I'm determined to have Mickey forget him and the only name she will remember from here on out is mine.

Once I tell her.

I morph into my humanoid form, treading the water to keep myself afloat. Lifting my hands, I flip them over, studying the dark scales and long claws. How will she react when it's hands like this touching her?

My wings act as ores, slowly rowing me through the water. My hands fold over my stomach and I'm left looking at the cloudy sky. Rain patters against my stone chest, soaking into the cracks to revitalize my body.

Once I feel like I'm charged enough, either by sun or water, I'll go back to the house.

I'm not sure how long I float, but I've managed to find myself in the middle of the lake, her house barely in sight. The lights are on and from here, they remind me of a candle wick flickering as it burns.

Flipping to my stomach, I dive under, swimming toward the bottom of the dark blue water. I pass a few fish that zoom away from me, recognizing that I'm a predator. My toes sink into the heavy sand, brushing over small rocks. When my feet are flat, my wings spread wide just as the moonlight breaks in the clouds for a moment and penetrates the abyss of the lake.

Stretching out my arms, the crocodile skin fades and gray replaces it. My forearms become larger, and my fingers lengthen, the claws curl and become sharper, my feet widen, and my gargoyle bursts free.

I crouch, then launch myself through the water. I break the surface, draping my wings down my back. The air whooshes by my ears, drying me instantly. Just as I lose momentum, I spread my wings, flying as close to the stars as I can get.

I'm angry that I can't steal one and give it to Mickey. The sky can be so selfish. All I want to do is hand her a star to prove I can feel her light anywhere, no matter how near or far I am.

Taking a hard left, I glide through the night in the direction of Mickey's home. I circle the perimeter, checking for any threats.

It's clear.

For now.

The man at the diner is someone I won't forget. As my eyes scan her property, it is his face I am looking for.

My stomach grumbles, reminding me I haven't eaten, so I cut through the nearby forest and land on a tree branch thick enough to hold my weight. My claws sink into the bark. Patience is not my strongest quality. I just want to break into my mate's house and watch her sleep.

Is that too much to ask for?

The sound of leaves rustling to my right makes me turn my head in time to see a deer step into the clearing. My night vision is crystal clear compared to the daytime. I'm able to see the deer's every move. It lifts its head, chewing annoyingly loud, and I decide to make a little noise.

I feel like a chase tonight.

I snarl long and deep, leaning forward. My claws dig into the tree to hold my body up. The deer's tail lifts, signaling danger before bolting through the woods.

"Finally." I leap from the branch, flying over and under other tree branches.

The deer jumps over a fallen log, and I snatch it mid-air by wrapping my arms around its throat, putting it out of its misery fast and painlessly with a loud snap of its neck. I might be a monster, but pointless suffering isn't necessary unless you're a bad person.

I eat what I can, clutch onto the carcass, then fly over the treetops to Mickey's house. Bringing her food is important. She needs to eat more. I will provide it. She will never go hungry again.

I hover just above the deck and drop the deer with an unpleasant thud. I hurry to the long grass to cover myself, but my foot somehow gets caught on my wings with my panic. I tumble forward, somersaulting twice before landing on my stomach, my face smacking against the ground.

I grumble, fisting the dirt in my claws, and shake my head to get the ringing to stop. There's dirt in my mouth which only adds to my murderous emotions. I spit it out, the tips of my damp hair dragging through the soil.

Now I'm dirty and will have to bathe before I see Mickey tonight.

"Hello?"

Her sweet voice cuts through the annoyance and I spin around, staying crouched so she can't see me. Mickey looks down and screams, covering her mouth with her hands when she sees the deer.

My smile fades and I scratch the side of my head with my claw. This isn't the reaction I was expecting. The deer is a gift. I can't remember food as a human. Is this not sufficient?

"Who did this? Who left this here?"

"What is wrong?"

I bite the air, wishing her brother's throat was close enough to rip out to silence him. What's he still doing here?

"Someone left a dead animal here. What if... What if..."

"No, don't go there. This isn't Ty's style and remember, he's dead."

I flinch being compared to him. He would never give her a fresh kill. I'm already so much better than him.

"An animal probably dropped it off. Think of it as a gift."

That's the smartest thing I've ever heard him say. Maybe I won't kill him after all. The decision is still up in the air.

Mickey sighs, crossing her arms. "I would hate for it to go to waste. Maybe I'll take it to the lake."

"Let me get changed and I'll help."

"No, it's okay, Milo. I can do it. You go to sleep. I'll just tie some rope around its legs, try not to cry, and not look at it in its cute face."

So my mate has a soft spot for animals. That makes my gift-giving a little trickier unless I keep them alive and give them to her as pets.

Yes, yes, that. I bet she would love a bear cub— something soft and cuddly. No, actually. I don't like that idea. It would want her time, invade her space, and take all attention away from me.

Never mind.

I'll be her pet.

"Mickey, let me do this."

"No, Milo. If you weren't here, I'd have to do it. I want to do it."

He backs away and gives a timid nod. "Okay. Let me know if you need me."

That's my cue. I shift into my crocodile and scurry to the lake, gliding into the water before she can see me. I'm not ready for her questions when I barely have answers.

Poking my head above water from a close distance, watching her tie rope around two legs, tie a knot, and begin to pull with her back toward the deer and the rope over her shoulder.

"I'm so sorry," she apologizes to the dead deer. "I don't know what else to do. I feel so bad. I can't leave you here, though. I appreciate your sacrifice. You'll feed plenty of fish, maybe even a crocodile. Don't ask me why a crocodile is in the lake. I have no idea, but you'll feed him, and that's good."

My mate is cute trying to reason death to a deer.

Mickey pulls and grunts, exerting herself when she doesn't need to. By the time she gets to the shore, she's exhausted, gasping for breath with her hands on her hips. Even from here, I can see the sheen of sweat glistening on her forehead.

I'd love to taste it.

She unwraps the rope and drops her fingers down into the water, splashing her fingers on the surface. "Here crocodile, crocodile, crocodile," my mate calls, ending with a whistle as if I'm some cat or dog.

I'll let it go because how else do you call a wild animal?

I slither through the water like a snake and when Mickey's bright blue eyes see me, her smile lights up her entire face.

"Hey, so I have a gift for you. I don't know if you want it." She takes a step to the right to show me the deer. "Ta-da." She stretches out her arms, wiggling her fingers happily. "It was on my deck, and I can't eat it, so please, it's all yours."

I come closer, the scent of the deer's blood making

my eyes roll, but there's something else. Someone else's blood.

Hers.

My claws drag the sand when I reach shallow waters. Her blood is a beacon to the vampire lurking in my DNA.

I'm suddenly very thirsty and yet, I can't tell where she is bleeding from. I roam my gaze over her, checking for any cuts. She squats, causing her legs to spread, and her aroma hits.

I purr, my cock becoming hard in this form.

"Okay, well, I'll see you later. Enjoy." She gives my snout a pat before standing, giving the deer a wide berth, shivering in disgust.

When she's gone and the door is shut, I snap my jaws around the neck and pull the deer in the water, giving it a few death rolls for the fun of it to subdue my prey— even though it is already dead. I have to get my kicks where I can. I take the deer deep, placing it in a thick brush to hold it there for me to come back to later.

The early night passes and the lights in Mickey's house are off. I crawl out of the water, shifting into my humanoid form seamlessly. Water drips off me, forming muddy puddles at my feet. The grass helps wipe the dirt clean and when I'm close enough, I jump onto her porch, crouching on the rail. I listen for noise, for any type of voice or heartbeat.

Silence.

Milo, her brother, is on a new couch that wasn't there yesterday. I can see him through the glass. I'm careful not to wake him as I slip through the door. One quick smother of a pillow and he'd be dead.

But then Mickey would be sad, and I don't want that.

"You live another day," I mumble, staring at him longer than I intend to.

He's cuddling a pillow, holding it tight like a person would another. Not wanting to waste any more time on him, I yank the blanket from his body, so he is cold and stroll down the hallway.

Her scent causes me to stop in my tracks outside the bathroom. The light is off, and the door is open, so she isn't there. I'm unable to keep my phantom form, the aroma is too strong. I'm not able to focus. Before I can think better of it, my plan changes and I've locked myself in the bathroom. Vibrations tremble my bones and I try to stay quiet, but a growl slips through my lips. The scent of her blood has me sniffing the air, my beasts going berserk. I follow the trail, kneeling on the hardwood floor until I'm staring at a trashcan.

I grip the bin, the plastic creaking in my hold. My muscles tremble as I try to remain calm. I bury my nose in the trash, groaning from the pheromones. My tentacles whip around the base of my cock, stinging the inside of my legs. My dick hardens, the tip leaking precome. A thick drop slides down my shaft and I stop it with my claw. I suck it into my mouth, knowing after tonight, being a ghost by her side won't be enough.

I pick up an item wrapped in toilet paper and unwrap it, my mouth watering when a blood-soaked tampon is revealed. My heavy, erect cock jerks from the sight.

Unable to stop myself, I suck the ruined cotton into my mouth. Her blood soaks my tongue and I whimper, falling onto my back. I bite into the tampon, sucking hard to get every drop out. The red fluid is like the finest liquor, drugging me, changing my fucking DNA all over again.

I'll never want to eat anything else again. Only her. Only her blood.

My tongue wraps around the spread material, licking down the seam. I imagine it's her cunt, bleeding, inviting me to feast and worship the sacrifice her body gives.

"Fuck." I stroke myself faster, my tentacles stinging my stomach. "Fuck, fuck, you taste so good, mate. I want your blood from the source. I want it fresh. This isn't enough." I sound like a madman desperate for more, but more will never be enough.

Even if I bleed her dry, I'll lick the inside of her skin to gather every drop.

I toss the tampon to the side and get onto my knees, rummaging through the trash for more. I find another and I could weep with relief while unwrapping it as if it is a present.

I'm a sick fuck.

I run my nose across the tampon, inhaling until my lungs can no longer expand. My entire body shakes. There is no fixing this side of me now.

She is doomed to be consumed by me.

The moment I suck the tampon into my mouth, I stumble backward. The corner of the counter digs into my back. I fuck my fist faster, hissing through my fangs. I rub the tampon over my lips, coating my mouth in her blood. I gasp for breath. Sweat beads at the base of my neck. My wings knock over the insignificant objects on the sink that are in my way.

My cock glows, and the jellyfish head covering my sack pulsates blue. My tentacles strike me harder, adding a bit of pain to my pleasure. I fucking love it.

I slide to the floor, my mind lost to bloodlust.

My reptilian eyes shift to the color red, the sharp tip of my fangs ripping into the cotton.

"Mmm, fuck, Mickey. I can taste your pretty little cunt too. So sweet." I'm not able to taste her blood though. I pull the tampon out and toss it, heading to the trashcan again. I dig through it, hoping for another.

Just one more.

I snarl, wanting to kill someone when I don't see another. I need more. I need her. Snatching the trashcan, I empty all the contents onto the ground.

There's one.

Just one left.

I shred the toilet paper with my claws surrounding my snack. Is this what my life has come to? Hiding away in a dark bathroom, stealing my mate's tampons just to taste her because deep down I know she will never accept me as... *this.*

A monster.

A deviant beast who wants her to sit on my face while she's on her period so I can taste her and have the warmth of the blood slide down my throat. The image has my orgasm right at the surface. My entire body buzzes, the tentacles dancing faster, stinging me harder, and I bite into the tampon, a gush of blood soaking my taste buds.

Needing my come to be saved, to be on her, so she always smells claimed, I let go of my cock for a second to open the cabinets, uncaring of how loud I am. The door on the left smacks against the wall.

I'm desperate. If Milo walks in here, I will kill him. I'll rip him to pieces for stopping me, for interrupting my process to make Mickey mine.

Something square and in a pink wrapper catches my eye next to the box of tampons. I unfold it, peeling the small piece of tape back to reveal a pad. It soaks blood too.

An idea forms.

A sick, demented idea that only makes me realize it isn't enough.

I unfold six pads, lying them flat and still safe in the wrapper. Kneeling, I fall forward on one hand, chewing the last tampon to gather every single drop of blood while stroking my cock. I peer down under me, the pads in my line of sight, and thrust my hips.

My long, thick, shaft slides effortlessly in the tight squeeze of my palm.

"Mickey. Mickey," I moan, spitting out the tampon as my orgasm ignites my blood.

Stream after stream soaks the pads. I aim in different directions, sending my come over each and every one of them. When she puts them on, she'll have no idea I'll be right there, marking my fucking territory.

My entire body shakes when the last drop of my orgasm falls from my slit. My claws dig into the floor, raking across the new hardwood she just put in as I try to control the burning need to head into her room and fuck her.

My chest rises and falls in unashamed rhythm while I attempt to catch my breath.

I fail.

Because even from here with the door shut, I can smell her in the other room.

I fold the pads and put them where they belong under the sink. They don't seem like they have been tampered with to me.

Smirking, I clean up the mess I made and toss everything I took out of the trash back in the bin, then notice a pair of panties.

I unravel them, simple and light pink, but it's the middle that cups her pussy that makes me hard again.

The small pair of panties are stained red, still wet with blood, and I suck the material into my mouth. I fall forward, catching myself on the wall with one hand.

A knock on the door sounds. "Mickey? You okay? I think I'm hearing groaning." The annoying protective brother with good intentions yawns, knocking softly again.

Not wanting to get rid of the underwear, I tie them around my wrist, the middle seam turned out so I can smell her anytime I want.

I drift into my ghost, unlock the door, and breeze through him.

"Woah, what the fuck?" He touches his chest, then pats his arms and legs. "I feel like I just walked into a spiderweb. I am not awake enough for this." He flips on the light in the bathroom and checks his hair for the eight-legged mini villains. Milo spins in circles, checking every inch of his body for the arachnid.

Well, at least he is occupied.

I leave him to his own peril, following the delicious scent of my Beloved's blood. I lick my lips, the taste of her dancing tangos on my tongue. I want more. My hunger has turned into starvation since the first taste. My stomach is an everlasting abyss for her blood, my veins flowing with her precious nectar, and my soul is being fed by her unknowingly.

Milo grumbles behind me, dragging his feet by the sound of it to head back to the couch, finally leaving me alone. I stop just outside her door, inhaling deeply and allowing her scent to stick to my lungs so it never fades.

"Oh, you smell so good," I groan, unable to hold myself back any longer.

I push forward, vanishing through the door until I'm in her room. My night vision allows me to see everything or everything she doesn't have as of yet. This room is not big enough for the two of us, but that's an issue for another time. My Beloved is currently on a small bed. There's no frame. It's just a mattress on the floor and calling it a bed is generous.

She deserves more.

I'm going to give her everything and she's going to wonder who would provide such luxuries for her. She'll be so confused but I'll watch the weight of the world lift from her shoulders as she experiences peace.

"No," she mumbles. "No!" Her arms lift in a defensive gesture, blocking someone. "Get off me. No. No." She begins to cry. "Stop. Stop!" Her voice becomes louder. "Snapdragons. Snapdragons!" She screams the codeword her brother spoke about earlier.

I crawl over her body, my invisible knuckles grazing her face. "You're okay, Mickey. You aren't with him anymore. You're safe with me." My jaw becomes tight when a tear breaks free from her distressed face.

I hate that he makes her cry when he isn't even alive to haunt her.

Good because that position is filled.

Her face relaxes when she feels me, a small smile playing on her dollish lips. Her lashes flutter shadows over her cheeks. She tugs the blanket to her chin and a long relaxing breath has her sinking further into the pillow.

"Such a good girl," I praise, clutching the blanket in my hand. "But you don't need this right now." I tug the blanket free, hoping it will expose her beautiful body. I tsk when I see she's wearing matching pajamas. The top buttons up and is long sleeve and instead of shorts, there are pants.

I growl from the unpleasant sight. "This will not work for me." With my index claws, I start at her waistband and cut down, the material ripping a small whisper in the room.

Her pants are in ruins, and I'm stunned by the view of a lifetime, a sight men wish and dream to see before they die. No man will ever have this view again, not as long as I am alive and breathing.

"This body—" I place my right hand on her ankle "This art of survival—" I lay my left hand on her left thigh "Belongs to me." I glide my palms up and down the smooth flesh, the bumps of the scars slide against the crocodile scales that make my hands.

Just for a few minutes, I allow my ghost form to fall so I can see what my skin looks like against hers. My claws glide down her legs, the skin dipping from the slight pressure.

The ugly crocodile scales against her beautiful human form leaves me unsettled.

"It's such a shame a beautiful woman like you has to be meant for a monster like me." I spread her legs with my knee, my tail slithering up her thigh. My tail looks like stone, but it is smooth like the crocodile scales so I can't hurt her, not that I'd ever want to.

I'd rather spend all my remaining eternities in stone than ever make her cry a single tear.

The tip of my tail slips under her panties and my entire core vibrates as a new thunderstorm flashes in the sky outside her window.

"I can't wait anymore, Mickey. You'll understand one day. You'll understand my need for you." I slide my tail up and down the seam of her cunt, teasing her and myself.

I want to know what I can get away with before having to be invisible.

With one claw, I slash her panties until they are nothing but shredded cotton on the bed. Her trimmed pubic hair feels good against my tail. Every stroke against the soft bush causes my cock to slowly drip precome from an orgasm that seems to be stuck mid-shaft.

It feels so good like fire is burning me from the inside out. Desire is its own animal right now, forcing the tip to slide across my stomach. Sticky residue is left behind and a soft buzz of electricity tickles my abdomen where the come is.

"Mmm," she whimpers the quicker I stroke her pussy.

My tail shines with her pleasure, the wet sounds becoming louder with every passing caress. She spreads her legs unknowingly, allowing me more access, and giving me a view of the pretty pink lips I can't wait to kiss. She's glistening with need.

"Look at you," I purr, biting my bottom lip as I roll over her clit.

She gasps, moaning in her sleep.

How long before I wake her up? How long before she realizes I'm not a dream?

I bring my tail to my mouth and lick her juice from it. I pierce my own lips, sucking the appendage clean. As I stroke it with my tongue, I wrap my hand around my cock, my eyes hooding from how good it feels.

I lower myself between her legs, gliding my tail under her shirt. The very tip plays with her nipple and her lips part, a sleepy erotic exhale falling from that pouty mouth.

My eyes shut as I press my nose against her cunt, inhaling her natural scent mixed with blood. My tongue slides out and I lick down the middle of her pussy while flicking her nipple. Her hands fist the sheets as she gets lost in her dream.

There's so much I want to do to her tonight, so much I want to say, and I already know where I want to start.

The strength of my tail rips the buttons from her shirt forcing the material to part enough for me to see her breasts. With every stroke of my tail against her tightened nipples, she moans, her chest rising and falling to catch her breath.

I morph into my ghost, not wanting to chance being seen. My tail caresses down her body, wraps around her thigh, and helps me spread her legs wider. Her body arches, her hands clasping at the sheets, she's moaning, and I haven't really touched her yet.

"You have something I want, Mickey." I slip my finger over her lips before circling her clit.

"Oh," she moans, turning her head to bury her cheek against the pillow.

"That's right," I croon. "I'm going to make you feel so fucking good that you'll always call upon the voice in your head to come fuck you." I slip my finger inside her, unable to get far when I notice a barrier in my way.

It's soft like silicone and I tug the skinny end, slowly removing the item. I'm careful, doing my best not to wake her, but I know that will be hard considering what I'm doing.

To my shock, it isn't a tampon, but a small cup, and when I have it free, she rubs her legs together, her eyes opening to see what's going on. Mickey can't see in the dark.

"Hmm," she hums before easily falling back asleep.

The cup is full of blood. My fingers are tinted with red. This is even better. It saves the blood. I'll have to always convince her to wear this for me so I can have a fix anytime I want. I shoot the blood back as if it's alcohol, licking the inside of the cup to get every drop.

When it's clean, I toss it over my shoulder, and it lands with a soft thud against the wall.

I'm feral now.

With a loud, fierce growl, I yank her legs apart again and dive between her thighs, plunging my tongue into her cunt.

Blood flows over my tongue.

And I fucking feast.

I snarl into her pussy, digging my claws into her body to keep a firm grip on her. I slide a hand up her stomach, the growl in my chest never fading and the vibrations become as loud as the lightning outside.

Cupping her left breast, I palm it softly, kneading it, loving how perfectly she fits. Pinching her nipple, I roll it between my fingers, giving it a soft tug before adding more pressure.

Her heavy breaths turn to pants. She tries to close her legs, but her attempt is for the weak. I keep them parted, fucking her cunt with my tongue and gathering every drop of blood I can get.

My night vision fades to red, my vampire coming out in full force.

Her hands run up her body, grasping the pillow on either side of her head before burying her mouth in it.

"Mmm, fuck, you taste so good," I murmur before licking up to her clit.

"Ohhh." She turns her head, rolling her lips together before squeezing her eyes shut in her sleep. "Ahh. Oh, oh," she exhales, her breaths becoming shorter.

My hand glides across her chest to her other tit, pinching the bead tightly which has her arching her back and rolling her hips against my face. She licks her dry lips, her tits slightly bouncing from her movements.

I suck her clit into my mouth, my fangs scraping the sensitive bundle at the same time I slip two fingers inside her and begin a punishing pace.

And that finally wakes her up.

Her body slides up the bed with every forceful fuck of my fingers.

"What? What—" she tries to ask, confused. "Oh God," she moans, her hand fumbling on the small nightstand.

The light flips on, illuminating the truth.

No one is here.

No one who she can see, anyway.

I grab her by the hips and yank her back down the bed, plunging my tongue into her tight channel, drinking all the blood that willingly feeds me.

Her hands grasp the sheets, twisting and yanking on them while she tosses her head back and comes.

"Oh, what is happening? What is—" She cries louder,

more blood and come flowing down my throat. "What is this?"

"You're dreaming, Mickey." I leave bloody kiss marks on her inner thigh. "And the next time you come, you better say my name."

Her eyes become heavy again, the cruel twist of exhaustion and confusion of not knowing if this is real or not pulls her under.

"I don't know your name," she whispers.

I suck the blood from my fingers and moan in approval, cleaning her from me when the light hits the makeshift bracelet I made with her blood-stained panties.

Curling over her, I whisper into her ear. "My name is Rhett Royals, My Timid Little Bloom. And I'll be back tomorrow. Be ready for me."

CHAPTER TEN

MICKEY

"You look exhausted." Milo leans against the counter, sipping on freshly brewed coffee. "I made you a cup."

"Thank you." I rub my burning eyes, trying to remember what happened last night, but I can't.

I know I had a wet dream. I know I orgasmed, but it is the phantom voice, the hands I thought I felt on me, and the tongue between my legs that give me pause. There were moments when it felt real. I remember waking up once and nothing– no one– was there.

It had to be a dream.

Or I had to be sleepwalking because I woke up with bloody sheets since I didn't put in my menstrual cup. I could have sworn I did, but I found it clean and on the floor this morning before I showered all the dried blood from between my legs.

He slides the mug across the counter and stares at me.

I lift my gaze from the surface of the coffee as I take a sip. "What?"

"You look like shit," he says bluntly.

I snort. "Where's my favorite sibling? She is much nicer than you."

"She is at work pulling a double. I just call it like I see it."

I roll my eyes, yawning for so long, Milo begins to laugh. "Shut up," I grumble. "I didn't sleep well last night." And I had to change the sheets on my bed and shower to wash the dried blood from my legs. "A nap is definitely in my future today."

"You don't have to go to the diner?"

I shake my head. "No, Demi dropped me to one to two shifts a week so I can focus on the renovation. She also said I can come in whenever I want."

"She is the best. We got lucky finding this town. I don't want to leave."

I sit my mug down, tapping the counter with my fingertips. "Did you plan to?"

"No, no, I'm just saying, I don't ever want to leave. I've never really liked a place so much before."

"You sound like you have one foot out the door."

He shakes his head. "I promise I don't." He downs the rest of his coffee, setting it in the sink. "What are your plans today with the renovation?"

"A few deliveries. They are going to finish the roof. I have people coming to get started on the main bedroom and bathroom. Hopefully, within the next couple of months, this house will be done."

"Busy day ahead. I'm proud of you."

I grin, blushing from words I have only heard a few

times in my life. "Thanks."

The doorbell rings and I jump, startled by the sound. I place my hand against my chest and we both chuckle.

"That scared me more than it should have." I slide from the chair and tighten the belt around my waist.

Opening the door, a delivery guy is standing there in a brown uniform and holding a package.

"Are you Mickey Bloom?"

I close the door slightly, so it doesn't seem like an invitation for him to come inside. "I am."

"I just need your signature."

"Sure." I sign for the package, and he hands it over. "Thank you." It's heavier than I expected and rattles. I'm trying to think about what I ordered that could sound like that. I've bought so much lately, I can't remember.

"No problem. Have a good day," he waves, hurrying to his truck. "Nice statue," he shouts.

The truck grumbles to life, drowning out my thanks, and I'm left staring at my gargoyle statue, only this time, something is different.

His cock can be seen. It's long, wide, and hard. My clit pulses between my legs and the memory of my dream last night tickles the back of my mind.

"Rhett," I say quietly, wondering who that is and why I remember it being whispered to me.

Maybe it's the voice in the back of my mind that I named.

"Because that doesn't sound crazy," I sigh to myself, taking one last look at the statue and bite my lip because I've never noticed how it– he– was naked before.

It's odd how he is there sometimes and not others. I snicker. "Maybe he is a real gargoyle." I kick the door shut, leaving the stupid words outside.

The jingle of keys clinks together. Milo stuffs them in his pocket before grabbing his phone and wallet.

"Your security system is being installed today so whatever you do, don't leave the house, alright?"

I set the package on the counter, cutting the seam open with a knife. "Where am I going to go? I like it here too much. I have everything I need, including a big lake. Maybe I'll go swimming today." And then I remember the dead deer I gave to the crocodile.

Okay, so I probably won't go swimming today since a dead deer is probably floating in the lake.

"Okay, text me when the security is in place. Maybe this house will actually look like a home soon."

I mock him playfully, parting the flaps of the box before peering inside. My smile fades. My stomach churns with painful memories. Bile creeps its way up my throat. Tears build and fall in an instant. My body shakes. Memories I've tried to forget resurface, and I remember the pain of every scar he gave me.

"No. No, no, no. No!" I scream at pandora's box and back away.

"Mickey? What? What is it?" He peeks into the box and his concern flips to anger in the next beat of my heart. "What the fuck? Is this some kind of sick joke? Who sent this to you?" He closes the panels of the box to read the label, then slams his fist on the counter. "There isn't a return address."

I curl against the wall, bringing my knees to my chest, and wrap my arms around them. "He is dead. He is dead. He is dead," I chant, replaying the day I escaped. "I killed him, Milo. I remember. I remember driving the bottle into his neck. He bled out."

"These can't be from him. Right? They can't be. You said…" He swallows, then clears his throat. "You said you were chained." He lifts the chains from the box, the metal clinking against each other has me flinching. "Are these the chains?"

"I can't look," I tell him, my bottom lip trembling. "I can't look. Please, Milo. Please, don't make me." I turn my head to the side, staring at the old fridge that came with the house.

His footsteps scuff against the new floors and he squats, his shadow playing on the wall. "I know you don't want to look, but I need you to, and then we are calling Jake, okay? He needs to know if these are the chains because then that fucking asshole isn't dead and that's a big fucking problem. If he isn't, I'm going to kill him myself. Remember, you aren't alone anymore, Mick. No one is going to get to you."

I shut my eyes and wipe my cheeks, taking a deep breath to gather the courage I need to. When I open my eyes, Milo is holding out the chains, and time seems to stop. He places the metal chain in my hands and the weight of them feels the exact same.

"So many chains are made, right? I mean, these couldn't be it."

"This isn't random," I say, running my fingers down the links. "These aren't new, and I know they are mine." I stare at the lock at the end of the chain, turning it over to show Milo the engraving.

Mickey, My Pet.

I toss the chains on the floor. "He's alive. This is him telling me he knows where I'm at. He's going to come looking for me, Milo. I should have died in that house. Everything would be easier if I had just died." My voice is monotone. My gaze is caught on the off-white refrigerator, staring into space. "I should have died."

"Hey, don't you dare fucking talk like that. Do you understand me? You shouldn't have died because Minnie and I can't live without you. You matter. Don't let that piece of shit win. He won't. He can come back, and he can try to take you, but he won't. Don't ever talk like that again. Ever." He turns my chin, forcing me to look at him. "Do you understand?"

I nod. "I'm sorry. I'm sorry. He just makes me wish I were dead. He has this—" I shake my head, staring at the ceiling to stop myself from crying. "He has this hold over me that I can't explain. Not in a good way, but like I depended on him for survival, Milo. There were plenty of times when I thought I was going to die, and he made sure I didn't. It's fucked up. It's like..." I curl my hand into my chest, holding my heart while the tendons begin to break. "I'm trained. He's trained me."

"No, you were abused. You are not trapped. You are free of him."

"Am I? Am I really?" I force myself to my feet, using the wall as leverage to pull myself up. "Look at me, Milo. I'm scared every day. I'm afraid to fall asleep because most of the time his face is in my dreams. I'm always scared. He has broken me. I'm ruined because of him. I'll never be the same."

"You shouldn't be the same. Not after that. And you are so far from broken. Do you know how in awe I am of you? You have started over. You bought this house. Look how much work you have put in. You are building your life back and that is not easy." His Adam's apple bobs, and he places his hands on either side of my neck where it meets my shoulder. Milo's lashes become wet and when he peers up from the floor, a singular tear breaks free.

He never cries. Ever.

"I'm so sorry I wasn't there for you." He wipes his cheek on his shoulder. "I should have been a better brother. I should have come to the house more. I should have—"

I throw my arms around his neck and hug him tight, crying with him. "Don't you dare. Don't you dare blame yourself. I knew when you came over. I heard you. I heard your voice anytime I was trapped in the closet." I pull away and cup his face. "You came to the house all the time. You called all the time. I was worried he would kill you. You pissed him off so much. You did everything you could, Milo."

He shakes his head, a loud sob escaping him. "I didn't. I should have done more. I should have done a better job of protecting you. That was my job!" he yells. "I should have killed him when I had suspicions about what was going on."

"You had to consider me too. There was too much at stake."

"No, I should have done more to get you out and that's on me. I'll have to live with that guilt for the rest of my life." He fumbles to get the phone out of his pocket. "I'm going to call Jake personally." Milo touches the screen a few times and places it against his ear.

"Milo—"

He doesn't let me say another word, giving me his back. He picks up the chains, tosses them in the box, and like the amazing brother he is, removes the package from my line of sight.

Ty can't be alive. I ripped his jugular apart. I stabbed him.

I sit back down on the floor, replaying all the pain and suffering Ty caused me.

"*Stupid Girl.*"

"*You should have known better.*"

"*Spread your legs. Don't make a sound.*"

I take a deep breath, trying to slow Ty's voice in my head, trying to think of Rhett's. Rhett might be a figment of my imagination, but he makes me feel better. He chases away the pain and suffering.

At this point of my mental downfall, does it matter if Rhett is real or not?

I close my eyes to focus, to try and hear Rhett, the man who gave me strength to swing at my pain.

He's silent.

And without his voice, one of the worst memories I have reels me in. I sink deeper into it, losing myself in the night when I tried to run to survive.

My legs burn. My throat hurts. My feet are cut from all the small twigs lying on the ground. I can't stop. This is my chance. I have to get away. Tears from pain and fear blur my vision as I sprint through the woods behind the forest.

Ty thought he locked the chain to the hook.

He didn't.

I had to take the opportunity. I had to run for my life.

I decided to take my chances in the woods behind the house. Thinking I would be able to hide more easily.

At the time, it was a good idea.

Now? I didn't realize how out of shape I was, how much weight I've lost, and my endurance is non-existent.

The pouring rain isn't making it easier. My bare feet slide against the dirt, my toes digging into the mud. I grip the chain attached to my neck, keeping it out of my way so I don't trip.

"You Stupid Girl!" His voice echoes through the forest, reminding me he is never far behind. "I'm going to fucking get you and when I do, you better be ready. I swear to God, I'm going to beat the shit out of you. Do you hear me? Stop now and maybe I won't make you wish you were dead."

I keep running, my nightgown soaked from the rain and completely sticking to my body. I want to yell for help. I want to scream. If I do, he'll find me. All I need to do is find a road, wave down a car, and I'll be free.

It's so much easier said than done.

I shout in pain when I trip over a small tree root sticking out of the ground. I grab onto my ankle, wanting to scream in agony, but that won't do any good. That won't save me. Pushing myself up, I use the nearest tree for support. The bark scratches my palm and I lean against the trunk, just for a second, just to catch my breath.

"You won't get far," he sings, coming closer. "Think about your siblings, Mickey! Think about what I'll do to them if you leave me. Do you want Minnie to take your place?" he yells, his voice an eerie haunt over my shoulder. "You want Minnie on my bed? Imagine all the wicked things I'd do to her."

I start running again, holding in my cries. I know he is lying. He wouldn't do anything to Minnie. I know that deep down. He'd get in trouble. He wouldn't be able to get away with it.

My fear says otherwise.

"You must really want your sister in my bed, Stupid

Girl."

I whimper with every stride, my ankle throbbing. The pain makes me fall. Mud flies against my face. Dirt embeds itself under my nails. I wheeze, struggling to breathe, inhaling rain and drowning slowly.

A car horn blows in the distance. The rush of the vehicles passing each other has me trying to get onto my feet. My arms shake with weakness and pushing myself up hurts so fucking bad.

"You're one Stupid Girl." He snags me by the back of the hair and shoves my face into the mud.

I can't breathe.

"You thought you could get away from me?" He straddles my legs and lifts my dress and I hear the zipper of his pants lowering. "You'll never get away from me."

"Mickey? Ms. Bloom?"

I blink the memory away, sniffling when I hear a different voice that isn't Ty's.

"Mickey?" Milo's voice is next, and his hand is cupping my jaw. "Mick, are you with us?"

I nod, pressing the end of my sleeves against my eyes to soak up the tears causing my vision to blur.

"Where'd you go?" he questions, eyes dancing over my face.

"You don't want to know."

He frowns, keeping his thoughts to himself. I know he understands. I don't want to talk about running for my life. I don't have the energy.

Lifting my hands, Milo understands and helps me to my feet.

The sheriff takes off his hat and presses it against his chest. "Mickey. It's good to see you again."

"You too. I'm sorry for the circumstance." Milo wraps his arm around me, keeping me close, and I let him.

Jake keeps a respectful distance. He knows about everything that has happened to me. Telling the police about my situation— minus the murderous details— was the first thing Milo wanted to do when we arrived in this town.

"Don't apologize. This is what I'm here for. Now, Milo, I understand you're about to leave. Mickey, if you feel more comfortable, we can go down to the station, so you are around people."

"I've texted Demi. I told her what happened. I'm not going anywhere, Jake."

"Okay, okay, great, but regardless," he gives me a reassuring smile, "we should leave the decision up to Mickey. Her comfort is all that matters right now."

Even having the choice brings me relief. "I'm fine here at home. This won't take long anyway. I know what you want, and I don't have any information. A package was delivered. It has to be from Ty. They are the same chains that he leashed me with. There's no return address."

His jaw ticks with rage as he writes on his notepad. "We are going to look into this. I'm going to take the box for evidence, run it for any fingerprints, and find the delivery guy that came here. We will get to the bottom of this, Mickey. I promise."

"I know, Jake. You're a good cop. I appreciate you trying." I know he won't find anything. Ty was an animal and dumb in many ways, but abuse? He was— is— smart. There won't be any fingerprints.

The doorbell rings and Jake's hand flies to his gun. He's a quick draw, aiming the gun at the door.

He holds up a hand to us. "Stay here. Don't move," he says so quietly, that I can barely hear him. His fingers come to his mouth, telling us to be quiet.

My heart thumps while I hold my breath, waiting for relief or a gunshot.

"What's your name? Give me your employee badge. I want your boss's phone number," Jake orders, keeping the man at the door.

My head begins to swim, and my lungs begin to scream, begging me to inhale.

I can't. I can't breathe knowing Ty is alive. I can't live every day looking over my shoulder.

"The guys are here to install the security system. They are vetted. I'll stay here with you until they are done."

"Me too," Milo echoes. "Why don't you go lie down and try to get some rest?"

"I don't think I could sleep right now. I have too much going on in my head. Plus, so much is happening with the house. I can't nap today."

"Yes, you can. I'll direct everyone. No need to worry, Mick. Plus, Jake is here. He won't let anything happen."

"I'll stay until I get a call saying I need to leave."

"See?" Milo says with a smile, trying to ease my anxiety. "We have this. Go."

"Okay. Okay. I'll go, but you'll wake me if you need me?" I tug on my sleeves before crossing my arms.

"No, probably not. Go. Go." He shoves me down the hall.

"Okay, okay. Jeez. It's like you're trying to get rid of me." I stop and snag Milo's wrist. "If you catch me sleep-walking, please don't wake me. You know it can be dangerous. It's only happened once since being in the house but with the added stress of Ty—"

"—I know what to do. You're safe, Mick. You have nothing to worry about."

"Okay. Thank you." I give my brother a tight hug, turning my cheek out the door to see certain parts of my gargoyle.

Between Milo, Jake, and Rhett, I should be okay, right?

Right.

CHAPTER ELEVEN

RHETT

The sun is about to set, and the moment is does, I'm sneaking into her room again, spreading her legs, and feasting on the blood that drips from her cunt.

This damn sunlight is my enemy. All it does is fucking rain but the day I don't want it to, it forces me to change into my gargoyle. My cock was hard all night, aching for my mate until the sun rose, turning me into a statue with proof of my need showing.

Being trapped inside myself isn't usually so bad. I typically fall asleep under the warmth, the charge of the hot rays giving me strength, but all day I've been awake. I've been pacing inside my mind, growling, and trying to shatter the stone that imprisons me.

I can't wait to break the shackles of this concrete and drift into her home, possess her body in her sleep, and maybe we can chase a wild heated dream together.

My cock is throbbing for attention, and I can't fucking

reach it. It's painful to be as hard as stone– literally– and unable to do anything about it.

The sun is taking its time to set. With every passing second, I become more irritated. The stars have decided to come out early and all I want to do is fly as high as possible to see if I'm able to feel how bright the light is just to understand how searing Mickey's is.

People begin pouring out of the house. Workers with dirty clothes and sweat-drenched skin walk with exhausted slow steps to their cars. A lot of progress was made on the house today, but I was able to hear the commotion from earlier.

The man that hurt her could still be alive and I can't wait to find him. I'll make him pay for what he did. All those scars. All that pain. All those tears she cried due to him.

They will be nothing compared to the torture I will inflict on the sorry piece of shit who hurt my mate.

"I appreciate you coming out, Jake." Milo shakes hands with the sheriff. "I hope this is some kind of sick joke. I'm not sure who would play it. He can't be alive. It's impossible. She–"

"–I know. We will get to the bottom of it, Milo. I won't let anything happen to Mickey."

A quake is trapped within my chest. Milo and Jake dart their gazes around to see where the sound is coming from before ignoring it.

"I don't recommend her going to work. She needs to be careful. The less she is seen while I get more information, the better."

"Good luck with telling her that, Jake. She refuses to be kept in a prison. Her freedom is everything. Being trapped because of him again is something she will refuse to accept."

"I'm only thinking of her safety. If she goes anywhere, she can't be alone." His radio goes off and he reaches to his shoulder, pressing the button to reply. "I'm on my way." He sighs, patting Milo's shoulder. "I know it's a lot to deal with, but she'll get through it. We will find him and arresting him will feel so good."

Arresting him? That's fucking cute.

Jake won't ever have the chance. He might find Ty's bones or pieces of his body, but he will never speak to Ty. He will never hear that man speak or breathe.

"I'll keep you updated," Jake speaks his final departing words before heading to his SUV that has Sheriff written across the side in big bold black letters. "Get some rest, Milo. I'll be sending a unit to watch the house."

What a waste of time and energy when I offer more protection than any officer could. They don't want to do what is absolutely necessary to protect people.

And that's kill.

I'll kill. I'll become murderous. I'll damn my wicked soul to Hell only for the devil to play with it for all eternity. I'll bathe myself in her abuser's blood. I'll skin his flesh from his bones. I'll pluck his nails from their bed.

I'll do all of this while he is alive, begging for mercy.

I'll show him none.

To get to Mickey, he'll have to get through me, and that will never happen.

A rumble shakes the stone that shells me again. Milo's eyebrows dance with confusion as he steps out onto the freshly cut grass. He turns left and right, peers toward the sky, then scratches the back of his neck before yawning.

He is a good brother. That's fortunate.

Or I would have killed him.

He takes so much of Mickey's time. He's so needy.

She's mine.

Milo heads inside and locks the door. It isn't a simple click that slides into place. The mechanism sounds mechanical. There are three dead bolts on her door and the only way to enter is to press three fingers on a keypad outside.

I chuckle internally.

All that money spent on security and it still won't keep me out.

Dark orange fills the night. The cool air begins to replace the warm sun, but I can still feel its rays. I have about thirty minutes before I'm free.

I listen acutely as the minutes tick by. Milo's even breaths tell me he is asleep yet there are footsteps in the house. My heart skips a beat with worry. Focusing on the inside of the house, the footsteps are slow, light, and slightly drag. There isn't another heartbeat in the house.

Only Mickey's and Milo's.

The locks on the front door click in release before the new red-painted slab of wood opens to reveal Mickey. Her hair is messy from sleep, tangled and sticking up in a few places. She stands in the middle of the doorway, eyes open, and her body just slightly off-kilter as she sways.

I try to burst free from the statue but I can't. The last remaining rays of the sun can still be felt and until it is dark, I can't go anywhere or do anything. Is she okay? I can't tell.

She strips off her pants, stumbling before catching herself on the doorframe. Mickey tosses her pants in the yard, followed by her panties. I slam against the concrete holding me, needing to take her inside before anyone sees the body that belongs to me.

No one else can see how beautiful she is. Every curve of her, every sound she makes, every drip of blood from that pretty cunt– is mine.

Her shirt covers her just enough, stopping on her upper thigh to cover and tease the world with her legs. I want them wrapped around my neck. I want her thighs to squeeze my throat until I can't breathe while I have my tongue plunging into her tight pussy. I want her to be crying out for me, trying to get away because the pleasure is too much. She won't be able to go anywhere because my arms would be wrapped around her legs, keeping her trapped and her pussy fucking my mouth.

She's walking toward me, a dazed, far-off, vacant look in her eyes.

Mickey is sleepwalking.

Oh, the fucking things I'm going to do to her.

Only for her not to remember.

Her hand slides up my leg before she grabs onto my knee and hoists herself up the statue.

Even through this form, I can smell her arousal.

"Rhett," she mumbles, wrapping her arms around my neck.

She remembers my name. I'm shocked.

I fucking love it.

Mickey, circles her legs around my waist, and the heat of her cunt hugs my erected stone cock. One of her arms dives between her legs, a small grunt leaving her when she pulls out the cup holding all that delicious blood.

She pours it onto my cock, drenching the stone in

red.

Mickey has to know I'm meant for her. Why else would she be doing this?

Hooking her arm around my neck again, she glides herself up and down my cock, letting the stone rub against her clit all while using the blood as a lubricant.

I groan inside my concrete prison, feeling every fucking wet slide of her cunt while she uses me in her sleep.

That's it, good girl. That's it. Fucking use me.

She rocks herself against me faster, whimpering with every roll of her clit against me. Mickey drags herself up and down, pressing her forehead against my neck while she sleepily ruts against her gargoyle statue.

Her tongue flattens against my throat, licking up the rough stone. Her groans become quick and broken as her orgasm gets closer. Her lips find mine, lazily kissing me even though I can't reciprocate.

Her tongue licks my bottom lip, then my fangs, working herself up and down. My mate's hips stutter, sliding herself long and hard on the very last stroke as her orgasm explodes through her.

"Rhett, Rhett, Rhett," she mutters my name in a broken moan.

A growl of frustration builds in my chest, wishing I could break free, slam her against the ground, and give her what she is seeking. Would my mate ever come to me awake or will I have to fuck her and breed her every time her eyes close?

As long as I get to have her, I don't care how.

Mickey lifts herself, pressing the crown of my head against her entrance.

My fingers finally begin to move, slowly as the sun

finally begins to fucking set. At last, I have my mate right where I want her and I'm not able to do a fucking thing. Mickey presses down, the warmth of her squeezing the head of my cock.

"So good. Wish you were real," she slurs in the depths of her sleep.

Oh, if you only knew, My Timid Little Bloom.

Blood mixed with her come soaks me. I feel it dripping down my shaft the more she's able to take of me. I spread her wide, filling every fucking inch of her in a way that piece of shit ex never could.

She takes me by surprise when she takes another inch, painful whimpers mixed with pleasure tease my ears. Her nails scrape along the back of my rock-solid neck, and her mouth is on mine again.

Mickey can't take all of me, not while I'm in my gargoyle form.

"Fuck," she groans, gaining the courage to move. "So big. Need you, Rhett."

Her pretty pink cunt grips my shaft, rocking herself back and forth, up and down. Mickey leans back, rolling her hips, her hair flowing behind her and nearly reaching the ground.

If Milo were to come outside, he'd be traumatized.

She fucks me faster, her little erotic sounds bringing me to life quicker than the night ever could. Mickey slips her hand under her shirt, playing with her nipple while crying out softly– or as loud as she can while she sleeps.

"You're going to make me come. He never did. He never could," she admits, making all my beasts roar in victory. "More. More."

The last of the orange from the sun is gone and night

has completely set. The moon is nowhere to be seen but the stars are out by the millions.

With a primal snarl, I break free from the statue, shifting to my humanoid body while I'm still inside her. My tentacles are freed, whipping her pretty cunt until red welts appear.

Wrapping my arms around her, I spread my wings, taking us into the air. My eyes roll to the back of my head as her muscles clench and unclench around me, nearly making me lose my train of thought.

I fly us over the house and into the backyard near the lake and then press her against the ground, the long grass giving us coverage from curious eyes.

"I came to life for you, Beloved, My Sweet Mate. Your gargoyle will always fuck you when you are in need." To keep her sense of control, I flip us until I'm on my back, giving her what she needs in her sleep.

She wants to take. She wants to be in charge.

And I will allow that if it helps heal her inner peace.

Unable to help myself, my claws sink into her hips, helping her rock back and forth. I gather the hem of her shirt and yank it over her head, tossing it in the water. Vibrations purr in my chest watching her tits bounce knowing it's because she's fucking me.

My curious hands travel up her body, cupping her small tits. I was right. They fit perfectly in my palms. I groan, my wings twitching to fly us up into the sky. I hold myself back, biting my lip until it bleeds while she uses me for my cock. My thumbs travel over her nipples, the beads sensitive and tight.

"Fuck, you take this cock so good in your sleep, Mickey. You are mine. You belong to me, but you know that, don't you? It's why you found me. You know I'm more than a voice in your head." I tilt my head back, roaring when she moves faster.

Her hands slide up my chest, then she flattens them on my pecs to use as support.

I dig my feet into the ground for stability, pressing into her from the bottom. "You feel so fucking good," I moan, watching where we are connected, witnessing my cock vanish inside her with every stroke her pussy gives me. There's blood on our inner thighs, her period heavy and warm, allowing me to slip in and out without worry. "Look how good you take my big cock, Mickey. Be a good fucking girl and look at us." I dig my claws into her scalp, fisting the roots of her hair, and force her to look down. "You can't take all of me yet, but you will, won't you? You'll be greedy for every fucking inch of me." My tentacles sting her inner thighs, one paying special attention to her clit.

With every slash of my tentacle, her body jerks from the electrical shock. I sit up, wrapping my arms around her, and tuck my wings behind my back. My mouth gravitates to her breasts. Wrapping my lips around one nipple, I suck it into my mouth, moaning at how soft her flesh is and how it gives under my attention.

My saliva paralyzed the guard but with my mate, it only seems to enhance her lust. I blow on the wet bead before moving to the other, not wanting to leave any inch of her body without attention.

Red flips my vision, the vampire inside me starved for her blood.

I don't want to sink my fangs into her neck, though. I want to drink from between her legs so I can also taste how much she craves me.

"There's so much I want to do to you and I'm not sure if I have enough time before you wake up. How much can I get away with before you come to your senses?" I rake the sharp point of my claws down her chest, over her nipples, and down her stomach. Red marks arise on her skin, and I hum in approval at seeing my claim on her.

Gently, I ease her onto her back. I glance down, obsessed with watching my cock sink into her. Mickey's arms settle above her head and with one hand, I keep them pinned. I drive into her drenched cunt, loving every high-pitched sound I ignite from her sleep-induced state.

I curl over her, dragging my tongue down her arm when I notice a long, skinny ridge. "What is this? Are you going to tell me, Mickey?"

"Birth control."

I snarl, not liking the sound of that at all. With my claw, I slice the skin where the narrow implant is. To my surprise, Mickey doesn't cry out in pain at all.

And I know why.

This pain doesn't compare to all the agony she's experienced. This is nothing.

I lick the blood dripping from her arm, ramming my cock into her so hard, she begins to glide across the grass. I wrap my mouth around the wound, sucking the meat of her flesh between my teeth. My tongue dives into the wound, searching for the implant that is stopping me from claiming her in every single way.

Growling deep within my chest, I apply more of my weight to her body to keep her still, plunging my cock into her soaking wet cunt while I suck the birth control from her arm. I finally feel it, like a small skinny twig, and

I snag it between my teeth. I pull it free and grab it with my fingers so I can get a good look at it.

"This little contraption was going to stop me from putting my child in you?" I scoff, snapping it in two between my thumb and index finger. "Nothing will fucking stop me." I plant myself inside her, groaning as my tentacles flicker in different directions.

I bite my wrist and force it into her mouth, the vampire whispering in the back of my mind to feed her my blood. Whatever my instincts tell me to do to her, I'm going to without question.

"Now, I'll be able to feel what you feel." I bend down and lick her wound, watching her skin heal.

She'll have no idea her birth control isn't there. There isn't a mark to prove what just happened.

"Who did this to you?" I whisper into her ear, punching my hips so I can bury myself into her cunt. "Who hurt my mate? Tell me his name. Tell me where he lives. Be a good girl and I'll give you what your body craves." I push her hair out of her face, my claws rubbing against her scalp. I kiss down her throat, focusing on the strong pulse jumping behind her skin.

She doesn't answer me.

"That's okay. I'm going to find him and I'm going to kill him for you, My Timid Little Bloom. I'll set your soul free." I sink my fangs into her throat, moaning as the fast rush of hot blood flows into my mouth.

She cries out to the stars as my bite pushes her over the edge of her orgasm, her muscles tightening around my shaft to milk it.

I dig my fingers into her hip, the sharp points of my nails breaking the skin. I hold on tight to her body, driving myself to the edge before I slow down and slip out of her heat.

"No!" she shouts from being empty.

I shove her onto the ground and kiss down her body, wanting to taste between her legs again.

"I'll give you my cock again. Just let me have a taste first." I place each leg on my shoulder and pick her up by her ass, chuckling as I latch my mouth around her swollen, tender clit.

She groans from the sensitivity. My tentacles really love shocking this little bundle of nerves. Before I plunge my tongue inside her entrance, I find myself cleaning her blood from the inside of her thighs, not wanting any to go to waste.

Giving a quick look at my cock, I become irritated that I can't bend until I'm sucking her taste from my shaft.

"Mmm," I hum, licking between the pink lips of her cunt, gathering every red trail I can see. I clean her well, licking up and down her seam before swirling my tongue around her clit again.

I moan when I latch onto her entrance, plummeting my tongue where my cock belongs.

"Fuck, Mickey, you taste so fucking good. I could be down here for hours." I give her clit a kiss before flipping her onto her stomach, wrap her hair around my wrist, and drive my cock home. "But I need to be inside you too. I'm going to fill you. You're going to take every fucking electrified drop of me. Fuck. Fuck!" I roar, planting my feet in the ground to get better traction, burying myself to the hilt over and over again.

My tail slashes through the air and glides down her spine, slipping through the crease of her ass.

She whimpers, her eyes still dazed with her sleep.

"I'm going to have your ass too. I'm going to claim every fucking hole so when you sit, you'll be sore. When you cross your legs, you'll gasp and think of me. When you swallow, your throat will burn from me fucking it." The tip of my tail slips through her puckered hole and that's all it takes for her to clench around me again, her orgasm spasming all of her muscles.

Pressure builds in my shaft, my own orgasm looming. I pull from her, keeping the crown nestled in her cunt when I notice a large bulk forming at the base of my cock.

I slam into her, the bulb becoming larger every time I manage to slip out. I notice the grayish stone pattern inching up the stalk as I drive into her one more time.

The knot, my gargoyle growls in victory, locks us together. My cock turns to stone, and I watch as her pussy spreads wider to accommodate me. It looks like if she moves, she'll split open. Just when I think there is no possible way for her to stretch more, she does.

Her come, blood, pleasure, her body beneath mine, it's all too much.

I toss my head back and roar so loud, that I disturb the calm lake water, and it ripples from the force of my shout. My tentacles shock her clit with every thick stream of come that I fill her with, leaving her no choice but to drink me into her womb.

"Oh God. Oh God!" she cries, her body tightening around me again. "Yes," Mickey groans, her fingers clawing the sand.

Another wave of come fills her and she orgasms again, her muscles clenching once more.

Then, it hits me.

She's being shocked from the inside and the out.

My tentacles on her clit. My come electrifying her g-spot. She can't stop coming until I do.

I wrap us in my wings and kiss the back of her neck. She turns her head and I wrap my hand around her throat, bringing her head up so our mouths can meet in our first kiss.

The feel of them against me has another jet of seed begging to find her womb. Our tongues meet gingerly before I sweep mine inside her mouth.

"Rhett," she whispers down my throat.

"I'm here," I tell her, kissing down her shoulder. "I'm never going anywhere, Mickey. I'm in your dreams. I'm all around you. You will never be alone again." I trace her scars with my claw. "You'll never be able to get rid of me." I kiss her shoulder again. "For every scar he inflicted, I will seek a thousand moments of revenge on him."

I stare at her throat where my bite is, another scar to add to her collection, the only scar that should exist on her body. It hits me as my knot deflates.

I fed her my blood.

I knotted her.

I bred her.

I've marked her.

We are mated and nothing in this world can ever change that. And if we can only have our life when she is sleepwalking, then I will gladly live my nights filling her pretty cunt under the stars.

CHAPTER TWELVE

MICKEY

A knock on my bedroom door has me groaning myself awake. I'm not a morning person and Milo knows that.

"Go away, Milo," I grumble, throwing a pillow against the door.

"It is nearly noon. I just wanted to make sure you were alive."

"Barely." I bury my face in the bed and bring the blankets over my head.

He chuckles. "Okay, well, I have to go to work. I'm covering for Minnie. She isn't feeling well so she's at home resting. There's supposed to be a severe thunderstorm today, so just be careful."

"I'll be going to work later. I'll see you there."

"No, you won't. Jake told Demi what was going on. You're off work for the time being."

I'm too tired to argue that right now but I do plan on fighting about how they are making decisions for me without speaking to me. I'm not some feeble victim who can't make decisions for herself. I don't want to be run out of my job. This was supposed to be a new beginning for me.

This town was supposed to be my starting point. Everything in the past was supposed to be forgotten.

Why can't I be free of him? Why can't I be free of the mental torment he has caused? Why can't he leave me alone?

I push myself to sit up, wiping the lone tear on my face.

And that's when I notice my hands.

"What?" I question lightly in confusion. I turn my palms up, then over again, completely lost about how they are so dirty.

"I left coffee in the pot. It's still warm. If you need me call me. Okay? I love you." He taps his knuckles on the door before departing.

"I love you too," I raise my voice so he can hear me, but the rasp to the words is impossible to miss.

The front door shuts, the locks click into place, and the beeps around the house inform me the windows are secured.

Dirt is buried under my nails. A trickle of warmth drips down my legs and I rip the covers off to see a fucking mess.

I jump out of the bed, staring at my ruined sheets.

Blood and dirt are smeared everywhere. I look down at my naked body, showing just how filthy I am. It's as if I trampled through a giant mud puddle. I dash to the bathroom to get a better look.

That was a bad idea.

My hair is tangled with pieces of grass. Mud is dried on my cheek. Long red scratches form down my chest. Bite bruises have me touching my breasts. There are three bite marks, and they don't seem... human.

All over my body, there are marks I can't explain. My toes are caked in dirt, blood is wet and dry between my thighs, and my heart hammers in my chest when I try to recall what happened.

I only remember going to sleep.

"Oh, no," I whisper, knowing what happened even if I don't want to admit it.

I was sleepwalking again. Do I need to put cameras in the house to make sure I don't do anything dangerous?

My sleepwalking has to be because of Ty or the anxiety of starting this renovation that has me losing not just time, but my actions. What if I hurt someone? What if I hurt myself?

I flip the handle of the shower and wait for the water to get hot, plucking grass out of my hair.

"What did you do? What did you do, Mickey?" I question myself, knowing damn well I don't have an answer. I need to try to jog my memory.

There's an ache between my legs too, the kind of ache that women have after they have had sex, and I know for sure that I haven't been doing that. There's no one here I want to have sex with.

Rhett.

My eyes roll when the name rings in my head.

"Rhett. Right," I scoff, chuckling hysterically. "I am losing my damn mind if my own thoughts are telling me to fuck the voice in my head I've made up. Jesus, Mickey." I step inside the stall, sighing when the hot spray lands on my shoulders. "Don't lose yourself. You're okay. This is just a moment. That's all. Nothing you can't fix. You'll be okay," I chant words of encouragement, leaning against the wall in exhaustion.

Every ounce of my body aches. Every muscle is tired. I gather my hair over my shoulder, squeezing the ends. Debris, dirt, and blood tint the white of the bathtub, the water swirling down the drain in a murky whirlpool.

I wash my body, scrubbing my skin until it hurts. I lose track of how many times I've washed, but the water finally runs clear.

Blowing out a breath after I've used half of a bottle of shampoo and conditioner, I stand under the searing water, my skin turning red from the temperature, and focus on what happened to me.

My hand slides down my chest, my fingers rubbing over the scratches left behind. I gasp, my clit throbbing. My mind is blank, but emotion is quick to fill the void in my heart.

Passion, desperation, and need have my hands sliding down my stomach to the soreness between my legs.

A loud, memorable growl has me snapping my eyes open.

Nothing is there.

I place my hand against my chest, willing my heart to slow. That growl in my memory had to have been from last night. It had to have happened. Did I get in a fight with, I don't know, a bear?

Did I win?

I cover my mouth and laugh, throwing my head back as I wrap a towel around my body.

"Right. You, Mickey Bloom, beat a bear. In a fight.

What did you do? Kick its knees?" I work another towel through my hair and step out of the stall, then pause. "Do bears have knees?"

Shaking my head, I grab the vanity's edge and allow my lungs to fully expand. Opening the cabinet, I grab a tampon– not trusting my damn cups to stay in– and do my business before washing my hands. I tilt my chin up to glance in the mirror, lift my hand to wipe the conden-sation off, and drop it to my sides when I see a message written on it.

Stumbling backward, I hit the wall, my throat becom-ing dry.

"You taste so good when you bleed."

And a small heart is drawn underneath it.

I wipe the message away with my palm, squeezing my eyes shut, and then clutch the counter again. A pounding begins to form in the middle of my forehead.

"It isn't real. No one is here. No one can get in the house." I'm talking to myself again. I need to get out of this house.

I've traded one prison for another.

I swing the door open and take one step out of the bathroom when I notice an odd amount of light coming from the entryway of the house. An unnerving sensation sets in, my stomach flipping, my instincts screaming at me not to take another step.

A creak in the living room has me holding my breath. I clutch the towel against my chest, the tips of my fingers digging into the semi-soft material. My middle knuckle pops and I gasp, shutting my eyes in hopes that whoever is in my house didn't hear it.

It can't be anyone. Milo has this place on lockdown.

No one is here. It's all in my head.

Just in case, with gentle and slow ease, I open the cabinet under my sink. I might have hidden a gun in every single room. I haven't told anyone. Milo nor Minnie know, and I guess I need to be honest with them if they are going to be here.

I pull the hammer back, wincing when the loud slide of the bullet slides into place.

"I have a gun!" I take a deep breath and stretch my arms out, gripping the simple nine-millimeter like how I was taught.

All those late nights when I was supposed to be in therapy– I was– but I didn't go to therapy every single night like I told Milo and Minnie. I was determined to never let a man take advantage of me again. Ty wouldn't win my resilience to live again.

And I won't let him take it now.

With therapy, I took self-defense classes and shooting lessons. I'm not perfect. Even with all the training, I'm shaking. I'm scared. I don't know if I remember a day when I was not petrified at one point or another.

"I'm not afraid to shoot you!" I yell from the bathroom, sliding my foot across the floor to get out of the bathroom.

Who am I kidding? I've never shot anyone. I'm terrified.

My entire body trembles as I step into the living room, aiming the gun in every corner. Nothing is there. Only the ridiculous half-dead plant I bought the other day.

"I won't call the cops if you get out of my house now. I won't cause a scene. I won't shoot." I might shoot.

On accident.

Because my fingers are shaking so much, I might pull the trigger.

"Please," I beg the intruder, spinning around when I think I hear a noise.

The front door is wide open, spilling in the light. Milo would never leave it open. He's too protective of me. I know him. He probably checked the lock three times before leaving.

Out of nowhere, the front door slams shut and all the lights in the house turn off.

My breathing becomes fast and heavy. I turn four different times, aiming the barrel of the gun in every direction possible, but nothing is there.

What closed the door?

"I don't know who you think you are, but this isn't fucking funny!" I scream, reaching for the light switch in the kitchen.

I flick it over, again and again with no luck. The electricity is out. There's no storm that could have done this. It's a sunny day.

My cellphone is in the bedroom. No one will be able to get here in time if someone is in the house.

"Listen, I don't want anyone to get hurt. I'm only trying to move on with my life. Please, just leave me alone." I hate begging but I'll do anything at this point to be left alone, to save myself, and what other choice do I have if it means Ty is alive?

He has to be. Although, this is unlike him. He typically is loud, demanding, and uses his brute strength against me before I can do anything.

The silence around me is screaming in new volumes I

didn't know existed.

I put one foot in front of the other, taking my time, and careful not to step on the floorboards that creak.

My towel is ripped from my body when I take my next step. I swing the gun, hoping to aim it at the intruder's face but no one is there.

Did the towel fall?

I swear I felt the tug as if someone grabbed it and ripped it from my body. I bend down to pick it up when a force grabs me by the hair and yanks it back. The gun falls from my hand, and it's kicked across the floor. The metal slides until it hits against the opposite wall where I can't reach it.

"Look how fucking pretty you are on your knees for me."

My mouth parts when I hear Rhett's voice. I know I'm not asleep. Am I? I fall backward, crawling away from the delusion.

"You have no idea what you do to me." Something snags me by the ankle and yanks me across the floor. "I'm desperate for you, Beloved. Every craving I have, only you can sate."

He's saying all the things I wish a lover would say to me. This is how I know it's all in my head. Men like this do not exist and my wish to be treated as if I'm the most important person in the world to my significant other has now damaged me.

I'm imagining Rhett. I've made up his voice.

"You aren't real." I crawl away again, tears forming in my eyes when the reality of needing more help than a therapist can bring, has my emotions breaking free.

"Nothing about this is real. Nothing about you is real. How you make me feel is just a dream."

I kick him away and stand, running down the hall to my room. I slam the door, locking it for good measure, and cover my face with my quaking hands.

"You're okay. He isn't real." The words are a broken sob as they escape me. Folding my hands into a steeple position, I stare at the door as if I'm waiting for it to burst open.

My legs become jittery while I stand here.

"You'll go check yourself into a mental health facility. Nothing to be ashamed of."

"You really think locking yourself away from me will work?" The depth of his voice travels up my spine. "Do you really believe I won't follow you everywhere? No amount of help. No amount of medication. No amount of therapy will be enough to keep me away from you." The phantom touch of his hand wraps around the back of my neck and I gasp. "No matter where you are, I'll find you. You belong to me, Mickey. I'll always be in your head." His finger taps on my temple. "I'll always be in your heart." The same digit slides down my chest causing me to inhale sharply. "And you better believe I'll always be inside you."

I gasp when his hand cups my pussy before two fingers slip inside me.

"If there is one person you don't need to be afraid of, it's me, My Timid Little Bloom."

I try to back away from him— it— whatever is controlling me right now— and I'm slammed against the wall. His long thick fingers slide deeper, and I whimper.

"You aren't real." I squeeze my eyes shut and count to

five.

"Oh, I'm real. Feel this?" He slides his fingers in and out, ever so slowly, curling them in a come hither motion.

I practically climb up the wall with how good it feels—even with how sore I am.

"That's fucking real, Mickey. And does it matter if it isn't? As long as you feel good, that's all that matters." Rhett begins to move his hand faster, fucking me harder.

I glance down and I see the same thing that helped me swing the sledgehammer. I'm able to see more of his body this time. My mind truly decided to make the man of my dreams a monster.

My delusion has come to life.

And he is beautiful. At least, the parts I can see are. Some areas are completely invisible while others have a faint outline and I'm able to see what my broken mind has conjured up.

One arm has me caged against the wall. His bicep is huge, flexing and showing the strength and definition of his form. His bottom half is too blurry to see, but his chest is wide, triple my size, and there are scales on his shoulders.

I understand my hallucination now. He's part crocodile, like the one I met by the lake, and from the cracks across his chest, he is a gargoyle too, just like the one in my front yard.

How sick am I that I would prefer a beast to a man because nothing in my mind could be more monstrous than a human being?

"You can try all you want to escape me," he whispers followed by a purr, a trill that vibrates in my own chest.

"But I know where you will be. I can smell you. I'll hunt you down if you ever leave me."

Flashes of what Ty did when he hunted me down have me denying every word this… hallucination is saying.

"No need to be afraid, Mickey. My sweet, sweet Mickey. I'm going to find the man who did this to you." The claw dragging across my scars is a stark reminder of how this moment isn't real. "I know he's alive." He runs those long claws through my hair before gripping it, forcing me to look at his face by tilting my head back.

He's so tall. His face is blurry for certain parts, truly ghostly and I'm unable to see all of him, but from what I can, he has a very square jaw and a strong defined nose. His eyes are reptilian, the same shade and shape as the crocodile in the lake.

I'm so fucking sick for dreaming up this man— beast— person. I'm horrified for myself and turned on because he hasn't stopped stroking my g-spot with his skilled fingers.

"I'm going to hunt him down and bring you his body. I'm going to kill him in your name, *for* your name, and we will fuck in his blood to celebrate our victory."

My eyes roll to the back of my head as Rhett speaks my deepest, darkest desires.

I have more. More that I've only shared with my therapist. A fucked up deep craving I've had ever since I escaped Ty.

With someone I trust, with someone who will allow me to control the situation, I want to be forced. The sick need has been building inside me, nearly breaking me without understanding why I'd want something so vile when that was one of the main reasons why I ran from Ty.

My therapist said I have a "force" fantasy which is very different than rape since rape holds violence and harm. Most women who want this want to replace the fear with pleasure that comes with the haunted term.

I'm still learning what it means, and I don't know if I'll ever have the strength to take my control back, but Rhett makes me want to try.

He isn't real. He is a figment of my imagination, so wouldn't I be safe?

"Stop."

"Stop?" he tsks, inserting another finger. "You don't want me to really stop, do you? I feel how wet you are for me."

I shove at his chest and with each push, I'm able to see him solidified for a moment. His chest is made of stone, and he has abs that have been carved to last forever.

His fingers slip free as he stumbles. I take the opportunity to run, but he grabs me by the back of the neck and throws me on the bed. I go to open my mouth to yell at him. Before I can speak though, his cock fills my mouth and hits the back of my throat.

A cock I can't see.

"Is this what I have to do to shut you up, Mickey? Do I need to fuck this pretty mouth? Do you know how hard it has been to be stone throughout the day and not see you? But now we are mated, and I can come have you any time I fucking want."

Whips of small stings on my chin and cheeks have me whimpering.

"Those are my jellyfish tentacles. Don't mind them."

Don't mind them? I love the slight pain. I want more. I cough and gag, slapping his thigh to get him away from me all the while I'm sucking him deeper.

Truthfully, I don't want him to go anywhere.

He reaches between my legs and drives his fingers inside me again before pulling them out, tampon and all. Blood drips down his fingers. I completely forgot I was on my period. He moans as he sucks them into his mouth, the red working its way down his throat.

His cock apparition invades my mouth and with every other thrust, I'm able to see the tentacles, the jellyfish appearance he spoke about. He has ribbon-like sides down his cock, his tip resembles the head of a jellyfish.

I bite down on his shaft and his tail wraps around my throat to stop me.

"Careful mate. That only turns me on more. Bite me, scratch me, fuck me up to the point where I'm bleeding, and I will love every second of it." His hands grip the sides of my head to keep me in place, flexing his hips back and forth as he uses my mouth.

"Snapdragons," he grumbles. "You'll say your code-word to tell me to stop. Won't you?"

I nod to my illusion, curious as to how he knows about the word that saved my life.

"But you won't say it because you fucking love this." He pulls out from between my lips. "Because you know in the chambers of your darkened heart, I would never hurt you." He flips me onto my stomach and pulls my ass up in the air. "But I'll let you hurt me if that is what it takes for you to live the life you deserve."

My visitant rams himself into me, pressing my head

against the pillows, the sheets still messy from last night.

"Last night..." I groan when it hits me that he is the reason for how filthy I was.

"You fucked me in my statue form. You can't get enough of me when you're sleepwalking."

"You aren't real," I say more to myself than him.

He thrusts deeper, gripping me by my long hair, forcing me to arch my back, and I cry out.

"Does this not feel real, Mickey? I'm stretching your pretty cunt wide. You feel every inch of my big cock."

"It's all in my head." I grip the sheets as he drives himself into me. Our skin slaps together, his heavy sack slapping my pussy every time he thrusts to the hilt. "You're only in my head. Fuck!" I shout from how good he is making me feel.

I try to kick him away, but it only makes him fuck me faster and harder.

He feels so much better than Ty ever did, filling me in ways Ty never could.

Rhett changes our positions, pulling me to his chest as he lies down on his back. I turn around, unable to see anything other than the messy bedsheet beneath me, but the cock making me squirm and moan lets me know something is there, allowing me to ride him.

Unless it's all in my head.

I jump off him from the bed, more blood smeared across my thighs.

I can't do this. I'm insane. I miss Rhett's cock inside me. I'm empty.

I'm sick.

I dash to the door again and Rhett is there, slamming

me against it.

"You can't get away from me. I know what you want. I hear your thoughts, Mickey. I know you want more than this." He fills me again, effectively stealing my breath. "Tell me. I'll make it happen."

He growls into my throat, banging us against the door with every long stroke. My orgasm is close, pathetically close due to the circumstances. I never had an orgasm with Ty because I knew with him, it meant violence.

Rhett means pleasure and my body knows that– my heart knows that.

"You love being fucked by what you can't see."

I do. I love it so much, but there is a part of me that believes I'm asleep and everything about this is living in my fantasy world, my dream escape.

"We are going to have so much fun, My Timid Little Bloom."

I slap my hand against the door, taking every brutal inch and thrust Rhett gives me. His claws dig into my sides, and the familiar vibration that led me outside sounds again.

"I'm losing my mind. I'm insane." The door slams against the trim, the hinges rattling and threatening to break.

"It feels so fucking good, doesn't it?"

I shatter, tightening around my imaginary lover. "Rhett! Oh, fuck, yes, more." My head thuds against the door, and I gasp as the orgasm tingles my entire body.

And then he slides out of me, forces me onto my back, slams me against the door again, lifts my leg onto his shoulder, and his face is between my legs.

He snarls as he feasts, and I roll my hips against his face.

"I'm— I'm— on my—" I pinch my nipples, rolling them between my fingers tightly until it hurts.

I want the pain.

"I know. And you taste so fucking good, Mickey. You feed the vampire. Don't ever waste your period when I'm here." His tongue warms my channel, tingling the muscles and threatening another orgasm as it builds.

He stands, wraps my legs around his hips, and thrusts in.

We moan together and he plunges his tongue into my mouth. I'm able to taste myself and my blood, and it is disgusting.

Yet, I don't mind as he kisses me as if he is trying to possess me.

"Take my fucking cock, Mate. I'm going to fill your cunt with so much come, you'll have no choice but to carry my child. You'll be bound to me."

I barely have a warning before he comes and the electric shock of it latches onto my g-spot, shocking it with every stream he burdens me with. I orgasm, the electric current causing multiple orgasms back-to-back.

"Don't move," he warns, his cock becoming harder and thicker. "You take my stone knot so well, Mate."

My eyes fall shut and I know when I wake up, this will all have been a dream and I'll have no reason to believe a ghost fucked me.

My torment reminds me of all the pain associated with my trauma, but so much more haunts me now than ever before.

CHAPTER THIRTEEN

RHETT

I love how much I hate not being inside her. There are many things I shouldn't have done and breaking into her house, scaring her in ghost form, is not one of them.

I plan on doing it again because while she smelled of fear, she reeked of desire. She loved being forced. I think there is more to my mate than she lets on. She'll be hon-est with me one day when she realizes I am real. I'll give Mickey everything she desires, no matter how much those desires scare her, I'll show her how safe they are with me.

My time of being her ghost is coming to an end, soon-er rather than later. She deserves the truth, and I won't let my indecision of her seeing the real me jeopardize her. If Mickey did ever check herself into a mental institution, I wouldn't ever forgive myself.

She has her fears and I have mine.

I like the new me. I like my beasts.

I dislike that I have to reveal them to her. I won't today

or tomorrow but I will *have* to. Not many things have scared me since being an experiment, but showing Mickey who I really am? Even my beasts rear back wanting to hide at the thought of my mate, my beloved, my matching statue, rejecting me.

She can't reject what she doesn't know, and right now, she's too confused to understand which is my fault, but a fault I will stand by until it collapses.

Until then, I'll watch her every move and I'll touch her every chance I get. Once she's about to fall over the edge of insanity, only then will I admit the truth.

The front door slams shut, and my claws dig into her new roof. I've been perched up here for a few hours to enjoy the warmth. I'm no longer bound by the sun during the day; I can move around freely if I choose. The stone in me makes my bones crave the sunlight still so after I watched Mickey fall asleep and dream, I came onto the roof to enjoy the sunrise.

Mickey freed me from only enjoying a portion of my life. I was arrested and chained to live the rest of my life in the dark.

She climbs into her car, the engine sputtering a few times before it starts with a grumble. The exhaust coughs black smoke and I fall forward on my hands, digging the tips of my nails into the new roof.

I snarl at the car, hating how unsafe it is. She can't drive that around when she's pregnant. When we have our children, they won't be safe. She needs something reliable.

She flies down the road, the tail end of her car slightly fishtailing before coming to a complete stop at the sign.

I scoff, placing my hand against my chest as my own heart stops at her recklessness. She'll be the death of me with all this newfound worry and stress. Can I die from being stressed out because of my mate?

Launching myself in the air, I spread my wings, and follow behind her from up above. My shadow falls just behind her car, the massive wingspan taking up the entire road.

I could choose to be in my ghost form but it's too fun to leave people guessing if they see me.

Every so often, her exhaust spews black, irking me further. I'll be slashing her tires, peeling back the roof, and tearing apart the engine beyond repair so she can't drive this piece of shit.

My mate deserves the best.

I'm going to get it for her.

Mickey pulls into the parking lot of Demi's Diner and even from up here, I can see her frustration with how hard she slams the door.

Oh, my mate is mad.

It's so cute.

I watch her enter the diner to ensure she's safe and around friends before I continue flying by. I soar over the restaurant and quaint town. It's almost humorous how sweet this town appears to be, not knowing the creatures that taint its innocence are here.

A few people enter the pharmacy, lifting their hands over their eyes to block the sun to see what is casting such a large shadow. I grin, rise sharply, and disappear into the clouds.

Closing my eyes, I enjoy the wind grazing my cheeks

and blowing through my hair. Freedom like this is impossible to have as a human. I'd never go back to such a fragile, weak body.

How I was made was cruel, yet the outcome is something I would never dream I would ever want for myself.

Wanting to have some fun, I flap my wings in a fast beat, gaining speed. I barrel roll, then decide to fall, my wings flush behind my back.

"Woo! Yes! Haha!" I smile, spreading my wings out to stop myself from getting too low. Using my vampire speed to help me fly, I blur through the sky, climbing toward the sun. The air becomes thinner. My lungs struggle to breathe, and I spread my arms and wings, maneuver onto my back, and fall.

The weight of my body has me piercing through the sky. I keep my tail safely wrapped around my leg, enjoying the danger of wondering if I'll hit the ground or not.

My sliver of humanity kicks in.

If I don't look where the ground is, if I don't double-check how close I am to hitting it, I'll make impact.

I'll most likely die from those wounds.

Mickey would be free. My ghost of her would no longer haunt every corner of her mind and body.

I growl at the thought, flipping over onto my stomach and flying higher to avoid death.

She'll have to fucking deal with being haunted because I'm never going anywhere.

Who am I kidding?

Not even death would stop me from consuming her. My soul would rise from the dead. I'd escape the clutches of Hell for her. In my afterlife, I'd choose to be burned by my sins over and over again in every attempt to get to her. When demons rip apart my spirit and piece it back together again, they will find her in my soul's light.

And even they will realize no amount of torture will hold me back. I'll earn my right to invade her life.

When I'm six feet under and the insects are eating my flesh, when the Devil himself is holding my sins, when my bones are forgotten and turn to dust, her light will bring me home.

My cage is not Hell, and I will fight my jailers for trying to keep me there. Mickey is my imprisonment, and I will happily serve my sentence for eternities to come.

Death is nothing but an obstacle if it ever were to happen. Souls live forever and I'd plague hers.

Noticing the car dealership down below has my sordid thoughts disappearing, and I nosedive, my wings flush against my back to gain speed. As I get closer to the dealership, I change my angle, placing my feet first. My wings help slow when I place them in the right position causing the right amount of drag.

My feet hit the hot pavement and I waste no time shifting into my ghost form. Trucks, SUVs, and cars are everywhere. A few salesmen have their hands tucked into their pockets, laughing at something the other said.

I lace my hands behind my back and begin to whistle while checking out the inventory.

No cars. They aren't big enough for all the children Mickey and I will have. I am going to keep her pregnant until she says she wants to stop. Even then, I don't know how I'll stop the craving for seeing her round with my son or daughter.

My cock plumps at the thought and I growl, reaching down to give it one long stroke.

"Did you hear that?" One of the salesmen asks his friends.

"Probably a storm coming."

"It sounded like a growl. An animal."

"It's just thunder, man. Relax."

I chuckle darkly. They should listen to him. An animal is here and is most definitely going to take. I could do this properly. I could pay in cash from the banks I've robbed, but that money is for Mickey.

Not these assholes.

I extend a claw and stare at them, waiting for their reaction as my nail drags across every vehicle I pass.

"What the hell is that? Do you hear that?"

I stop, a sly grin tilting my lips when one of them comes over. He runs, mouth parting when he sees the damage.

"Fuck– guys–"

I cut him off, dragging him behind one of the SUVs, and shift so he can see me. His eyes widen in fear, and I cover his mouth in time, to catch his scream.

"It's okay. I'm not going to kill you." I feel the moment he is caught in my gaze. He relaxes. His brown eyes hood, taking on a glazed appearance. Similar to Mickey's when she is sleepwalking. "You aren't going to make a sound. You aren't going to remember this." There are drops of paralytic beads on the tip of my nails. It doesn't work on Mickey, which makes sense since she is my mate, but everyone else?

Mmm, they are in danger.

I swipe it on his skin. "You're not going to be able to feel your body. You'll be fine in a few hours." His knees buckle and I step back just to watch him hit the ground, his head smacking against the pavement. I click my tongue. "That sounded painful." I shove his body with my foot to see he is immobile and unconscious.

Perfect.

"Sean? Hey man, you okay?"

I sigh in annoyance. "I have to go take care of your other friends now. Don't move." I snicker to myself. "You know what I mean." I blur to the other salesman, slashing his arm with my nail, then the other, and another.

Until all that's left is one.

I snag him by the collar and throw him against a car, denting the door from the force.

Whoops.

He's locked in my gaze, and I take advantage. "You're going to get the paperwork written up. You'll say the car was a giveaway prize or maybe you'll pay for it, I don't care how you do it. See that pretty blue SUV over there? I want it for my mate. You'll give it to me. Okay? And then, after you give me the keys, you won't remember a fucking thing about what happened here, will you?"

"Not a thing," he slurs from my vampiric influence.

"Good." I release him. "Go get it done."

The blue SUV matches her eyes. It looks like it has everything she needs including three rows of seats for our kids.

"And get me a big fucking bow!" I shout over my shoulder.

He takes forever. I have to paralyze the other salesmen two more times and the sun is setting before he comes dragging his feet out of the building with keys and a big bow in hand. The bow is dragging on the ground behind him because it's so massive.

I grin, plucking each from him. "Thank you." Then I slice his arm, inserting the paralytic in his system. "Sorry. I just felt like doing that. You won't remember any of this." I bend down and pat his bald head. "So at least you'll have that." I make my rounds to each downed salesman, mystifying them to alter their memory.

See, if I had no soul, I'd kill them, but my way is so much more fun. For the rest of their lives, they will wonder what happened today, and they will never know. It will bother them. It will be the itch they can't scratch.

Makes me giddy.

I stand in front of the SUV and click the buttons. The door opens automatically, and the car starts.

Climbing inside is another issue.

I can't fit.

"Mother fucker," I snarl, trying a new angle.

I turn, bend over, and back up so my tail has space. My wings get caught on the door frame. I stop and take a minute to gather my patience. I'm one second away from throwing this SUV over a cliff.

My hands are on my hips and my tail whips behind me in anger as I stare into the driver's seat.

Tucking my wings flush against my body, I scoot the seat all the way back, then open the moon roof for the tips of the wings to peek through. Rolling down the window, my tail slides up my back and then slithers out the window.

I barely fit in this damn vehicle.

Peeling out of the parking lot, I leave six men paralyzed, and the only thing I'm thinking about is getting back to Mickey. I'm a few towns over and I won't be at her house for a few hours. Flying is faster and according to the sign I just drove by, I'm nearly two hundred miles away.

I growl, pressing my elbow on the edge of the window, needing to get back to Mickey as soon as possible.

Two hundred miles is too far. What if Ty attacks while I'm gone? How could I be so irresponsible? I lose my mind when I'm flying, a peace falls over me, and I lose track of time.

Pressing my foot against the gas pedal, the engine purrs. I speed down the highway, the trees on the side of the road blurring as I pass them. My wings itch to fly after being trapped in this tight space. The damn bow takes up the entire back seat and trunk.

Red and Blue lights flash behind me, and my fingers curl around the steering wheel, gripping it so hard it creaks.

Snarling, I pull to the side of the road. I'm going to kill this fucking cop for keeping me away from Mickey even longer.

"Don't kill him. Don't kill him," I chant to myself. "Don't get blood on the new car. Mickey won't like that." I take a deep breath in, then release, my thirst for murder easing.

Slightly.

Thinking of Mickey is what will keep this cop alive.

"What the fuck? Are you into cosplay or some shit?" he asks when he gets to my window.

"Something like that," I growl, flashing my fang.

"Do you know how fast you were going? I'm going to need to see your license and registration."

I turn to him, giving him a full view of my face. My eyes bleed red, and he's caught in my gaze.

"You're going to let me go, Officer. You pulled over a man on the way to the hospital with his pregnant wife. She's in labor. You won't remember me, and you let him go because you understood."

"I understood," he echoes in his trance. "That's really nice. I hope the baby is healthy."

"Aw." I pucker my lips. "Aren't you sweet?" I tap my claws on the side of the door, debating if I want to make him bleed. Just a little. Instead, I'll have fun. "You're going to get naked, turn your siren on, and dance in the middle of the road until the sun comes up, Officer."

"That's an awfully long time," he drowses, slowly un-buttoning his shirt because he has no choice but to listen to me.

"It is, but it's either dance or I kill you for keeping me away from my mate even longer."

"I understand. I don't want to die."

"Shame." I suck my tongue over my fangs, wishing this were a different day. "Have fun dancing and use that baton in..." I smirk "A special way. Won't you like that?"

He begins to undo his belt. "I don't think so, but I'm going to try."

I slap his arm and put the car in drive. "Thatta boy. Have a good time." I wrap my tail around the baton, hand-ing him the weapon. "Careful. Seems big."

He holds it to his chest, his Adam's apple bobbing.

"Have a great night, officer." I ease forward, keeping a safe speed so I don't accidentally kill him.

I want to kill him, though. I want to hear him scream. I want to hear him beg to live.

Cracking my neck, I growl at the thought of him crying and yelling, the smell of his fear permeating the air and it has me speeding down the road again.

Miles vanish between me and Mickey with how fast I'm going to get back to her. I turn on the radio to help with the last hundred miles, my claws making it difficult to change the station.

I could file them down, but then I couldn't drag them down Mickey's body and leave those bright red lines on her flesh. The marks are a symbol that she belongs to me. They are too important.

And then it hits me.

I have no marks of her on me, which is a shame be-cause I belong to her too. I am hers. She owns me in ways no one can understand except me, except her. I am hers to do what she wants with.

"Thank you for tuning into Cove Top Hits. This is Jerry Z, your radio host for the evening. If you're new here, we do emergency messages from loved ones on every break. We have an urgent message for everyone out there from a worried friend. His name is Fitz. If you're Rhett Royals, this message is for you. I'll play his voice message. Trigger warnings, folks. Be prepared to have your heartstrings tugged."

When I hear the name Fitz, I swerve off the road and yank the wheel to the left, then right, trying to get control of the SUV. I slam on the brakes. Grass and dirt kick up from the tires as I slide to a stop.

My arms are straight. My hands are wrapped around the wheel. My fingers hurt from how hard I'm gripping it. I can't breathe.

And when I hear his voice, every memory I have of him has tears welling in my eyes.

"Hi Cove listeners. My uh—" He clears his throat, emotion already heavy in his voice. "Ah, man. I can't believe I'm doing this, but I'm calling every radio station in the country and I'm desperate."

I stare at the screen, Cove Top Hits scrolling to the left, and a tear breaks free.

"I'm looking for my best friend, my brother. Rhett Royals. He's been missing for... months." He sounds so resigned as if he's lost all hope that I'm out there. "I refuse to give up looking for him. He was supposed to meet me for drinks, and he never did. He never showed and that isn't like Rhett. He's the kind of friend that shows up no matter what. So, Rhett," he calls out to me, my name a shattered breath. "It's Fitz. If you're out there and you're listening, man, please, come home. Call me. Let me know you're..."

I place my head against the steering wheel, more tears dripping down my cheeks as memories and emotions I have completely forgotten about take over me when I think of Fitz.

"Let me know you're alive." His words become higher before they turn into sobs. "Please man. Someone, even if he is dead, I'll get his body. I'll bring him home. He's..." he sniffles. "He's tall, a big guy, over six foot three, built. He owned Royals' Garage, so he isn't weak. He did a lot of manual labor. He has blonde hair. Blue eyes. He's kind. He'll do anything for anyone. He was last seen wearing oil-stained jeans and a light blue T-shirt that had his name on it. I'm not going to give up. I don't care what it takes to find you, man. I know you're out there. I'll find you. It kills me to know something terrible happened to you and I wasn't there."

Fitz is a mess now, trying not to cry but he's failing. He was always the kind of guy who didn't care about showing his emotions.

If I remember correctly.

"Anyway, call this number—" he rattles off his phone number "And here is my email. My home address. Every-thing. Please, anyone, call me with any information. Rhett, you haven't been forgotten. I love you, brother. I won't stop searching. I promise."

The voice message ends, and Jerry Z comes back on the radio.

"Wow." He clears his throat, obviously affected. "That's a damn good friend right there. If anyone has someone in their lives who cares about you that much, hold onto them. Rhett Royals, if you're out there, we hope you're safe. We hope your friend finds you. You have a lot of listeners hoping for the best."

I slam the power button on the radio with my palm to turn it off.

"Ahhhhhh!" I roar at the top of my lungs, the vibra-tions shaking the car, and I grip the wheel and repeatedly hit it with my fist. I slam my back against the seat and let out a tortured, soul-wrenching shout, my cheeks wet with my agony.

What am I supposed to do? Call Fitz and tell him where I am? Tell him that I'm... this? I hold a hand to my chest, grabbing my heart from how much I didn't know I missed my friend.

It's better if he believes I'm dead.

The Rhett he is looking for doesn't exist anymore.

He died the day I was taken.

And he's never coming back.

CHAPTER FOURTEEN

MICKEY

"So you've never seen this car before?" Jake asks, standing next to me as we stare at the brand-new bright blue SUV.

It is beautiful and it has a big red bow on the roof. I never trust gifts. There are always stipulations. Gifts are a kind of manipulation. It's subtle. People think that presents are so kind, so thoughtful, but are they? It's just another delusion the gifter is creating.

It's a cycle.

The giftee will think, "Wow, that was so kind of them to get this for me." And then that person with the gift is bound to the person who gave them a present, thankful, skewing their mind with fake kindness.

No, there are always strings attached to gifts. "I don't want it," I blurt out.

And lie.

I do want it.

I want this car so bad, especially since mine is trashed and there is no way of fixing it.

Jake and I look at the heap of metal that used to be my vehicle. The roof is peeled back, the seats are ripped and shredded to pieces, and the windshield isn't even there. It's gone as if someone stole it.

"Found the windshield!" One of his deputies yells from the side of the house. "It's by the lake."

"Well, that answers that," Jake mumbles, grabbing his belt as he adjusts his stance. He lowers his sunglasses to the tip of his nose. "What do you mean you don't want it?"

I lift a shoulder and stutter before finding my words. "I don't want it. It has to come with strings." A tire on my old car pops and I jump from the loud noise. Jake protects me by slinging an arm out across my chest.

And then the long high squeal of air leaving the rubber is drawn out for too long and now it's awkward.

"You sure about that, Mickey?"

I sigh, knowing I don't really have another choice.

He points to what used to be my car. "I mean, there are deep gashes in each side, dragged down from the front fender to the back." He is next to the wreckage, placing his fingers on each gash. "It's like claws or something."

"I know, Jake. I can see it too." I don't mean to sound so sassy. Jake is being a good friend and sheriff, showing me all the issues as to why I have no choice but to accept the new car.

"And you have no seats left. The seats are barren. I can see the car's frame underneath them. Something peeled back your roof. Do you know how hard that is to do? Your engine is in literal pieces. It's impossible to put back together. And your tires are flat. One is off the rim and the other was also in the lake. Someone really didn't like you driving this car."

"This car is registered to you. Temp tags and everything. This is your new car, Mickey." Jake points to the blue SUV. "Whether you like it or not."

"Can they check for a tracking device or something?"

"Are you thinking it's from Ty?" Jake questions, walking toward me in hurried strides. "I don't think this is his M.O. He doesn't seem like the gifting type."

I bring my left hand to my mouth, biting my thumbnail with anxiety. "It isn't. He would never do this, but just in case? Can you check?"

"You got it, Mickey. I want to know too." Jake whistles and stalks over to his deputies, leaving me to stare at the vehicle that I paid a couple hundred bucks for when I moved into this house.

It's almost bittersweet.

My phone vibrates and Milo's number pops up. Already stressed, I run my fingers through my hair.

"Milo. Minnie. I'm fine. It isn't a big deal."

"Isn't a big deal?" Milo yells.

"It's the biggest of deals. Are you okay? Did they hurt you?" Minnie shouts too close to the microphone and I have to pull away to rescue my ear.

"There's no reason to worry. Whoever did this left another car, a newer one. Oh, look. Jake is coming back over. I gotta go. I gotta—"

"Mickey, don't you dare."

"Oh, no. I'm losing you." I stretch my arm in the air.

"I'm losing service. Milo?"

"Mickey, you brat. I swear when I get—"

I hang up the phone and blow a raspberry, relieved I've dodged that conversation that would leave me exhausted. I love that they worry, I do, but they worry too much.

"Losing service, huh? In your own yard?" Jake pokes at my horrible excuse.

"They don't need to worry when you're here. They have been sweet to me and kind, and I know I bring so much stress to them. I'm ready for my brother and sister to let go a little. I can do this. I can start over."

Jake grabs my shoulder, giving it a slight squeeze. Most other guys, I'd flinch, but Jake is different. I feel safe with him.

"And you're doing great, Mickey. You're doing the damn thing and I have never seen you speak to your sibling the way you did just now. Your personality is coming through. It's good to see. I'm happy for you and I'm glad you trust me. That means a lot because I know it isn't easy. It's such a gift to me to know you feel safe with me and my officers here."

"You've been such a great friend to us since we moved here. You've been kind to me. You've had my back."

"I do and will. That's why I'm going to try to track where the SUV came from. There's no tracker on the vehicle. It's clean. So far, this is safe. I don't think this person is out to hurt you. In a weird way, I think they are protecting you."

"From what?" I ask more of the universe than Jake, but he answers anyway.

"The world, it seems. Your old car wouldn't protect you from the wild drivers out there like this new one will. It's thoughtful, even if it is questionable."

"Questionable? Jake, it's an eighty thousand—"

"One hundred thousand."

I roll my eyes at him. "Whatever thousands of dollars' worth SUV. I'm supposed to just accept it? It's a trick."

"Trick?"

I nod, kicking the ground with the tip of my shoe. "To get me to trust them. It's like a promise already dipped with the intention to lie. You can't see the intention, the person who made the promise has already tainted it. And then eventually, you notice they broke the promise they never meant to keep."

"I can understand that, Mickey. You don't have to trust anyone but keep the car anyway." He winks just as his radio goes off. His playfulness falls the longer the dispatcher speaks. "Sure. Yeah, I'll be there in two minutes." He lets go of the button on the radio, his face falling. "We have to go. Another robbery downtown."

"Another?"

"I have no idea what's happening. We look at security footage and it's just this blur. There isn't a person. Nothing is there, but money is being stolen. This is the third bank. He or she has hit the only banks we have here. There's nothing left for them to steal."

"Wow." An unsteady feeling works its way into my stomach when I think of the ghost I see. "Go. I'll be fine. Be careful."

He grips the front of his hat, pinches the brim, and gives me a slight head tilt. "I'll leave an officer."

"Don't. Go." I shout as he is midway to his car. "Truly. I'll be fine."

Jake's jaw tenses. He runs by my ruined car, and I know it bothers him that he doesn't know who did this. He doesn't want to leave me unprotected. The reality is, I can't depend on Jake and my siblings forever. I have to start depending on myself. They can't be at my beck and call. It's wrong.

One by one the sirens wail, and the tires spin on the grass as they speed away. Dust kicks up creating a heavy cloud before the slight breeze steals the dirt away.

The loud murmurs of conversation are gone. The sirens get quieter the further away they get.

And the silence is loud.

I grab my upper bicep with my left hand and look around, that too-familiar sensation creeping up my spine again.

Someone is here... I can feel them watching me.

"Hello? Who is out there?" I stomp forward, heart pounding in hard jabs against my ribcage. I spin around, not seeing a damn thing. "Ty? Is that you? Come on!" I yell, spreading out my arms. "Come on. Come and get me, you son of a bitch!" Birds fly from the trees, my voice echoing all around me.

"I know you're there," I whisper into the darkness of the forest. "And I won't be afraid of you." I scan from left to right, searching for anything between the shadows the branches cast. "I can feel you."

A loud snap echoes from the belly of the forest. The wind kicks up, tangling the ends of my hair. The sun disappears behind the graying clouds, thunder rolling nearby. The storms here build so fast and out of nowhere. The weather changes keep me on my toes.

Rain begins to fall. The dirt beneath me turns from a light red to a dark brown. As seconds tick by, the hiss of rain becomes louder, as the drops make impact with the ground as if they hate one another.

I rush to my newly covered porch, leaning against the oak-stained beam. There's nothing here but my paranoia trying to get the best of me. I take one last look at the worthless car before scanning my fingerprint on the handle and going inside.

Only to see the back door open.

And because I was here with Jake, I didn't bother to reset the security system.

"One of the police officers must have left it open. Doesn't mean anything," I tell myself, heading toward the other side of the room to shut the door.

I toss my damp hair in a messy bun and appreciate the progress I've made on the house. The kitchen is complete with new stainless steel appliances and open to the living room just like I wanted.

An oversized deep burgundy rug lies in the middle of the space. Built-in bookshelves line the wall, framing the fireplace. A seventy-inch flat-screen TV is mounted on the wall in the gap the contractors measured to fit the monstrosity. I got it for Milo. He loves watching sports.

The windows on the wall where the back door is are large, allowing light in. There are benches under them, perfect for storage or sitting and drinking a hot cup of coffee or tea, looking out the glass, and watching the rain fall.

My house is starting to feel like a home and there is a warmth to that I didn't know I needed.

It's safe and it's mine.

I reach for the handle to close the door when I catch a reflection in the window that doesn't belong to me.

Steven. The man who said I knew him from high school.

We stare at one another for a long beat before he reaches for me. I dive to the right, but he snags me by my hair and yanks me to his chest.

"I have a message from Ty." He keeps a tight grip on my hair, then wraps a hand around my throat, squeezing it so hard I can't breathe, and spots begin to dance in my eyes. "I can understand his obsession with you." He inhales, his hot breath puffing against my ear. "You are fucking beautiful."

"Fuck. You."

"Oh, we'll make that happen. Ty said I get to have fun with you too, but he told me to tell you, you're a stupid fucking girl for thinking you could ever get away from him. I didn't think those cops would ever leave. By this time tomorrow, you'll be with him, I would have fucked you, and I get a nice lump sum of cash. I'm curious what else he sees in you. I didn't know one person would cause so much trouble." He licks my earlobe, chuckling. "He has paid me a lot of money to find you too. You made it difficult. I'll give you that, but I guess at the end of the day, you're exactly what Ty said you are. A stupid fucking girl."

I shake my head, inhaling to get as much air in my lungs as possible, then dig my nails into his arm around my throat. "I am far from stupid." I slam my foot down on his and bite into his arm until I taste blood.

"Fucking bitch!"

His arm loosens enough for me to get away, but I don't run because I know he'll catch me— they always do.

I lift my leg and kick him between his legs, but he catches me by my ankle right before I make contact.

His dead eyes meet mine. "Nice try."

"My efforts are far from over." I jump-kick, smacking him across the face with my other leg.

I knee him in the stomach, slam my elbows down on his back, and he wraps his arms around me, tackling me to the ground.

The air is knocked out of me and my shoulders ache from the contact. I groan.

"You fucking bitch." He wraps his hands around my throat again and I snag his wrists, this time, he intends to kill. "Do you really think I give a fuck if you're alive? I'll deliver you alive or dead to my client." His brown hair falls into his face, his cheeks turning red from the energy used to strangle me. "You're nothing but a piece of ass, and that's all you'll ever be, according to the stories Ty told me." He reaches between us and unbuttons my jeans. "I hear you feel better than any whore he has ever fucked, and I want to know what this pussy is like after hearing so much about it."

I grip his wrist harder and rasp through the constriction. "That's too... fucking bad." I rear my head back and throw it forward, smacking his nose with my forehead.

"God damn it." He cups his nose, blood dripping from between his fingers.

I roll to my side, pushing myself up, all while shaking

my head as it spins. Getting up is difficult, considering the room is spinning. I don't care if trying to get away from him kills me.

I will never go willingly.

I will never stop fighting.

I am so much stronger than the girl I was before.

And I was never fucking stupid.

Falling onto my hands and knees, I crawl to the loose floorboard where I keep the gun.

"You broke my nose," he groans.

I ignore him, ignore the pain throbbing between my eyes, and the tears blurring my vision. The room spins and spins. Everything seems so out of reach. I stop moving, squeezing my eyes shut as the dizzy spell passes.

Looking over my shoulder, Steven is getting up, which means I only have a few seconds to get what I need. Blood is wet on his chin, and he spits red, nostrils flaring from my damn audacity.

Audacity I plan to always keep.

"I like it when they fight," he says, wiping his mouth with his hand.

"Good. I never plan on stopping."

He digs into his waistband and pulls out a knife. The blade is thick and long with serrated edges.

"We'll see." I swallow, eyeing the blade. If he stabs me, I'm done. I'll die.

I stomp my foot on the floorboard, snatching the piece of wood with my hand since I can't bend down to grab the gun. If I do, he'll take the split second to stab me. I can't turn my back to him.

He lunges and I dive left, lifting the board into the

air and bringing it down on his wrist with every ounce of determination I have.

The knife doesn't escape his hold.

Wasting no time, I backhand the board across his face and blood-tinted spit flies across the room.

Along with a tooth.

It clinks against the floor.

Once.

Twice.

I bolt to the back door, jumping down the stairs.

I'm three steps into my getaway and a sharp pain stabs me in the back. I gasp, the pain unbearable.

"You really are a stupid girl." He grabs the handle of the knife and buries it deeper.

I scream at the top of my lungs. Flames lick the wound and burn my insides.

"If I pull this knife out, you'll bleed to death. You'll do as I say if you want to stay alive."

"Being alive and living are two different things." I suck my tongue over my teeth, tasting blood, and spit the wad into his face. "And I would rather die than ever be with Ty. So go ahead and kill me."

"I'd be glad—" he is cut off as he is tackled to the ground.

I fall to my knees, swallowing as much air as my body will allow. Blood drips down my back, my shirt warm and wet. I fall forward, catching myself on my left hand before falling to my side.

My breaths come out loud and hoarse. Every inhale is audible.

I'm going to die.

Laughter bubbles free. Out of all the torment I've lived through, the agony, the abuse, the neglect, and a fucking knife is going to kill me?

At least I'm in my own yard, by my own house, getting one last look at the beautiful lake I love so much.

I blink, tears breaking free as I watch two men fight.

Well, one man is fighting– the other doesn't look like a man at all. Snarls and growls have hope building in my chest.

"She is mine!" The beast with wings warns. "How dare you try and take her from me. How dare you take her life when it is so much more important than yours."

"No. Please! Please, I'll go. I'll leave."

The beast's tail whips out, wrapping around Steven's neck, then picks him up and off the ground. His feet dangle, searching for support that is not there.

Breathe.

I remind myself, inhaling through the pain.

"You're out of your mind if you think I'm going to let another man's mate be at risk because I let you live."

Breathe.

I know this voice. I know this beast.

"Rhett." His name gets lost in the sound of the long grass swaying together.

His wings spread and he lifts into the air. Steven screams at the top of his lungs. Rhett still has him by the neck when they dive into the water. Steven's cries end the moment my monster takes him underwater.

Breathe.

Steven screams again, crawling his way out of the lake. Water pours off his soaked clothes as he gets to his feet. He doesn't spare me a glance when he takes his next step.

The crocodile launches out of the water and snaps his jaws around Steven's leg. From here, I can hear the bone break, and a normal person would turn away from the violence.

Not me.

I want to watch the man who tried to kill me die with my last few breaths.

He claws at the ground, wailing for his life. "Someone, please help me! Someone help!"

The crocodile's stare aims directly at me, a softness, a love flutters over his eyes for a split second before they darken.

He death rolls.

Water splashes from Steven trying to break free, to get one last breath. Steven manages to get free again, swimming to the shore. And then the crocodile is there again, nearly jumping into the air. The large jaws with rows of teeth clamp on Steven's neck.

The crocodile death rolls again, choosing to drown Steven instead of breaking his neck.

Breathe.

I don't know a lot about crocodiles, but I do know from watching educational shows growing up that death rolls are to kill and dismember their prey, then they eat pieces that have broken off, whole.

The splashing of water stops and there is no crocodile or Steven to be seen.

I groan, my breathing changing pace, and I glance up to the sky as the rain continues to fall, feeling the cold drips of rain on my face.

"I wish the stars were out," I say to no one but myself as the pain becomes nonexistent.

It doesn't hurt anymore.

"Hey, hey. My sweet mate. No." A wet hand slides under my head.

And I'm left staring at someone who isn't human.

My mind is still playing tricks on me in death.

"Rhett." I touch his cheek with my hand, grazing over the crocodile scales before sliding my fingers over his nose, the rough stone skin tickling my palm. "You're here."

"I'm always here for you, Mickey." He pushes my hair back, the kind softness returning in his eyes. "He is dead and soon Ty will be too. I promise." He bends down, leaning so close I can almost feel his lips against mine. "This is going to hurt."

He yanks the knife from my back, and I cry out, the pain unimaginable. Black spots dance in the sky.

Rhett bites into his wrist and shoves it into my mouth. "I won't live without you. Drink. Drink, My Brave Little Flower. Drink to stay with me."

With every drag, energy returns to me. He holds his wrist against my mouth, and I groan at how good he tastes.

He purrs, a constant vibration in his chest that's calming, as he runs his claws through my hair.

This must be death because nothing in my life has ever felt so peaceful.

"Take what you need. Take all of me."

My lungs can fully expand now, so I slide his wrist from my mouth. Blood must be covering my chin.

"I know," I whisper, half-drunk off nearly dying, and his blood.

Or slurring because I'm sleep-talking. I'm not sure.

"What?" he whispers.

"I know what you are." I graze my knuckles over his high cheekbones, then trace the large pout of his lips.

"I'm a monster."

"You're not the monster that hurts me but the one who slaughters for me."

His mouth parts in shock, and his reptilian eyes blink at me.

"I know what you are," I repeat, sighing as the ache in my back disappears. "And I love you anyway."

CHAPTER FIFTEEN

RHETT

"*And I love you anyway.*"

The words echo as I hold her in my arms. She's so small in my embrace. I'm afraid if I move her, I'll hurt her. I am more than two-feet taller than her and even though I've been inside her, in this moment, I've never felt closer.

Her lashes are long and wet, speared from the rain. Her ice-blue eyes are brighter than anything around us. Everything, the grass, the water, the clouds, has darkened, and her eyes are the light.

It's impossible for her to love me. She doesn't know me. If she did, love would be the furthest thing from her mind.

The wind blows her scent to me, and I growl when I smell her attacker all over her. She's only allowed to smell of me.

How long has it been since she's swam in the lake? I've released my musk in there, so every time she swims, she bathes in me.

And I can't smell myself on her at all. It's him. It's fear. It's Death still clinging on to her soul. Death won't win this time. My blood is stronger.

"Rhett," she manages to say my name one last time before closing her eyes.

"Mickey? Mickey!" I shake her but she doesn't respond. In a panic, I rest my ear against her chest, clutch her small ribcage in my hand, and release a breath when I hear her heartbeat.

"You're lucky."

I place Mickey under my body as I curl over her, protecting her like a shield.

A black shadow figure is a few feet away, drifting in and out of skeleton form. He's leaning against a nearby tree, arms crossed, ankles over one another then pushes away. He floats toward me. He disappears and reappears every few seconds until he is in front of me.

"You're one lucky ducky, Mick." He reaches out to touch her and I roar as loud as I can in warning. I place my hand on her side, curling my claws into her body, then push her against me protectively.

"Easy. Down boy." He holds out his shadowed hand. "Lorcan. Pleased to meet you."

I curl a lip, sneering at the gesture.

"Grouchy fella, aren't you? Jeez. It's like—" he lifts his hands and mocks "—Someone tried to kill your mate."

"And I'll kill you if you try to take her from me."

"Eh, I'm not here for her." He waves his hand in disinterest. "I'm here for the guy you just killed. You know, the body floating face down in the lake." He points over to where I left Steven.

"I'd kill him again too."

"I know. He wasn't a very nice guy. Don't worry, where I'm taking his soul, he'll never know peace again."

I grunt with a nod. "Good. No one harms my mate and lives."

"Oh, I know. That's how it is for all paranormals but you're special, huh? All those different DNAs." He boops my nose.

Boops it.

"I'll have to tell Hell's Harvesters about this because it's you, and they are still learning about your... kind."

"They know?"

"You aren't the only DNA experiment here. You think you're the first cute little monster with a fluffy soul for his mate?"

"Creed," I say with realization. "The man at the diner with a feral pet on his shoulder."

Lorcan snickers. "He isn't a pet. That's his son."

I lift a shoulder before scooping Mickey into my arms so I can feel her against my skin.

"If you have questions, you should go to him. He is... crankier than you are though. I suspect it's because of the dragon DNA. Dragons are always ready for violence."

"I'm not angry about what happened to me. I accept who I am now. I like who I am now more than I ever did when I was human. I'm only angry for Mickey."

He tilts his head, tapping his chin. "Why?"

I stroke my claws through her hair, then trace the delicate edge of her jaw. "Because she's had to deal with enough monsters in her life. She doesn't need another."

"Being a monster isn't about how you look but how you act."

"I've done things to her I shouldn't be proud of." I touch the mating mark on her neck, my fangs itching to make a matching set on the other side.

"But you are?"

"Very," I growl, lifting her into my arms. She buries her face in my neck, her breath causing goosebumps to arise on my skin.

"I see." He floats over to the body, plunges his hand into Steven's chest, and rips out his soul. "I am taking him to Hell. Remember that when you think of monsters." His eyes land on Mickey, an envious expression crossing his face for a brief second before it's gone, replaced with a toothy grin. He waves his fingers. "Tootles, Rocky."

"Rocky?"

He blinks at me, then eyes me up and down. "Duh, dude. You're made of stone. What else would I call you?"

"Rhett. My name is Rhett."

He crinkles his nose. "I don't like it. It sounds so human. Rocky is better. See ya later, Sidewalk."

I growl at him and debate on ripping his shadows from his damn skeleton, but he snaps his fingers, and he's gone.

Before standing, I grab the knife that got embedded into her back because I wasn't here. I robbed one last bank. I just wanted enough for us to start our lives and not to worry about our future. I'm not sure how I'll ever be able to work again looking the way I do, and it shouldn't be up to Mickey to work all the time because she's stuck with me as a mate.

I don't care how many banks I have to rob. I don't care if it means I have to travel from state to state. I'll do it. I don't care if I'm a criminal or committing a crime. I've busted my ass before when I owned my business and look where it got me.

The blood on the knife is still wet and I can't help myself. Mickey tastes so good. I can't let any go to waste.

I press the flat side of the blade against my tongue, licking the blood from the metal. The moan that escapes me is loud. I flip the knife over, cleaning the other side.

"Fuck, My Brave Little Flower. You taste so good. How will I ever get enough of you?" I lean down and kiss her forehead.

I need to get rid of this knife. She doesn't need to see it when she wakes up. The memory of almost dying will be enough trauma. I rear my arm back, and with all my strength, I throw the knife in the air, and it flies across the lake.

A normal person wouldn't be able to see where it lands, but I can. It's in the deepest part of the lake and when I'm in my crocodile form, I'll bury it under miles of sand.

Mickey whimpers, wiggling in my hold before pressing her nose against my neck and inhaling. It's as if the scent of me calms her.

"You're okay. I'm sorry I wasn't here. That will never happen again." I walk up the steps of the back porch, open the door, then slam and lock it shut behind me.

I take her to her room, bypassing the spare she's been staying in because the primary bedroom is complete.

Milo took care of the dead animal as promised and

now it's her dream room. A large king-size bed sits against the left wall so she can have a view of the lake when she goes to sleep and wakes up. The windows are more like a solarium. There is no drywall but thick glass from one end to the other, giving her a massive view of the environment she owns.

The storm continues outside regardless that Mickey almost died. The world doesn't notice moments. It will always continue to spin, whether someone had their worst day or their best. Everything continues as if you never existed.

I stand in the middle of the room, taking in Mickey's existence.

The world doesn't know, but it is a better place with her in it, and if she were to be gone, a darkness would fall over the planet because I would forever be altered.

I hold on to her harder, needing to feel her flesh give under my fingers. I gently place her on the bed, appreciating the dark four-post frame with a sheer white net over it. Every corner is tied to a post. Pillows upon pillows stack up on the bed, taking up too much space.

I bet they don't get used.

Her comforter is an emerald-green, soft and warm.

"I'm starting to think your favorite color is green, Mate." I tuck her hair behind her ear and smirk. "That's good, considering most of my body is that color." I sigh, stroking her arm. "What are we going to do now? I don't know if letting you believe I'm real is a good thing or not. I don't want to play with your mind. I truly don't. Mickey, I haven't felt the emotion of fear since I was kidnapped and tested on. I've lived every day since not being afraid of anything. And then you happened. You've seen me, and my God, Mickey, that scares me so much. You have no idea all the things I want to be for you. Your protector. Your lover. Your provider. Your strength. But your monster? Something you've already been running from? I'm not sure how to give that to you without losing you."

She turns to her side, the ruined blood-stained shirt catches my eye and I snarl, ripping the shirt from her body. I toss it on the dark hardwood floor, forgetting all about the material when I begin to count the scars on her body.

There are so many.

Too many.

I trace every one I see, starting at her lower back and working my way up. There's no scar from the knife wound. My blood took care of that, and our mating faded her scars slightly, but I'm afraid they won't ever be gone.

"I'm going to bring you his head, Mickey. Even if you only ever love the ghost of me, I will always love you in any form. And you deserve to mount his skull on the fucking wall. I'm going to make it happen. I'd go the core of the earth for you, Beloved. I'd walk through the fires of Hell and kill every demon who stopped me from getting back to you. I'd gather all the stars in the night sky just to prove to you your light shines brighter to me than they ever will. Is that what you want, Mickey? Do you want someone to give you the stars? I could gather them all, leaving the night a dark void, and wouldn't regret leaving the world in an abyss if it meant you were happy. Yet—" I sigh, tracing another scar given to her from hate.

The only scars I want to give her are out of love and

obsession.

"—There would not be enough stars in the sky to amount to the love I have for you. The world would dim and still, I would be angry I didn't bring you enough light. I could steal the sun and it wouldn't compare to your soul. Nothing, no one, equates to you, Mickey. "

I curl over her body, the body that's endured too much in one lifetime, the body I vow to protect because it is mine now, and I press our lips together. I just need to feel them, the give, the softness, the way they make me hold my breath. I squeeze my eyes shut, cupping her face, my hand engulfing her jaw. I break away when I have to breathe and press our foreheads together.

Drifting my hand down her chest, I stop at the button of her jeans, flicking it from the hole. "Let's get you in more comfortable clothes." Tugging her pants off, she's left in a simple black bra and gray panties, nothing fancy, but the vibrations build in my chest again. My cock hardens just from getting the privilege of looking at her.

Thunder claps outside, followed by a strike of lightning. I dig my claws into the bed, breathing deeply to control the urge to mate. Every time it storms, all I want to do is knot her pretty cunt.

I push myself away from the bed, taking one last look at Mickey, her body calling to me to claim it. Spinning sharply on my heel, I stomp my way into the attached bathroom. My wings scrape the ceiling and dust falls all around me.

"Oops." I wipe the dust from my shoulder, my brows rising when it hits me how big this bathroom is.

The shower is huge with black tiles, and no curtain.

There are two shower heads and a long bench.

A bench I am going to fuck her on. I'm going to fuck her on every fucking surface of this house. I reach for my cock to give it a stroke, then drop my hand, remembering I need to focus on Mickey.

The long vanity nearly takes up an entire wall, with a mirror to match lined by LED lights around it. Two sinks.

My heart skips wondering if she put in an extra sink for me or hoping she'd have a partner in the future. Me, obviously. No one else is coming into my house, sleeping next to my mate, or fucking the pussy I've claimed.

I'm the monster of this house and anyone who dares to enter is as good as dead.

An emerald bathtub captures my eye, the anger of another man in the house dwindling when a mental picture of me and Mickey in this tub together infiltrates my mind.

It isn't the color of an emerald, it is an emerald. My mate must have splurged for this. It's beautiful with different shades of green, glittering against the faint amount of light peeking in from the window overlooking the forest. The faucet is gold and there's enough room for me and her with some to spare.

I stroke the edge of the tub, surprised by how smooth it is, and grin like a fool. I know when she had this house renovated, she probably didn't have me in mind, but everything is three times the size it needs to be. It makes me happy thinking that maybe I'm in her subconscious.

Tapping my claws against the tub, I open all the cabinet doors, including a linen closet, where I find a cloth. I dampen it with warm water and hurriedly walk back to Mickey, my wings scraping against the ceiling again.

"Fucking, son of a bitch—" I mutter in annoyance, flicking the annoying flakes of dust off my shoulder again. If they were only a half of an inch higher, this wouldn't be an issue.

When I get to the bed, Mickey is still on her back. I bite my lip as my eyes roam her body, focusing on the way her panties cup her lips. I can see the indentations and they are fucking begging me to slip the material aside to feast.

I inhale, wondering if she's still on her period, and when I smell it, I almost fall over. I wrap a hand around my cock, squeezing it so hard it hurts to stop the orgasm threatening, but one stream shoots free and lands on her bedding.

Reaching to wipe it off, I stop just before the rag hits the rope of electric white.

I'm going to keep it there so her bed smells of me.

With every breath, my growls and vibrations become louder, my need almost taking over. All I want is to do right by her.

I wipe her feet, then the dried blood from her side, and then the corner of her mouth where Steven must have slapped her. No bruises. No sign of assault. All because she's ingested my blood.

"I just—" I moan, dropping to my knees while spreading hers. "I just want to smell you. I need it. Fuck, My Brave Little Flower, watching you fight like you did made me want you even more. Nothing about you is timid." Dragging my nails up her legs, I pause at the apex of her thighs, staring at the gray material, a red dot appears.

She's leaking.

I groan, burying my face in her cunt, clutching her hips, and I yank her to me until my ability to breathe is fucking gone. All I smell is her. All I want is her. All I fucking crave is her.

"Mmm," I moan too loudly, my tongue flicking out. "I don't have control of myself. Just... just one little taste." I suck the material into my mouth, soaking it with my spit. My fangs tear the material and that's when I realize I've bitten her underwear, ripping them from her body.

"Look at you. A sight for monstrous eyes." Her pubic hair tickles my nose as I inhale her again, and my control falters, licking down her cunt until I get to the string. "You're full, Mate. This must be so uncomfortable." I suck the string into my mouth and groan when her blood hits my taste buds.

My control snaps.

Her blood belongs in my veins.

It's meant to pump through my heart.

She's meant to keep me alive.

What else am I to do but devour her in order to keep my breath?

I lightly tug on the string, watching, waiting to see if she wakes up. She scratches her nose and turns her head to the opposite side. Her eyes are still closed, in a deep sound sleep, and I pull harder, the tampon easily slipping free from how weighted it is.

My mouth waters.

I sink my fangs into the cotton, sucking the blood free, and at the same time, I orgasm when her blood coats my tongue. The iron seeps into my taste buds and a fucking whimper escapes. Come shoots from my cock, the tentacles stinging my thighs and lower abdomen.

My eyes bleed red, my vampire taking over, and when the blood runs dry, I toss the useless tampon over my shoulder.

And dive into the source.

My tongue plummets the warmth of her cunt and she moans, fisting the sheets once more. I slide one hand up her body, rip the bra down, and knead her breast. I rock my hips, my dick rubbing against the side of the bed with needed friction.

She whimpers, tossing her head to the left, then right, her mouth parting with pleasure. I wonder if she thinks she's having a dirty dream.

My other hand reaches around, pinching and rolling her clit.

Her moans and whines fuel me. I growl into her, licking her depths to get every fucking drop of the blood that feeds me.

Mickey's thighs begin to shake, and she lifts her head from the mattress, a sleepy mewl signaling her orgasm.

"Such a good girl for letting me eat," I whisper, kissing the inside of her thigh. The rush of blood in her artery casts a spell on me and I drag my lips across her inner thigh, peeking up at her to see if she's still asleep.

After her orgasm, she isn't moving.

This bite will wake her.

I shift into my ghost, unable to deny the need to bite her and sink my fangs into her flesh.

Mickey screams in pleasure, my bite causing her to orgasm and sweeten her blood.

"What... what? Oh God, yes." She arches her back,

fists the sheets, and tilts her head to the mattress. "Rhett. Rhett. Rhett!" She chants my name as I drink, doing my best to remain quiet.

Removing my fangs, I lick the marks to heal them.

Her eyes hood again with sleep, but it doesn't stop her from staring right at me as if she can see me.

"Rhett?"

I remain quiet, letting the doubt creep into her mind that I'm not truly here. It's better for her.

"Rhett," she whispers before falling asleep again.

I stand, reeling in my anger, the storm outside gaining wicked fury, and the need to mate hits me again. I trash her drawers looking for underwear. I snag a pair, grab a pad that has my come soaked into it, place it in the middle, and dress Mickey again.

Crawling onto the bed, I stay invisible, and I don't sleep. I can't sleep.

My anxiety is too uncomfortable and the only thing that makes it better is looking at Mickey.

I watch her. I memorize her. I obsess over her every beautiful fucking detail.

She doesn't love me like I love her.

Mickey probably loves the idea of me, but my love for her?

It's more than an idea. It's reality. It's action.

It's a catastrophe.

CHAPTER SIXTEEN

MICKEY

It's been two days since Steven attacked me, and the body is just now getting pulled out of the lake.

I didn't call it into the police station when it happened so someone else must have. I would have had to explain to Jake what happened and who would believe that Steven stabbed me, but I have no wound to prove it?

I'd look guilty or at least be a suspect, so I kept my mouth shut.

I know Rhett saved me. He fed me his blood. He changed my clothes. He put me to bed.

And I know he tasted me again.

Yet, he hasn't been around. The voice in my head is gone for the time being and now I can't help but wonder if I truly imagined it all. Did Steven really stab me? Did I almost die? Did I see Rhett for the first time?

It all seems like a dream and all of my doubts are clouding it.

It's why I'm on the front lawn. I've ripped up all the weeds and now I'm planting snapdragons in every single color. For the most part, they will take up most of my yard. They were delivered an hour ago and planting them seems like a stepping stone for me.

They bring me hope when I can't seem to find any.

I wipe the sweat off my forehead with my arm, staring up at the hot sun. I can't remember the last time a day went by when it didn't rain. My knees are wet from kneeling on the ground, the soil still wet from the storms coming and going every day.

And you know what's in my yard again?

The gargoyle.

I swear, his pose is different. His head is down, his wings wrapped around him, and I think there might be a tear running down his cheek. He looks sad.

"I know you're real," I tell him, digging into the ground with more force than necessary. "I don't know why you're doing this but I'm not stupid and I don't appreciate you making me feel stupid." I stand, wiping dirt from my knees. "And you know, I really dislike that you think I don't notice anything different with my body. I have new marks, my old scars have faded, and every time I look at you, I get this feeling. It's a rush, a warmth, and a need. Yet you hide from me. You are always hiding from me, but I saw you. You saved me." I march up to him and cup his perfectly sculpted face. "You can hide from me all you want. I'll find you every time."

I expect him to move, to explain himself, to answer me, but he stays still.

I let out a long breath before backing away. I'm talking

to a statue in hopes he will respond. If anyone were to see me, they would think I'm crazy.

It might be time for me to accept who I am.

I pick up a bottle of water and chug it before getting back to work. There are so many different types of my favorite flower and I arrange them up so that not one area is ever the same.

Rocket snapdragons grow tall, so I mixed them with Tahiti snaps which grow to eight inches. Black Prince, Sonnet, Madame Butterfly, La Bella, and Chandelier Snapdragons are planted too. My entire yard is full of flowers, and I can't wait to see them in full bloom.

My favorite is the Night and Day Snapdragons. The petals are a deep red, nearly black, and the body is white. They can get as tall as eighteen inches and can grow more than a foot wide.

"Excuse me?"

I scream, holding a hand to my chest when I see the mailman.

"I didn't mean to scare you. I have a package for a Mickey Bloom?"

I stand again, wiping my palms on my shorts. "That's me. Do I need to sign for anything?"

"No, you're all set." He looks around, taking in the scenery. "The place looks great. It's really coming together."

I smile, tucking the envelope under my arm. "Thank you so much. I've put in a lot of work. I'm glad someone noticed."

"Hard not to." He has a flirtatious grin on his face. "You know, I've been by a few times and—"

The sound of concrete grinding makes him pause to look over my shoulder.

"–And I was hoping I could take you out sometime."

The concrete grinds again, interrupting my conversation. I glance over my shoulder and now the statue has turned his head to the side, his eyes peering over at us from above his wing.

I *think*, he moved.

The familiar fear wraps around my insides, tightening like a snake wrapping itself around me. Nervousness begins to set in, wondering how long it will be before this man I don't know is angry. "I'm not really dating. I wouldn't want to waste your time. It's not that you aren't handsome or anything–"

"–You don't have to explain why you aren't ready for something. A no is a no. No explanation is needed. I'm happy to just deliver you mail or be a friend." He holds out his hand from behind the fence. "I'm Nicolas, friends call me Nikki."

My chin tilts to my chest as I stare at the hand. Too many thoughts are running through my head. If I take it, will Nicolas only shake it? Why am I imagining him forcefully pulling me closer and yanking me over the fence? What if this is his way of manipulating me just so he can toss me in the mail truck? He'll probably take me to a location where no one can find me.

"I'm not trying to be rude. I don't like to be touched," I say, holding out my knuckles instead.

He grins, fisting his hand to give my knuckles an easy, pressureless tap. "Thanks." A cute dimple shows up on the left side of his face.

"For? I'm the one being rude."

He shakes his head, tucking his scanner in his pocket. "No way. You found a way to meet someone today within your boundaries. I respect that. I have to go. Mail won't deliver itself."

I lift the envelope in the air to wave goodbye and he lifts a peace sign in return before driving away.

"I'm making progress," I say to myself and do a little celebratory dance. I swing my hips in a circle, sticking my tongue out, and smack the statue with the envelope. "Don't think I didn't hear you get curious. I heard. Sounds like someone is jealous."

I don't bother to see if he reacts. At this point, I'm only feeding my delusion and I'm oddly okay with it.

"Let's see what's in the mail, shall we?" I rip the package open and frown when I see a small piece of paper fall to the ground at my feet. I bend down, picking up the square post-it size paper.

Stupid Girl.

The note drifts from my hand, floating through the air only to get caught in the tall grass.

He knows where I live.

I press a hand against my stomach. My tongue sticks to the roof of my mouth. The snapdragons I just planted wither and die in front of me, the skull-like flowers manically laughing at my terror.

"Not real. Not real. Not real." I press my palms against my eyes and take a deep breath.

I dash inside the house and open the security system box on the wall. With a scan of my finger, the door slams shut, the powerful locks groan into place, the windows beep, and I press my sweaty forehead against the wall.

"Breathe. Just breathe. You're okay. You're better than you were now. You're stronger. He can't hurt you any-more. You'll fight. You won't let him win." I tell myself the same pick-me-up mantra to help me settle.

My fingernails dig into the drywall, scraping against it as I drag them down to make a fist.

The phone vibrates in my back pocket, startling me out of my process. I don't bother looking at the screen. The only people who call me are Jake, Milo, and Minnie.

"Hey," I answer, waiting for Milo's happy greeting.

A tick of silence follows.

"Hello? Is someone there?"

The static of heavy breathing has me double-checking that my door is locked.

"This isn't funny. Don't call me again." I hang up, my nerves rattled from the note and Rhett.

Rhett being real plagues more than anything right now. I miss him. His presence always made me feel safe. If he is only a voice, a hallucination, then where is he? Why can't he be here now? Why is my mind so broken?

The phone vibrates again. Unknown number flashes across the screen. Angrily, I press my finger against the ignore button.

My phone vibrates again.

I sit on the couch, holding the phone in my hands, debating if I should answer. No, I won't give them the satisfaction. I hit ignore again, toss my phone to the side, and turn on the TV.

My phone rings again.

"What? What the fuck do you want?" I shout answering it, proving all my anger.

"Woah, hey, what's going on, Mick?" Milo's voice is soft with a hint of concern.

I flop back, sinking into the oversized couch cushion, and groan, tossing my arm over my eyes. "Milo. Thank God it's you. Someone keeps prank-dialing me and it got under my skin."

He's quiet for a moment. "You're sure it was a prank call?"

The note comes to mind. It's on the tip of my tongue to tell him Ty has found me, that he knows where I'm at, and it was probably him on the other end of the call.

I don't want to talk about it. I don't want to admit my worst nightmare is still haunting me.

"I don't think it was him. Really. I'm going stir-crazy. I think I need to go back to work, Milo."

"I don't know. I understand, Mick, I do, but we can't put Demi's business at risk like that. She'd never say that. She'd agree to give you hours, but imagine if Ty found out? What he could do?"

"Creed wouldn't allow it."

"Creed is dark and fucking twisted, but not even he can save everyone, Mick."

"Demi is lucky to have someone like Creed."

"Way to switch topics."

"I just mean, it must be nice to have that sense of security. If Ty did enter the diner, I have no doubt Creed would do something about it."

"But it wouldn't be for you. It would be for Demi. He doesn't do anything for anyone unless it is for Demi. He is an asshole. Did you know he burned my customer's order? I don't know how he managed to turn it to a crisp as I was walking to their table, but he did. He said it was because he didn't like that they didn't say hello to Demi when they entered the diner." He raises his voice. "Because they didn't say hello!"

I giggle, liking how intense Creed is for Demi.

"That guy is off his damn rocker."

"Yeah, but he means well."

"No, no, he doesn't. And his son? It's like having a feral cat running around the diner. It needs its damn shots."

"Milo!" I toss my hand over my mouth and laugh. "That's terrible."

"When I walk, he bites my ankles, Mick! I have bite marks on my damn legs, and you know what Creed says? It's cause his son is teething. Please. What a joke."

I cover my face with a pillow to smother how loud my laugh is.

"Yeah, it's funny now. Wait until you come back. You'll see."

"Or maybe I'll leave," I whisper, playing with the frayed edge of my shorts. "Maybe I should run."

"What are you talking about? You aren't running. We are done with that."

I let the idea play in my head liking it more and more. I won't admit it to Milo. It's best he doesn't know. "You're right. When will I see you and Minnie again? I miss you guys."

"We miss you too. Minnie is sick so you won't see her leaving the bed. I'm beat. I'm picking up double shifts."

"But why? Don't you still have some insurance money? Why kill yourself working?"

"Because money always runs out, Mick. I won't be foolish, and I won't ever think I'm good enough not to work."

"I understand. I just worry about you. You're working so much, and the diner is picking up. It's packed nearly every night."

"I'm fine. It's you who I'm worried about."

I'm so close to telling him about the note. He'd call Jake. Jake would come here with more questions than answers. I'd be left exactly where I am now except with more people worrying about me.

And I'm so sick of people worrying about me.

"I know. I'm fine. I have to go. When are you planning to stop by next?" So I can plan my escape and disappear where no one can find me.

"Tomorrow. Promise."

"Okay. Sounds good. I love you."

"I love you too. And hey—"

"—Yeah?"

"You'd tell me if something was wrong, right? You'd be honest with me."

I pick at the string hanging from my shorts again and stare at the plant in the corner that's in dire need of water.

"I'd be honest," I lie.

I'm not proud of it. There comes a point where I have to protect the peace of those around me.

"Okay, good. This weekend, movie night?"

"Sounds perfect." I clear my throat when my eyes begin to water, my plan stitching itself together.

I'll leave the house to Milo and Minnie. I'll drive as

far away as possible, the farthest point on the map in the country, and I'll throw my phone away. I'll change my name and my hair, and only work jobs that pay under the counter.

I'll live the rest of my life hiding if it means my family has peace.

"I love you. I'll talk to you later."

"I love you too."

I hang up before I can spill my soul to Milo. He's good at digging his claws into someone's soul and forcing them to say what's been weighing on their mind. He's a truth seeker and hiding it from him reminds me just how broken I am.

I turn on the TV and flip the channels. Finding nothing on, I toss the remote to the side and stand, not bothering to look at what is on. I'm three steps from the kitchen when I hear something I couldn't have.

Spinning around, I hit the button on the remote that takes me back a few seconds, then press play.

A man is standing outside a mechanic shop with his hands on his hips. In big retro font, it says, "Royals' Garage." He's wearing a black hat that says, "Rescue Rhett" across the front with a phone number underneath.

My fingers move fast, pressing the volume button as high as it will go.

"I'm looking for my friend Rhett Royals. He used to own this garage."

I take a step forward, wishing I could get closer and step through the screen to talk to this man.

"We won't stop looking for you, Rhett. If anyone has any information, please call this number on the screen."

I believe in coincidences, and I doubt it's the same Rhett.

"Just ask for Fitz. You'll talk to me and give me all the information. Here is his photo." He points to the left-hand side of the screen, and a picture comes of a man looking under the hood of a truck.

His head is turned to the camera, a big smile stretched across his face.

This Rhett is different.

I pause the screen, staring at the man I've seen— I think I've seen. It's impossible. It— it can't be. This Rhett is normal, no wings, no claws, no split pupils, no scales, nothing out of the ordinary.

Yet there are similarities that can't be ignored.

His hair is blonde but it's shorter in the picture. It has a shag to it, and the ends flip out as if it's been too long since he's had a trim. His jaw is square still, the cheek-bones arched and defined. There's the same intensity in his eyes, a determination I've only ever seen in him.

Now, his hair has grown out to his shoulders, from what I remember when I was dying.

He's so different now but I know this is the same man somehow.

Something horrible happened to Rhett Royals.

My Rhett.

My monster.

My ghost.

And I plan to find out what it is.

I dial the number flashing across the bottom of the screen.

"Rescue Rhett. This is Fitz. How can you help me find

my friend?" he answers immediately. It sounds like he has said it a thousand times.

"Hi," my voice croaks and I press my hand against my neck while clearing my throat. "Listen—" I start to pace my living room. "—I can't promise I've seen him, but I think I have?" I can't tell this guy that his friend looks like a monster now with wings and I'm positive he has fed me his blood.

Fitz, this amazing person searching for his friend, would have to be in a straitjacket. I wouldn't blame him. I don't think I can even say it out loud without wanting to commit myself.

"He looks familiar to someone I've seen around..." my personal space.

I can't say that either.

"Town."

"Where are you? I'll scope the place out. Is he okay? The person you saw?"

I roll my lips together, thinking about how to word this. "No, I don't think he is. I think he's been through a lot."

"Tell me where you are. I'll be there as soon as possible."

I might be making a mistake. I could be wrong. I could be giving this man hope for no reason.

Staring at the picture again on TV, I know it's for a reason.

The voice in my head is real, and somehow, the man on the screen is the same beast I've been dreaming about.

And I won't rest until I prove it to myself.

CHAPTER SEVENTEEN

RHETT

I want to take.

I want to fucking consume. I want to invade her bones, possess her brain stem, and be one with her entire body.

How does she expect me to be when she's standing at the shore, naked, the moonlight dancing on her skin, the stars trying to shine as bright as her entire being– which is impossible in every fucking version of this reality.

In my crocodile form, I swim closer, my tail drifting back and forth to help me cut through the water. Musk emanates from my pores, seeping into the water.

All she has to do is step forward. All she has to do is swim and bathe in me.

The scars on her body are illuminated and the reflection from the water rippling under the moon casts upon her. The small amount of light sways and dips on different parts of her.

Even from here, I can still see the brand on her arm. The ugly two letters T and Y stand out. I hate his mark there, him trying to prove his claim, that she belongs to him.

She's never belonged to him.

She was born *for* me. She was always meant to be mine and I'm upset I'm only finding her now. If I met her before, she would have never had to endure the abuse Ty gave her.

I creep closer, wanting a better look at my mate, and vibrations tickle my chest. They can't be stopped. I'm calling her to me.

Mickey continues to sway, proving what I thought.

She's sleepwalking again; only this time, she isn't covering her body– she's showing it off for me.

"What a good girl," I growl, closing even more space between us.

She knows who she's meant for. Life has been so hard staying away from her the last few days. I've had to wrap my mind around the fact that once again, her life will be changed forever because of a monster.

Because of me.

Things like me take what we want.

Does that make me a thief? If I steal her body will it be enough to earn the love she blindly confessed to having for me?

I vibrate again, the water slightly splashing around my body from the strength of the reverberations.

Mickey steps into the lake, her fingers tickling the surface of the water. The lake engulfs her, her breasts covered by the silky liquid of my home. She ducks her head under the water, slicking her hair back and the inky strands blend with the sinister cauldron she's found herself in.

She is broken by evil, and she'll be put back together by sin.

My vibrations are loud. Frogs bounce off lily pads to get away from the predator claiming the lake as his. Crickets become silent, not wanting to compete with me.

She swims with elegance, the water acting as a silk robe around her body. I'm jealous of the lake being able to touch her everywhere all at once.

I move closer to her, nudging her shoulder with my snout.

"Rhett," my name is slurred on her sleepy tongue.

She runs her hand over my nose, scratching the space between my eyes.

I groan the best I can in this form. I can't lie, it feels fucking good to get scratches.

Pressing my nose against her, I inhale, there's something slightly different about her scent. I don't know why, but it has my blood boiling to a feral degree. I snap my jaws and dive under the water, needing her more than I've ever needed her before.

The plus side to being what I am is I can hold my breath underwater for a very long time.

I shift into my humanoid form, spreading her legs so her pretty cunt is on display for all of the lake to see. Her legs wrap around my neck just as I suck her clit into my mouth.

Fuck.

I love eating her. I could live between her legs, night

and day. Time could stop, the world could stop spinning, and I'd want to be right here, feasting upon my mate. My claws dig into the meat of her plump ass, and I grip her flesh, pulling her cunt closer to my face.

This is where I want to die. Suffocated between her thighs. I'll sink to the bottom of the lake and rot, allowing my bones to turn to sand. In the afterlife, I would still be able to taste her on my tongue because Mickey would be the last meal I have savored.

Her thighs tighten around me. Her moans are muffled by the barrier of the water between us. I suck her clit, then slide my tongue down to her entrance before coming back up, circling it around the bundle of nerves.

She isn't on her period anymore, perhaps that's the difference in her scent.

No, it can't be. She's warm on my tongue, her body heat can be felt through my palms even in the cool temperature of the lake. The longer I'm around her, the harder I become, and the more desperate I am to be inside her.

I'm not sure what is happening, but I'm reacting to her differently. The tentacles around my cock stretch and try to swim to her. A neon glow fills the darkness of the water, the jellyfish impatient to sting and pour come into her womb.

My tail slithers up her legs, prodding her slick entrance.

She comes, tightening her legs around my neck, and I continue sucking her overly sensitive clit. Her thighs tremble. Her hands push my shoulders to get me away from her.

I hear up above, "I can't. I can't." Her actions next are hypocritical. She grips me by my long hair and uses the strands as reins, tugging me closer to her cunt. Her pheromones spread in the water, sticking to my skin, and invading all my senses.

Growling into her body, my attempts to make her orgasm again become more intense.

Almost violent.

My claws drag across each ass cheek as I hold her in place, refusing to let her leave. She can fight me all she wants but with every attempt to get away, my tongue sinks into her more, licking all the places she wishes she could escape from.

Blood tints the water from the tips of my sharp nails splitting her flesh. The reptilian eyes I have shift to red, invoking my surroundings in a crimson hue. My cock pulses, my orgasm flooding the water, and I moan into her.

I've never come untouched before.

And I feel like I didn't come at all. It didn't relieve the ache, the fucking craving to be deeper, to be inside her fucking skin is still there.

My fangs nip dangerously at her clit, the soft pink bud giving ever so slightly from the pressure. Her cries become louder, and those pheromones become heavier, drugging my beasts into their primal nature.

My scalp burns, her nails digging into the roots of my hair, tugging harder with each wave that passes through her.

And every wave is bigger which means every pull she gives is closer to ripping my hair from my scalp.

I love it.

I'm not sure how long I've been underwater. My lungs begin to scream at me to surface. My hands glide up her body as I kick to the surface, inhaling much-needed air.

I already miss being between her thighs.

Mickey's eyes are closed, floating on her back in peace.

I'm far from peaceful.

If anything, I'm on fucking fire. I'm in fucking need. Her scent becomes stronger, my beasts begging me to knot her, to breed her, and to not stop until she's pregnant with my child.

"Mickey," I growl her name.

She opens her eyes, a glazed expression still on her face. Surely, she can't still be sleeping?

"Let's go inside. I'm not done with you."

"I want you." She rolls onto her stomach, swimming toward me with heated, flushed cheeks.

"You look like you have a fever, Mate." I press my hand against her forehead, and she moans, using the water's buoyancy to wrap her legs around my hips, her cunt flush against my cock. The moan from my lips can't be stopped when she begins to slip her pussy up and down the long thick oral arm of my jellyfish stalk.

The tentacles around me begin to sting her, wanting her to come closer, pulling her to my cock. A jellyfish uses its tentacles to sting and kill its prey while the oral arms bring food to the mouth.

And the food I want is very close to being devoured.

"Rhett. I need— I need you so much." She cups her breasts, palming them, teasing her nipples.

The flush travels down to her chest making the faded scars more prominent.

I roam my hand up the middle of her chest, encompassing her throat.

"Such a pretty necklace for such a pretty fucking girl," I rumble, her scent becoming stronger. Sweat breaks out over my forehead, my tail whipping in the air from how potent her scent is.

My fucking God, what is this damn scent?

I look down, watching her rub her pussy on my cock. My tentacles take turns stinging her clit, one by one they attack her in fast whips. Her lips are parted, giving her moans to the universe.

And I'm jealous of the fucking stars again for absorbing them.

My hands move from her hips, stealing a squeeze of her plump cheeks before my palms travel up her back. The scaled pads of my fingertips caress every divot in her spine. When they reach the space between her shoulders, I apply enough pressure to make her sit up.

I groan with a deep, low growl, in a baritone that gives a slight curl to my lip, that tickles my throat. I inhale, dragging my nose across her jawline, the thunder in my chest becoming louder from the potency of her scent.

She smells of fire, of heat, of the same flames that become the sun, and I want to seep myself in her warmth until we both melt.

"Fuuuck," I groan against her fragile canvas, my entire body trembling. I have the urge to fuck her into the ground. To take her six feet deep, creating our own graveyard.

My tongue flattens along her cheek, gathering the lake water on my tongue. I capture her lips too desperately, controlling her body by pressing my hands against her back to deepen the kiss.

"Wake up my pretty mate. Wake up. I want you to see what is about to fuck you." I steal her lips once more before pulling back so she can breathe. "What's about to claim you." I plunge my tongue over hers, letting her throat feel the powerful rumble of my growl. "What's about to mark you." I glide my claw across her fragile collarbone. "Just here." I tap the side of her throat, kissing my way down the curve of her neck.

With careful, impatient pants, I drag my lips across the area that will have my mark. "Wake up, Micky. Let me see your blue eyes. I want to see the horror that will cross your face when you realize you're trapped in another nightmare." I suck her flesh, nibbling, nearly breaking the skin so I can drink. "It's selfish of me, but I won't let you escape me. I won't let you figure out a daydream that doesn't include me." I pass my lips down her chest in tandem with my index claw.

Her skin arises in goosebumps. Every scar I pass over, I kiss, thankful my mate is a fighter. Sucking her nipple into my mouth to bring my favorite, high-pitch whimper from her, my fangs nip and threaten.

Mickey's scent becomes more intense. Come doesn't shoot from my cock, but it drips constantly, the sparks tickling the dense shaft.

I trail wet kisses up the middle of her chest, then her chin, before consuming her lips again. Since she's sleepwalking, her kiss is languid in her dream state.

"Oh, I fucking love knowing I'm your dream right now, but I need you to wake up." I dare look into her eyes, but they are still glazed over.

Her scent rises again, her moans becoming louder as she rolls her hips. I grip her thigh, clench my teeth, and help her slip her cunt up and down my cock. She's trying to get herself off and I've never been so turned on.

"Let me help you use me, Mate. Let me get you off again before I bury my knot into your pretty cunt."

My orgasm looms. My tentacles strike her clit and then latch onto her, giving her a constant shock. Her pleasure skyrockets, a scream echoes across the pond, and I have no doubt the stars heard it.

Her aroma becomes too much. My wings spread wide, and my crocodile spine spears from my back. My vision is hazed with scarlet. My fangs drop longer and thicker. I had no idea they could do that. The phantom takes over me too, only it engulfs the entirety of my body.

I glitch.

My being shoots from invisible to solid in milliseconds.

My beasts are stronger, her scent urging them out of me further with every passing second.

"What is happening?" I snarl.

"Want," her sleep-drunk voice barely penetrating my mind. She sounds so far away.

And hearing it breaks me.

I swim us closer to the shore and when I'm able to stand, I throw Mickey over my shoulder. Her ass is in the air for the moon to see and I spank her.

Still, she doesn't wake.

And I know in a few moments, I won't care. Not with this need to breed her burning me from the inside. I'm begging to hurt her all over.

I lie her down on the bench settled in the gray sand right offshore. I roll my head around my shoulders, trying to gain some composure. Mickey spreads her legs and liquid drips from her.

A lot of it.

Clouds fill the sky in the next moment, lightning veining in unpredicted patterns. The trills in my chest become the loudest they ever have been. Paired with the thunderstorm and whatever is happening to us, I stand no chance of denying my mate.

Regardless of whether she's sleeping or not.

I press one knee between her legs and lean over her until I'm staring her in the face. Reaching down, I slip my hand over the wet puddle forming on the bench.

I bring the nectar to my nose and inhale, her aroma so potent, that I begin to pant. Unwilling to deny the curiosity, I suck them into my mouth, thunder rattling the sky at the same time.

"You taste." I blow out a growl. "Unlike anything I've ever tasted. You aren't going to wake up, are you?" I ask, lowering myself further.

"No," she replies quietly, small lustful pants shaking her chest.

"I'm going to possess you." I blow out another growl.

She stares at the sky with a dreamy shine in her eye. "Anything."

My ghost allows us to align ourselves in her form. We truly become one— as much as we can— in this form considering I'm so much bigger than she is physically. Our minds are locked together, and the most important body parts are lined up.

"I'm going to force you to do things to yourself if you don't wake up, Mate," I speak to her in the farthest corner of her mind.

I've heard not to wake sleepwalkers but with what is happening between us, the heat, the slick glistening of her cunt, my own body on fire with desire, has the sincerity of keeping her safety in mind dwindling.

She needs to wake up. She has to for this.

The thunder becomes louder, urging the trills in my chest to become louder, the ache becoming too unbearable. Tonight will be the night we claim one another in a different way. This feels different. The storm is feeding me, her scent is stronger, my cock is harder than it's ever been, and my knot is already starting to form.

My body continues to glitch, unable to maintain my solid or invisible form. When I lift my arm, her arm lifts, when I spread my legs wider, her legs follow.

Perfect.

Possessing her is one of my favorite hobbies.

I slide my hand down our bodies, the rain glitching my form even more with every drop. Her hand follows mine and a sleepy moan comes from her.

"You love this, don't you? I think you stay asleep on purpose because the reality of what is happening is all too much. I think you like not knowing what happens to you when you sleepwalk." I trail my claw around her nipple, forcing her to roll the tight bead between her fingers.

Another whimper.

"Yeah, you do. And I don't mind claiming you in your sleep because look." I turn her head, forcing her glazed eyes to stare at the sky. "I'm going to have you under the stars again. Let's make them jealous of how bright you truly are when you come for me." I cup her pussy, forcing her to do the same.

Every move I make, she has no choice but to follow.

I slip our fingers inside and her back bows, taking me with her.

My tentacles in ghost form continue to sting her and her clit.

"Mmm, Rhett," she mumbles sweetly, pressing her legs together to ease the overstimulation.

I don't think so.

I fight her urge, keeping my thighs apart which forces her to do the same. Moving my hand faster, she gasps, our fingers sliding in and out of her. The sounds are wet, mixing with the rain.

The faster she fucks herself, the more I want.

With a snarl, I sit up and stand, taking her with me.

"This isn't enough for me, Mate. I need to see you with more than our fingers fucking you."

As we stroll through the overgrown grass, my tentacles continue their onslaught of whips. She's a shaking mess by the time we get to the back door. Her body temperature rises. I feel the warmth as if it were my own.

I graze my hand on the side of her neck, her fingers following my movements. Small touches here, brazen caresses there.

There is one spot that has her standing on her tiptoes and it's right underneath the curve of her breast at the top of her ribcage. With every graze, her breathing speeds up, she licks her lips and pants.

"I wonder if I could make you come for me just like this. Petting your body with all the love you crave for it. It's okay." I kiss her cheek, grazing her ribs back and forth, loving how she has no choice but to mock me. "I'll give your body the attention it truly deserves. I'll give it the care it should have gotten all these years. You'll see, Mickey. A man nearly broke you but this monster– your monster– will put you back together again."

I open the door, lifting her leg by moving mine to enter her house. Possessing her body is taking too much energy. I'm not sure how much longer I can last. Since she's sleepwalking, it's like trying to move mud.

I lock the door behind me, lift her hand, and set the alarm to the house. The scanner reads her fingerprints, locking the doors and windows.

She's safe from everyone and everything.

But me.

"I want to see you against the solarium. Palms against the window. Legs spread. I want the world to see you knowing they will never be on the other side of the glass. I want you to wake up when I have my knot locked inside you and you're forced to see my reflection. But first, I want to play, Mickey. I love to play."

I also feel like it's part of the mating process to play with her body before claiming her during a thunderstorm. As the storm outside strengthens, so does the urge to mate. Something is telling me when the storm is at its peak, I will be too.

"Where are your toys, Mickey? I know you have them.

I know you've given this cunt relief when he couldn't. Show me."

Without saying a word, she lowers us to the floor, pointing under the bed. I bend us down, reaching under the bed to pull out a box.

"Naughty little mate." I open the box, surprised to see an array of different toys. Most are clit stimulators.

One is in the shape of a flower, with a hole directly in the middle. I turn it on, a smug smirk tilting my lips to the side when it vibrates.

"Oh, this is going to be fun. What do you think, mate?" I walk us to the solarium, sit down on the ground, and spread my legs.

If anyone were to look up and through the windows, they would see her pretty cunt on display.

The clouds thicken to black in the sky, lightning flashes every second, and rain slams against the glass. Leaves are torn from the branches as the wind picks up and I place the toy between her thighs, spread her lips with my fingers, and align the toy with her clit.

With a growl, without a warning, I flip the toy on and immediately she tosses her head back and moans.

Which means I do as well.

The pulsating vibrations have her pleasure becoming my own. My cock leaks come, dripping down the length.

"Spread your legs wider, My Brave Little Flower." I slide my feet across the hardwood floor, my body glitching.

"Oohhh," she moans as I press the button on the toy to a new level, increasing how hard it sucks her clit.

"Fuck that feels so good." I slap our hands on the floor,

groaning.

Every pull the toy gives, it's as if my own cock is getting sucked. No wonder she likes it.

I love this. We will have to do this when she's awake. Why won't she wake up? I've tried everything. What else can I do?

Lightning cracks right in front of us, charging my fucking body, the constant rumble beneath my breastbone becoming more intense.

The peak of the storm is near.

I increase the level of the toy again, roaring from how fucking good it feels. We begin to rock together, searching for more.

"Fuck, Mickey. Fuck." I watch the slick pool on the floor, the aroma of her fertility becoming stronger.

I run our hands up our chest, tweaking our nipples, tugging them with harsh pulls.

Her screams escape my throat just as she squirts all over the toy, and our thighs shake uncontrollably.

"Mickey," I fucking whimper her name. It sounds pathetic, desperate, a plea for her to come so I can too. "Come for your mate, Mickey. Come for me."

She listens so well.

Feeling her orgasm through my entire body is like a constant warm static tickling my bones. The pleasure is too much, too good, too everything. I practically hump the toy, wanting.

I come too, painting the sex toy with ropes of come. Its electrical current short circuits the flower. The hum powering the powerful object slows until it dies.

I'm wrecked. My arms shake as if I've worked out for

far too long. The ends of my hair stick to my glitched sweat-teased skin. We struggle to catch our breath, in and out, panting, gasping, small groans leaving us as small shocks of our orgasm roll through us at a lazy pace.

"What— What is happening? Why am I here? Why am I naked?" she asks through a dry throat. "Oh, God," she moans, reaching for the toy that will no longer work. "Why am I on fire?" Mickey lifts her hand, flipping her arm over to watch as we glitch together. "What— oh fuck." She lies on her back, screaming as a cramp rushes through her body.

She slides our hands down her body, then up again, cupping her tits.

"Everything is so sensitive. I need... I need... I don't know what I need. I need to be filled. I hurt. Rhett, I know you're here. Please... Please!"

Thunder and lightning clash. A rumble shakes the ground, the loud pierce of lightning rings my ears, and the vibrations become too much. Everything becomes too much.

I part from her body and throw her against the glass, clasping her hands above her head. I don't give her time to ask me questions or to look at me. We're both in need and only fucking through the storm will ease the swell of lust.

Risking everything, I shift into my humanoid form, wanting her to see me for who I am.

For what I am.

Even if I scare her, that terror won't stop me from sliding in to the hilt and pouring my come into her fucking womb. She can close her eyes and plead for it all to be over, but until then, she's going to have to wait.

The night is young. My cock is rock solid. Her pussy is drenched.

We aren't going anywhere until we show each other the stars.

CHAPTER EIGHTEEN

MICKEY

His reflection in the glass has me holding my breath. His one hand wraps around both my wrists, his claws touching easily. Rhett has me pinned against the glass.

We lock eyes in the reflection, and I hold my breath, staring at the most beautiful creature I have ever seen.

"I knew you were real," I whisper to the glass. "It wasn't all in my head." His red eyes glare at me, the pupil's sharp slits. His blonde hair is bright against his unique features. Cracks pepper along his skin that resemble con-crete. It's hard to see him all, as he is in and out of solid form, but I see the crocodile skin on his shoulders, down his chest, and abs. His tail slithers up my shoulder.

His. Tail.

And it wraps around my throat.

His wings spread with a whoosh.

"Do you wish I wasn't?" he whispers, inching closer until his cock taps my ass. Rhett kisses my shoulder. So gentle. So unlike the beast he looks like.

I think about his question. My heart pounds so loud, I hear the blood rush in my ears. I have so many reasons to say yes to him. I could push him away. I could scream and yell. I could be afraid of him.

But the truth is, he doesn't scare me at all. He doesn't entice fear. My instincts scream to fall into him, to let him protect me just like he has done so far. I have too many questions. I should be appalled by his actions while I've been sleepwalking. Everything I've been confused about; Rhett has to be the answer for the time I'm missing.

His cock slips between my thighs, probing my entrance and I gasp, unable to look away from his intense gaze. Small stings begin to lick my ass. Nothing too painful.

Actually, not painful at all.

I moan, tilting my head back until I'm resting it on his shoulder. "What... What is that?" His arm is still caging me in, his hand still pinning my wrists against the glass.

"That's my cock. My tentacles love touching you. You've only seen them while you've been sleepwalking."

"You're what happened to me when I was asleep?"

"I am. You loved every second. You'd search for me and who am I to deny my mate?"

There are so many questions racing through my mind, so much to think about, but the desire fogs my train of thought. I inhale a sharp breath, a wave of heat and pain curling my stomach. "What is happening?"

"I don't know." He inhales, growling as he buries his face in the side of my neck. "But if I don't take you right now, I might fucking die."

Lightning strikes the lake, cracking so loudly my ears begin to ring. The vibrations from Rhett's chest have my body responding. Warm liquid drips down my thighs. I glance down, confused at the wetness forming.

"We will talk later." I lick my dry lips. My vision sways as sweat beads across my forehead. "I can't... focus." I push my ass against him, the head of his cock slipping inside me. "Oh, fuck, Rhett," his name is a loud groan.

"You're burning up for me, Mate." His free hand clutches my hip, his fingers lying down one by one. His claws pinch my skin. "I'm going to fucking claim you all over again. I'm going to breed that pretty cunt."

I slip down his cock further. He stops me by applying pressure to my hip.

"You can't. I'm on birth control. Just fuck me already," I seethe through tight teeth.

A dark, sardonic chuckle shakes his body. He lifts my arm, eyeing where my implant is.

"You mean the small stick that kept your body free of me? I took that out." His tail wraps tighter around my throat and his fangs flash in the window. "Nothing will keep me from you. Nothing will stop me from knotting you, binding you to me, tying you to me in ways only we can understand. Your womb, your pleasure, your body—" he slides his hand up to the middle of my chest and presses it flat. "And your heart are mine."

He doesn't fight me as I spin around. Rhett presses me against the glass, wraps my arms around his neck, and lifts my legs around his hips. I still feel as though I'm in a dream. Like I'll wake up any second and he won't be real— a nightmare I don't want to face.

I press my hand against his, holding it in the middle of my chest, tilting my head in wonderment. "It was you," I whisper, cupping his face. "You were the pressure on my chest when I felt panicked." Pressing my forehead against his, my lips hover above his. "It was you who calmed me. It was you."

"And it will always be me." He eases himself into me, inch by inch he takes my breath away. "It will always be me," Rhett repeats himself, moaning when he has reached the hilt.

His tentacles waste no time sliding through my lips, curling around my clit, and then stinging me. My entire body jerks.

"Fuck," I curse. I'm about to ask if this is normal when it happens again.

And again.

Every lash has my body trembling and I moan. "Oh God, Rhett." I dare to look down, my eyes widening when I see the glowing neon blue tentacles shocking me. Slowly, I take in his entire body, sliding my eyes up his stomach.

My hands drop from his neck, wanting to feel his scales. My fingers trace the ridges of his abs, quaking with every inch I explore. The scales are smooth, and his skin has a slight roughness to it from the stone.

"You're my gargoyle, aren't you? The one in front of my house."

His trills become louder as I travel up his pecs. His blonde hair falls down his back, as he tilts his head. Rhett doesn't mean to, but he exposes the thick muscles of his neck.

"I'm so much more," he answers just as I kiss the middle of his throat.

Tasting his flesh on my tongue ignites desperation in me. I kiss up his neck, licking and nipping the skin before finding my way to his mouth.

His lips match the stone color of his skin just slightly darker than the rest of him. They are perfect, not too thin, not too thick, and I trace them with my fingers, in complete awe of the beast in front of me.

"I know you are," I whisper, tiptoeing my fingers up his cheek.

The wind outside howls. The rain is hammering against the glass, beating against it angrily as if it wants inside. Sweat drips down the middle of Rhett's chest. His body turns hot to the touch and his brow ridges furrow together.

He steals my lips with his, kissing me for the first time while I'm awake. The vibrations get so loud, I can't hear the rain outside bulleting the windows. Rhett snarls down my throat, his fangs nipping my bottom lip. He pulls his cock out until all that's left is the thick head.

And he slams back in, causing a groan to pour from me into the quiet room.

"You're so wet for me, Mickey. Your cunt is so tight, hugging my cock, taking it like a good fucking girl." He pins my wrists above my head again, curling his hips to find a way deeper.

My back slides against the glass. The cool temperature of the rain against the glass eases the heat on my back, but it does nothing to ease the flaming desire aching in my bones.

"Fucking soaking me, Mate. You love this monster

cock, don't you?"

"Yes. Yes. Yes." The words loud after the pause. "So thick, Rhett. Oh God, you're going to ruin me."

His claws sink into my thighs as he drives his girth in and out of me, stretching me to the brink of pain. My head swims with pleasure. The heat between us grows until I'm slipping against the now-fogged window.

"I can't believe this. I can't believe you weren't just in my head."

His massive hand wraps gently around my throat, his thumb claw pressing into my lower lip.

"Make no mistake, Mate," he growls, thrusting harder. "I was in your head. I was in your body. I possessed every inch of you, and I have no fucking regrets. I'll do it again." He thrusts again. "And again." Thrust. "And again."

"Rhett! Oh, God, I'm going to come. I'm going– I'm going–" My mouth parts to breathe and moan at the same time.

"Come for me just like you did when you were asleep, Mickey. You couldn't get enough of my cock. If you only knew the things I did to you. You wouldn't be here right now, spreading your legs like my good little slut."

He slaps his hand against the glass, his nails screeching down the surface as he uses the leverage to fuck me. He growls constantly, his beasts at the surface, and his entire body continues to glitch.

I tilt my head back, my hair sticking to the condensation of the window. Rhett takes that as an invitation. He strikes, a rumble from his chest shaking my bones. He grunts, pounding his cock into me while stealing drags of my blood.

I don't know how. I don't know why.

I don't care.

He feels too damn good.

"Rhett!" I scratch my nails down his shoulders, my orgasm squirting from me, drenching us where we are connected. "Yes, more. Take more. Oh, Rhett!" Another orgasm has me squeezing his cock, my body craving his come. "I can't take it. I can't," I shake my head, knowing I have no choice because those orgasms did nothing to ease the ache.

It's only worse.

He holds me against the glass by my throat, growling into my neck as he feeds. When he releases, blood drips down the corner of his mouth, and I wipe it away with my thumb, sucking it into my mouth.

His nostrils flare at the sight. "Do you see why I'm so addicted to you now? You taste better than anything this world could offer me, and I'd choose you every time." Rhett bends down, flattening his tongue across my neck. "I have a paralytic I can use but you know what? It doesn't work on you. Could you imagine what I could do to your body if you were completely incapable of moving? Would you be afraid of me?"

I shut my eyes, enjoying the affection as he gathers every drop on his skilled tongue.

"No," I rasp, clenching around his cock.

He licks up my jaw, the trills louder than the thunder shaking the sky. "Why? You should be. I could hurt you like he did," he sneers, hooking his hands around my shoulders.

"Because you would have already."

His wine-colored eyes meet mine. He flips me around, bends me over by placing his palm in the middle of my back, and drives himself into me again. My hands catch on the glass, sliding through the moisture.

My head is yanked back by my hair. He shoves his fingers into my mouth, making me gag.

"I'd never hurt you. Not even if you asked me to." He hammers himself in me, his cock pushing deeper than Ty had ever been. "Hurting you is a crime and those who are guilty will be punished, Mate." His heavy sack swings from between his legs with every fast powerful force of his hips. "I promise."

His vow is a heavenly whisper across the back of my neck, somehow etching its way into my skin and becoming more important than any mark on my body.

The window cracks, the glass splintering under my hand. We have no time to move before the solarium shatters. My body falls forward, rain drenching the top half of my body.

Rhett doesn't hesitate. He wraps his arms around me, his cock still begging my womb to open for him. His wings save us from falling and he flies us through the air, the rain soaking us.

He lands right by the lake, lays me on my back, and he pummels my pussy. I can't hear his vibrations anymore. In the thunderstorm, they mesh with the wind, rain, and lightning.

"You fucking belong to me, Mickey." His arms wrap around my legs, and he slides me to him, the back of my thighs meeting the front of his. "Feel this? It's all for you. Look what you do to me, Mickey. Fuck, I'm so goddamn hard, it hurts. I can't wait to fill you with every drop of my come. I won't stop until you're pregnant. You're mine. Nothing, no one will ever get in the way of that, if they do, I'll kill them."

My fingers dig into the mud, clutching the grass as the pleasure becomes my new enemy. It's too much. How can he make my body feel so good? I can't handle anymore, but I don't want it to stop.

The rain does nothing to cool the fire beneath my skin. Him fucking me isn't enough. I need more from him.

His wings curl over us, protecting me from the heavy beating of rain. With every hard thrust, we slide across the grass. He growls in discontent, plants a foot in the mud, and tilts his head back, a roar louder than a lion cursing the sky.

"I can't get deep enough. I want more." The impact of his cock has me clawing at the ground.

I arch my back, the appetite for his cock growing stronger with every damn groan he allows to slip between his fangs.

"I want to be closer. I want to lick your fucking bones," he snarls, perching the tip of his wings by either side of my head.

I risk looking down. My stomach bulges with every driving force he gives, my body adapting to his size. His claws scrape over my nipples, and I whimper, wanting him to grow somehow.

He wants to be deeper. I want him to stretch me more, and I don't know how that's possible. He is already on the verge of splitting me open.

"I want to see you use me."

He flips us fast. His wings tuck under my knees so they don't sink into the ground.

"Fuck, yes, that's the view I want. Look at you." His palms gently grab my breasts.

I press my hands against his chest and rock my hips. I don't go slow. I hate slow. I can't orgasm that way. I want to be fucked hard. Slow and steady does not win the race for me.

His sharp teeth bite into his bottom lip, his head lifted from the ground to watch me take his cock.

"That's it, Beloved. Ride me like you hate me. Fucking use me. You can anytime you want. This cock is all yours. No one else's. I belong to you. I am yours. You fucking own me, Mickey. Fuck. That's it. So fucking pretty sitting on your throne, proving who is in charge."

Those damn tentacles shock me, pulsing my clit with stings every second. I'm about to convulse.

"Need more. Faster," I whimper.

"How fast, Beloved?" His red eyes are eerie in the darkness.

"Fast."

The rain drips against his exposed fangs. He grips my hips, the tips of his talons breaking the skin, and he helps rock me.

Only his face, his body, the trees, the lake, everything is a blur. He's moving me at an unreal rate, a speed that can't exist, but oh God, it works.

I scream, slapping my hands on his chest. I dig my nails into his flesh and draw blood as I come. Stars invade my eyes, the world slows, and fireworks set off in my body as the most intense orgasm of my life has me in spasms.

Partnered with his tentacles on my clit, the orgasm rolls into another, and another.

I can't take anymore.

"I might… I might pass out." I sway on top of him, struggling to remain upright.

"Go ahead." He blurs us again until we are on our sides. "I'll knot you anyway. Unconscious or not, this cunt is mine. I'll fill this pussy until you leak with my come." He nips my shoulder. "Mmm," Rhett's rumble vibrates against my back. "I love the sound of that."

The idea doesn't bother me at all.

I couldn't sleep, not like this, not when I'm wide awake and know how good he feels.

"Fuck, Mickey. You're going to make me come." His forehead presses against the back of my neck, his breath hot puffs against my wet skin, and he wraps his arms around me to hold me close.

Pressure begins to build. "What− What is that?" I moan, my vision blurring yet again as another orgasm− yet again− threatens to kill me.

"My cock is turning to stone, thickening, and my knot is filling."

"You have a stone cock? And knot?"

"Yes," He grumbles with desire. "Fuck. Oh− goddamn it−" The knot applies pressure to my hole, popping in and out as it expands. Eventually, when it's almost too large, he shoves forward, the knot locking inside me as it con-tinues to grow.

Another primal roar from my savage beast ignites the night, his come filling me just as he promised. I can feel every hot stream jetting against my sore, soaked walls.

Then, I get shocked from the inside out.

I clench around him and groan. "Oh God, you're shocking me."

"It's my come. It locks onto your g-spot and shocks it until you give me what I want. You'll come for me again and your muscles will spasm, dragging my come deeper to claim your womb."

I wrap one arm around his neck, panting loudly, an erotic whimper pathetically leaving me as I'm shocked repeatedly. Between his come, knot, and tentacles, there's no hope.

At the top of my lungs, I scream at the same time lightning cracks.

And I lose all consciousness from pure orgasmic bliss.

CHAPTER NINETEEN

RHETT

I'm awakened by the warmth of the sun on my shoulders, birds chirping in the trees, and her pussy wrapped around my cock.

The fire blazing in my blood is gone but the want for her is still there like always. I kiss the groove of her neck, rubbing my knuckles down her arm to wake her up, but my mate sleeps like she's dead.

"Mmm, fuck," I groan, slipping out of her, and come begins to trickle out of her.

Immediately, I push it back in with my fingers. I need to get her a plug so that at all times she's full of me.

I know she has to be sore from the mating last night, so I refuse to take her again if she's in pain. She might not even be in her right frame of mind. Whatever fever happened last night, what if Mickey wakes up, the fog lifts, and she realizes what I really am?

There's so much to talk about and I don't want to talk.

I'm too afraid to lose her. I slip my arms under her, stretch my wings to get the aches out and roll my neck.

The sound of glass breaking has me turning to look up. The solarium is ruined. I watch as another sheet of glass falls, shattering on the ground. I'll have to fix that for her. Luckily, we only need the supplies and I'll be able to do the rest.

I miss working with my hands. If I don't use them, I can't fail though. This isn't about my life anymore. It's about Mickey's. I refuse to give her anything less than the best life possible.

Gently, I hold her on my chest, a purr of contentment building from her cheek against my pec, and I lightly flap my wings. Ever so slowly, I lift us higher in the air, taking us to her bedroom.

My feet land on the new floor, glass crunching under me, and I have to breathe in to relax my body at the memory of her bent over, pressing herself onto my cock, and taking every inch so beautifully.

She mumbles something incoherent, burrowing her face into my chest. I brush her hair out of her face. Mickey is too beautiful for the likes of me. Every angle of her face, every flutter of her eyelashes, every small puff that leaves her lips proving she's alive, I'm obsessed with.

Mickey could sit there with a lampshade on her head and not move a muscle all day, yet I'd be fascinated with her. Taking my eyes off her would be like someone deciding not to look at a shooting star.

You simply don't miss the opportunity to see something extraordinary.

"We are filthy, My Brave Little Flower. We have mud

all over us. What do I do with you?"

"Let's shower and then take a bath so we can talk?"

She startles me. I expected her to still be asleep and I nearly fall backward out of the giant hole in the wall that is completely my fault.

"You're awake."

"Barely." She yawns, blinking those big beautiful blue eyes at me.

I turn away, not wanting her to look at me. Fear replaces all my confidence and now she might reject me because of my appearance. I can't say I would blame her.

My eyes remain forward walking us to the bathroom. I sit her on the toilet seat and prepare the shower, letting it warm up before we wash the night away.

I don't want to wash away the best night of my life, especially if it's the only one I'll ever have with her.

"You won't look at me. Do you regret what happened?"

I spin around, lowering myself to my knees as I take her hands. "No. I could never regret anything when it comes to you. You're my mate, my beloved, you're meant for me. I'm just...cautious. I know I'm not what you expected." I continue to look down at the floor, nervous to even take a peek at her.

Mickey's fingers slide under my chin, forcing me to look at her and apprehension has me swallowing.

Her eyes travel all over my face. Her fingers brush my ears, rubbing the pointed tips, and those vibrations sound in my chest.

She giggles. "You like your ears scratched?"

"I love you touching me. Anyone else, I would kill

them."

Her hands continue to wander, tracing every scale she comes across.

I snag her hand and kiss her inner wrist. "Come on, let's shower, then take that bath."

She nods, standing up on trembling legs which makes me puff my chest a bit.

The floorboards creak under my weight as I step into the stall. Her eyes can't seem to leave my body. It's impossible to miss the curiosity in her gaze. She has a lot of questions and I have so many answers.

To my surprise, she doesn't seem upset at me.

Yet.

This must be the calm before the storm. She's going to yell at me soon, curse me, and probably kill me with all the guns she has in the house.

"May I?" I ask her when she grabs the shampoo bottle. I pick a few pieces of grass from her hair. She nibbles her lip in uncertainty before handing it over to me.

Squeezing the bottle it spurts into my hand, making an awkward noise.

"Um, that... that wasn't me. That was the bottle. I swear–"

She snickers, holding her hand over her mouth to laugh. "Likely story."

"Playful little mouth on you, isn't there?" My claws scratch her scalp. I'm careful, sudsing the shampoo through her hair.

She tilts her head back, moaning softly. "That feels so good. I've never had anyone wash my hair before."

"You'll never have to wash your hair again now that

I'm here. I enjoy taking care of you."

"Don't make promises you won't keep, or I'll be very disappointed."

"I don't make promises. I make vows. I make oaths." I tug her head by her soapy hair, forcing her to meet my gaze.

"What's the difference?" she asks, eyes closing from how relaxed she is as I wash her hair.

"Promises are for children. Vows and Oaths are for the ones who put their hearts, and their lives on the line. Not even death is safe from vows and oaths. A soul is tethered to them once they are made. Break it, and I believe the soul is damned."

I rinse her hair out, grab the loofah, and squeeze the come-ridden body wash onto it. I debate on telling her it's tainted.

I decide not to.

The rest of the shower is in silence as we wash, when it's my turn, she snags the loofah from me.

"I want to."

I lift a brow. "And how will you reach my shoulders, mate?"

"You'll figure out a way." She washes my entire body, and I realize I'm being bathed in my own come.

I don't care.

When she slides the loofah to my wings, they jerk in response, and my cock hardens.

"Does that hurt? I don't want to hurt you."

"The opposite. Don't stop." I turn my chin to my shoulder. "It feels good."

She starts from the bottom of my wing, the loofah

adding the perfect scratch, My hands slap against the wall, my claws digging into the new tile. I growl with every stroke she gives.

"You have to stop," I grit.

One more swipe and I'll come.

"Why?"

I show her why by turning around. "That's why."

She looks down and her eyes become fucking moons. She points, opening and closing her mouth. "That's a jelly-fish."

"I am. I'm many things, Mickey. And that's something we need to talk about."

In a coy gesture, she slides her attention to the left, not looking at anything in particular, and toys with the loofah in her hand.

"I like that you're not human." Her attention slides to my cock and she steps forward, wrapping her hand around my shaft. "And I love how unique your cock is." She strokes it and I moan.

I try to step away but my back hits the wall. There's nowhere for me to go.

"Mickey," I growl her name in warning. "You don't understand—" I stop mid-sentence when her thumb rubs over my slit.

"—No, I don't think you understand me." She strokes me harder and faster. The tentacles sting her hand, naturally, nothing I can do to stop that, but the stings don't seem to bother her.

Her blue eyes become hard, a bit darker, a raging sea in a storm, and I'm caught in the middle of it.

I wrap my hand around hers, snarling at her insistence. "I'm trying to be good, Mickey. I'm trying to make you see what I am— who I am. You're making that difficult."

"Good." She nips my chin, tightening her fist.

Her fingers can't touch around the girth. It's a gorgeous fucking sight to see.

I stop her, my jaw clenching with the need to come, but I can't do that to her. "Mickey—"

"—Rhett."

My head thuds against the wall. I can't seem to remember my argument with her hands on me.

"Turn around?" she asks in a soft voice.

Who am I to deny when she sounds so unsure? I smell the anxiety from her and something else, something… sweeter that hasn't been there before. My mouth waters for her blood.

I want to show her that I'll always listen to her. I'll never fight her for something she wants to do to me. I don't care what I have to do to prove she can trust me, I'll do it.

She deserves trust. It's a powerful emotion.

One she's never had before, and I am happy to be the first to give it to her.

"You really turned around," she whispers, rubbing her soft fingertips down my spine.

Every muscle flexes as her touch passes over every nerve.

"I'll do anything you ask me to," I answer, still waiting for her to realize who is truly in the shower with her.

One hand squeezes the base of my tail, then glides down, stroking it just like she would my cock. Simultaneously, she scrubs the loofah over my wings.

It's stimulation I had no idea would push me over the edge. My knees buckle and I groan, pressing my cheek against the wall as she has her way.

"Are you going to come for me, Rhett?"

"Yes," I rumble.

"Good. Consider it payback for all the times you've made me come, but at least you're aware."

"I'm— I'm—" I try to apologize, but my orgasm silences me. I stand on my tiptoes, roaring my release as it paints the walls. "Mickey," I moan.

I expect her to say something, to say anything. Silence falls over us instead, my heart still racing from the pleasure she gave to me. Spinning around, I try to apologize again, but she rinses me off, then the evidence on the wall.

I take her lead. I know she'll talk when she wants to, and I want to listen. I want to give her time to gather her thoughts. Her life hasn't been easy, and while I want to make it easier, I know as of now, I'm not helping.

I'm new to her.

I'm still getting used to myself and it's been months. It might take her forever to get used to the mere idea of me.

And I'll be here, patiently waiting for her to sleepwalk again.

We take turns washing off. When we are done, I step out and hold my hand out to stop her.

"Let me get the bath ready." I sit on the edge of the giant tub, twist the gold handles, and hot water begins to fill the emerald bath quickly.

"Don't forget the bubbles." She points excitedly, the

slight bounce she does jiggles her tits, and my eyes are locked on them. She giggles, covering herself playfully, and kicks my shin. "Rhett. The bubbles."

I shake out of my trance, smirking. "You can't expect me to focus when you're standing there, wet, naked, and beautiful."

"I do because I want bubbles." She gives me big, playful, yet somehow pouty eyes, blushing as she twists back and forth.

"And I'll always make sure you get what you want."

"Always?"

"For eternity, Beloved." I pour the bubbles in, placing my hand in the water to slosh it around. I hold out my hand. "Come on. Sit in it while it fills. Do you need anything before I join you?"

"My phone? Just in case my brother has called. And get us a glass of wine?"

"I'll bring a bottle. Can you imagine these claws wrapped around a wine glass?" I lift my hands, wiggling my fingers.

Her cheeks redden, unknowingly licking her lips as she stares at each finger. Can she remember how they felt when they were inside her? Mickey sinks into the tub slowly, inhaling when the hot water engulfs her, and the bubbles hide the body I so much desire.

I snag her phone on the nightstand, then head to the kitchen, grabbing the bottle of wine from the small stand she has on the counter. I put a pep in my step to get to her quicker, the bland walls capturing my attention. I imagine us filling the bare bones of her house with pictures of us and of our kids.

The floor creaks under me and I wince when I see the hole I made to peep in any time I want. I'll have to fix that now that I'm allowed in the house when she's actually conscious.

"Here you go." I set the phone on the ledge of the window where she can reach it, stab my claw in the cork of the wine bottle, then twist it free.

"That's handy," she notices, grinning at the sound of the cork popping.

"I think so too." I hand her the bottle first and she takes a very long gulp.

I slip into the tub, my knees piercing the bubbles. I probably look like an overgrown child.

She passes the bottle to me, and I take a swig, hoping it calms my nerves. The last time I tried to get drunk, the alcohol didn't do its job. I think my new form burns it too fast.

"So now that all that—" she blushes. "—is out of the way. I have many questions."

I tap my claws on the tub. "I know. I'm ready for them."

"What are you?"

I snort and look out the window, wondering how to answer that. "I— don't know what I am. I do know what I was created from. I don't know what to call myself except a monster."

Her hand lands on my knee. "You aren't a monster."

"I am," I correct her. "I am very much a monster, Mickey. I fucked you while you were sleepwalking. I fucked your mouth while you were sleepwalking. I've fingerfucked you." I grab her arm and point to where her birth control used to be. "I took that out because nothing was going to get in the way of binding you to me."

"I don't remember you doing that."

"Because you were asleep. You wanted me when you were sleepwalking. There was one time, you came outside when I was in gargoyle form, and you fucked my stone cock. You loved it too. I knew right then, if I could only have you in your sleep, I would be happy. I burrowed under your house and watched you through small holes I created in your floor. I broke into your house and smelled the blood on your tampons." I lean forward and growl. "And I sucked every drop from them. I pulled your cup out once too and shot it back like it was my favorite fucking drink because I am a monster. No normal man would do that."

"You'd be shocked at what normal men do," she whispers, her voice small and distant.

I rub a hand over my face and shake my head. "Why aren't you angry?"

"You never answered my question. What are you?"

I sigh, rubbing my thumbs across her ankles. "I'm a vampire, gargoyle, crocodile, jellyfish– obviously–"

"–Obviously."

I smirk. "–And ghost."

She stays quiet for a minute. "I had no idea vampires, gargoyles, and ghosts were real. What happened? You must have been so scared." Mickey places her chin on my knee, not running out of fear which only confuses me.

"I was. I remember a little about what happened, but all the experimenting really fucked with my mind. I'm very much more beast than man. The urges I feel are animalistic and controlling them seems impossible. I still feel my humanity, at times, especially when it comes to my feelings for you." I gulp down more wine and my mind wanders as I look out the window again, not wanting her to see the anguish in my eyes. "I had a mechanic shop. I owned it– back when I was human– and things were going well. Then, the economy changed, and my business went under. I couldn't climb out of debt. This salesman," I snort, shaking my head more in anger at myself than anything.

"This salesman," I sneer with a curl of my lip, doing my best not to squeeze the bottle until it breaks. "Says he was looking for volunteers for a clinical trial. He said he was searching for failed businesses to give people a chance to get back on their feet. One hundred thousand dollars. It was hard to say no to, but I did because while I couldn't make it as a business owner, I'm not fucking stupid. He drugged me. I woke up in some unknown place and they did…" I blow out a breath. "They did things to me that made me scream." I finally look at her, tears welling in my eyes, and her lips tremble as she clutches onto my legs.

Her brows pinch together as she listens.

"I screamed for help every time they strapped me down. They cut me, beat me, prodded me, fucked me, had women fuck me, and had men fuck me, all for their 'data.'" I make sure to point that out in quotes. "All of it hurt so bad, but then I evolved into this thing." I flex my wings that are hanging out of the tub. "They didn't like that I could shift into my beasts separately, that I wasn't just one mixture that could do everything without shifting. They tried to kill me, and I broke free. I used my paralytic on the guard, who had come into my cell to fuck me—"

"—Oh my God, Rhett."

"—Don't feel bad for me when I did the same to you," I reply. "I won't apologize. I can't. My beasts—" I tap my chest. "They won't let me. You are a primal, feral need of mine, Mickey. You are my mate."

"What does that mean?"

I raise my brows and toss my head back, bellowing my laughter. Water sloshes over the tub.

"Ahh," I sigh on a half groan. "I have no idea. I just know it means something profound. You are meant to be mine and no one else." I lean forward and touch either side of her neck. "I've marked you. Those are my claiming bites."

She reaches for her neck, and I know she's going to be furious. Another man scarring her for life, another man claiming her as his, just another man taking advantage of her.

I wouldn't blame her if she killed me.

"So you see, I'm no better than Ty."

"You know about him?" She rears back.

"I do. I've watched you from afar." I tap my pointed ears. "I listen. You thought he was dead, but he isn't," I growl, wanting to rip his throat out.

"So you did kill Steven."

"You remember? I didn't think you would."

"Hard to forget a knife to the back."

I take a swig of wine. "That's very true."

"You shifted into your crocodile? If I remember cor-rectly."

"I death-rolled that mother fucker until he couldn't

breathe."

She bites her lip again, her eyes falling to my chest then my face. "And then I think I told you I loved you."

It's my turn to blush. I adjust my sitting position in the tub. "You did, but you were dying, and how could you? You don't know me and now you know I'm just as bad as Ty."

She frowns and leans back, taking her hands from my legs and I miss her touch immediately. "Why would you say such a terrible thing? You're nothing like him. You never have been. Even when you were in your statue form, I was drawn to you, and I thought I was crazy. Actually, you made me believe I was losing my mind. You would talk to me in your ghost form. I think that's what I'm mad at you for the most." She splashes water on me, and it hits me right in the face. "I'd wake up so confused. Dirty. Bloody– which I understand now– but why– why would you let me believe you were a voice in my head?"

She splashes water on me again.

Some gets into my mouth, and I spit it out immediately, rubbing my hand down my face.

"I believed I was losing my mind."

"I was afraid to reveal myself. I didn't intend to but when that man was there and he stabbed you, I knew I couldn't hide myself any longer."

"Afraid? But–"

"–Look at me, Mickey. Why wouldn't I be afraid? Am I supposed to reveal myself to the woman who I love, who my beasts yell at me in mind that you are my mate, mine, that you belong to me, and have you look at me with disgust?"

"Am I looking at you in disgust now?"

I swallow, playing with the bubbles to form a shape. "No."

"And I said I loved you, so I obviously fell in love with you in my head, while I was asleep. I fell in love with you before I could overthink. I've always wanted someone who wasn't a man. I'm afraid of men. I won't lie to you."

"Most of my human DNA is gone," I add.

"I love that," she whispers.

"How can you love me? I'm a monster. I've done unforgivable things."

"But they aren't unforgivable. You didn't chain me, beat me, rape me, torture me, whip me, throw me in the closet for days, starve me, and so many other things. You... protected me. And while you made me feel crazy, I understand. You're forgiven."

"But I scarred you too. I–"

"Marked me because your beasts wanted it, to show everyone I'm taken, right?"

"Yes," I growl. "Mine."

"You didn't do it to punish me."

"I'll never punish you." I pull myself forward by the edges of the tub. "Ever."

"And you'll never beat me, scar me to inflict fear and pain? Starve me?"

I snarl. "Never. You'll never go hungry again."

"Then I love you."

"But..." I lean in closer. "I'm a real monster. The kind people warn their kids about."

She cups my jaw, and a sad smile pinches her lips. "No, you aren't. I've lived that life, and you are nowhere near the warning my parents gave me."

"I'm not... human. I won't act human."

"Good. I've had enough of that in my life."

"I'm..." I'm finding it difficult to express myself, to find the words necessary. "But I'm a beast, Mickey. I look like a beast. I won't ever be able to work a normal job."

"And I love you anyway."

"But–"

She silences me with her finger. "No buts. And if anything, you can just rob a bank again." She quirks her brow when she takes a drink of wine. "That was you, wasn't it?"

"All the cash is under the house in my burrow."

"Because crocodiles burrow, right?"

I tap my claw on her chin. "That's right."

"You'll love me anyway?" I tuck her hair behind her ear, suddenly serious.

"I'll love you anyway."

The moment is perfect. Everything is right until the front door slams.

"Mickey!"

I growl, sneering. "Milo really likes to interrupt."

"Mickey, you haven't been answering your phone."

"Oh my God." Mickey's hand grabs the top of my head and pushes me down.

"What are you doing?" I ask, stopping myself from going under.

"I don't want my brother seeing me naked with my also naked mate."

"Right. Probably not a great introduction. You won't remember this, but I can hold my breath for fifteen minutes. You happened to like it in your sleep."

"Oh?" She pushes my head down. "Help me remember it then."

I hold my breath and go under, wrapping my wings under her. Her pretty pussy is right there for the taking so I spread her legs and latch my mouth onto her clit.

Her thighs clutch my neck in warning, but I don't stop.

"Mickey! What happened to the window?" Milo's voice is closer now, easily heard in the shallow water. Luckily, the bubbles hide me.

I get lost in her taste. Sliding my tongue down, teasing her hole before licking my way up to wrap around her clit. I ignore their conversation, listening to Mickey's heart instead.

It's beating faster.

Her body heat rises.

I'm not sure how much time goes by, but she's patting my shoulder in warning.

A second later, I hear her whimper and moan my name, running her fingers through my long hair before she grips it. Mickey grinds on my face as she comes.

I kiss her lips before coming up for air.

"You almost had me orgasm in front of my brother." She tilts her head back, throwing her arm over her eyes. "That would have been horrible."

"I had a great time."

She peeks under her arm, takes her free hand, and splashes me with water again. "You should use that talent more often."

"Happily, Mate," I snarl. "I'll happily go down again."

She pushes my head down again just as her phone

rings. "Let me get that first. It's probably Minnie. Hello?"

The smile on her face fades.

"What?" I sneer. "Who is it?"

"This isn't funny stop calling me." She puts the call on speaker and heavy breathing has my murderous instincts come to the surface.

"Stupid Girl. I told you your family would die if you ever left me," the voice mutters with a dark promise. "You. Are. Mine."

The call ends, the dial tone louder than Mickey's cries.

CHAPTER TWENTY

MICKEY

"No. No. No. No!" My hand trembles, the phone threatening to fall into the tub. "He said... he always warned me. He always did, Rhett. He said he'd kill Minnie and Milo. He said... oh my God." I can't breathe. My stom-ach turns. My breaths become shallow and short.

Rhett slides his hand over mine to keep me steady. "Look at me, Mickey."

I shake my head, tears falling rapidly into the water. My body shakes and bile creeps its way up my throat.

"Look. At. Me."

His demanding tone holds a soft quality to it still that has me peeking through my wet lashes.

"Call your siblings. We will go to them now. Ty is probably bluffing."

I shake my head. "He doesn't bluff. He doesn't do that. Every threat he ever gave was a real one. It's why I have these scars. It's why I have nightmares of him. Everything he says, everything he threatens, he does."

"And when I get my claws on him, he won't ever do them again." He wraps his arms around me, picking me up easily out of the tub. His strong arms wrap me in safety.

I'm not afraid when he holds me. Now that I think of it, when he is around, nothing and no one can touch me. I've always felt like that, ever since I saw him in statue form in my yard.

"Call Minnie. Milo just left. He is okay. I'll dress you."

I don't think about how ridiculous it sounds for him to dress me. I can do it myself, but as he dries me with a towel, I realize I don't want to do it myself.

Taking a deep breath to calm my nerves, I dial Minnie. Rhett is combing my hair as the phone rings.

And rings.

"She isn't answering. Oh God." I sob, hanging up when I hear her voicemail. "Please, please," I beg, trying for Milo next. As the phone rings, I hold my breath, hoping he'll answer.

Rhett is using his vampire speed to get us ready, blurring through the bedroom to find my clothes.

I think about why I'm not more angry at him, why I'm not disgusted, and so many other reasons why I should not want to be with him.

He did everything out of love and not hate. He didn't hurt me. He didn't punish me and while he is unconventional, I love that about him.

Milo doesn't answer either, so I redial, releasing a breath before holding it again. Rhett holds out a bra and I slip my arms through it. He clips it in the back as if he has done this a hundred times.

He probably has.

My phone vibrates and it's Milo.

"Milo! Milo, where are you? Are you okay?"

"I just pulled into the parking lot of the apartment complex. What's wrong? You sound upset. It's the solarium, isn't it? It wasn't a tree branch like you said."

I ignore his statement completely. "Minnie isn't answering her phone."

Rhett slips on one of my oversized T-shirts.

Short sleeves.

I can't focus on that right now. It doesn't matter. Only Minnie and Milo matter.

"She's probably asleep. She hasn't been feeling well, Mickey. It's okay."

"It's not okay!" I yell at him. "Ty called me. He said he hurt one of you. You're talking to me, so it's Minnie. Milo, please."

Rhett helps me slip on a pair of leggings. Wind and rustling cause white noise on the other end of the line. Milo is running. I can hear his footsteps. He climbs the steps, and all the chaos stops. His breathing is the only thing that can be heard.

"Milo?"

"The door is open," he whispers.

"Don't go inside," Rhett says out of nowhere. "Stay there. We will be there soon."

"I can't stay here. Minnie could need me."

Rhett braids my hair with fast fingers, snapping my hair tie at the bottom.

The door creaks open. "Minnie? Minnie!" Milo shouts. "Oh God," his voice shakes.

"What? What is it? Milo!" I stand from the bed, covering my mouth with my hand and then Rhett is there, wrapping his arms around me.

"The apartment is trashed. Everything is broken. Minnie! Oh my God, Minnie!" he yells, the phone clattering to the ground. "Mickey," he sobs. "There's blood everywhere."

A blood-curdling, "no" escapes me. My knees buckle. Rhett catches me and brings me to his chest.

"Is she breathing?" I dare to ask.

"Yes, she is. She has five stab wounds and… God, Mickey. There's a message for you. I have to call 9-1-1. Meet me at the hospital."

"We'll be there," Rhett says before ending the call.

"She's going to die because of me. She's lost blood. He said… he said he would kill them. I should have listened. I shouldn't have been so stupid!"

Rhett grips my shoulders and gives them a shake. "You are not stupid. Nothing about you is stupid. Nothing about this is your fault. This is on Ty. This is because of him. Don't you dare take the blame for someone else's actions. You are smart because you found a way to escape. No one should be bound to anyone because of fear. Your life is just as important as anyone else's. You are not stupid!" He raises his voice at me, his eyes softening. "Do you understand me? I don't ever want to hear you say that again. Now, let's go to the hospital."

"We can take the new car—"

"I have a quicker way."

My phone dings, notifying me of a picture sent from Milo. I click the message to open it, heaving broken sobs that make a stabbing pain rip through my heart.

Written in blood, it says, "Stupid Girl."

"We need to go. I want us to be there for Minnie."

I nod constantly, freezing where I stand, and stare at my hands that won't stop shaking.

His massive palms cover mine, stopping me from trembling. "She'll be okay."

"You don't know that."

"I do know that." He swings me up in his arms and cups the back of my head so I'm resting my cheek against his chest. "And if she isn't, I will find her soul to bring her back to you. I'll search the stars for her *for* you." He jumps out of the broken solarium and parachutes his wings to bring us down steadily. "I want you to shut your eyes and trust that I have a hold on you, okay?" He kisses the top of my forehead. "Close them, My Brave Little Flower."

"I'm scared to."

He wipes my tears away. "I know you are, but I won't allow anything to happen to you."

I press my face into his chest, shut my eyes, and blow out a breath before the air whips around us as he sprints to the hospital. Every second I don't talk to Milo, the pit in my stomach becomes worse, somehow deeper and heavier.

I'm not sure what I would do without either one of my siblings. I only stayed alive for them when I was with Ty. There were so many times I nearly killed myself, so many times when I asked myself, "What's the point?" But I thought of them and seeing them one day.

They kept me going.

My sadness, my guilt, it all turns to rage. I want to kill Ty. I want to watch him bleed and beg for his life. I want his skull on my fucking mantle. I want a part of him to be stuck watching me living my best life with someone who isn't him.

I want him cursed to see my happiness for all eternity.

"We're here," Rhett says, easing me to my feet. "How do you feel?"

"A little unsteady, but I'm fine. Keeping my eyes closed was a good idea."

We are in the parking lot of the hospital. The building is giant outside, with so many windows, and so many halls. Minnie will be in one of those rooms if she got here first.

"How long did it take us to get here?"

"Ten minutes, maybe? Probably less," Rhett replies.

"She might not be here then."

"That's okay. We're here, that's all that matters."

Sirens wail in the distance and as they approach, I bounce on my heels, bite my thumbnail, then peek at my phone.

Nothing from Milo.

The ambulance stops in front of the emergency entrance and the driver jumps out of the rig, running to the back.

Milo jumps out first. His eyes are red, tears dripping down his face, and his clothes are soaked in blood.

They pull the gurney out, one paramedic over her doing chest compressions.

"Oh my God! Minnie! Minnie, we're here. Oh my God, please. Please, no," I sob, watching as they take her into the entrance.

"Female. Twenties. Multiple stab wounds. Extreme

blood loss. We lost her pulse just a few seconds ago."

"No!" I scream my agony, launching forward to be close to her, but Milo pulls me back.

"Listen to me. Listen. The doctors have it now." He pushes my hair out of my face, but I can see the worry in his eyes. He doesn't believe that. "She's a fighter, Mick. She's just like you. She'll pull through this."

Milo's attention finally lands on Rhett. "Who are you? Why are you with my sister?"

"He's my ma— boyfriend," I correct myself, not wanting to give Milo a reason to have a heart attack by explaining that the paranormal is real.

I took it in stride because I've always believed. Milo? He's more of the world is black and white. He doesn't believe in shades of gray.

"I'm Rhett." Rhett holds out his hand and Milo takes it. "I'm sorry about your sister." He wraps his arm around my shoulders, tugging me to his side. "But this one is safe with me."

"Yeah." Milo narrows his eyes, his wet lashes sticking together. "I've heard that before." My brother tucks his hands in his pockets and rushes inside the hospital.

"Why didn't he freak out?" Rhett asks. "About how I look?"

"I don't know. Others don't mind Creed. Maybe this town is used to it?"

"I don't believe that."

"Oh my God, Mickey!"

Demi's voice pierces the air. I look around and see her pink hair walking fast toward me with Creed by her side. Their child, Storm is on a leash, running to fly, but Creed yanks him back.

"You know what I said about flying. Not here, Storm."

Storm hisses at Creed.

"Hiss at me again and I'll make sure you don't fly for months."

Storm growls, hanging his head as he accepts defeat, then climbs up Demi's body to perch on her shoulders.

That kid is wild.

"Milo called us while he was in the ambulance. Is she okay?"

"No," I answer honestly, gulping down my reality. "They lost her pulse when they arrived. She lost a ton of blood."

Creed and Demi finally notice Rhett. Creed steps in front of Demi and snarls, Rhett takes the same stance.

"What the fuck are you?" Creed asks.

"I could ask you the same," Rhett growls. "I'm patient zero from the facility. I'm assuming you were there too."

Creed straightens, his defenses down, and his eyes are wide. "I didn't... I didn't know that." He truly seems perplexed. "I thought I killed them all."

"I was before you.

"I wasn't what they wanted so they tried to kill me. It didn't work out."

"Okay, we can unpack all of that trauma later. We need to go inside and focus on Minnie." Demi loops her arms through mine and helps me inside.

The men trail behind us. Storm on the other hand jumps onto my shoulders.

"He must like you because he hates everyone else. He always bites them."

"He's fanging right now, Demi. You know it can't be easy for him. Those fangs hurt coming in."

"Fanging?" I question, taking a seat, my eyes following my brother pacing a trench in the floor.

"It's what we call it. Like teething, but his fangs are coming in and he is so grouchy."

"Oh." I lift my hand and scratch under Storm's chin. "He's so cute."

She places her hands on her very round stomach and pats it. "He is. We didn't know how the children would be considering how Creed was tested on. Storm is a bit feral right now but we're hoping he grows out of it," she chuckles. "If not, that's okay."

"You're trying to take my mind off my sister."

Demi wrinkles her nose. "That obvious?"

"A little," I give her a small smile. "I appreciate it."

Storm flies off my shoulder, soaring through the waiting room, and Creed tugs on the leash, catching Storm in his arms.

"You are flight grounded, young man."

Storm bares his teeth. Creed growls back.

"Test me, Little One. My teeth are much bigger than yours."

I place a hand over my mouth, staring at Demi, but she just rolls her eyes.

"What happened?" Caden flies through the doors with Holt. "I just got your message. I shut down the diner. Is Minnie okay?"

My eyes fill with tears. My lips tremble. "We don't know."

Storm crawls over to me, the retractable leash buzzing to give him more slack. He climbs up my leg and curls in my lap. I pet him like I would a dog or a cat. He seems to like it.

"Can I ask why Milo didn't react to Rhett?" I whisper to Demi.

"Caden knows a witch. She put a spell on the rain, making everyone believe our monsters are normal. All the storms are because of Caden. He's a kitsune. That's how it recharges."

"So Rhett can show his face in town?"

"Oh yeah," Demi waves. "I don't think the spell works on mates, which is why you were able to see him for who he is."

The nurses freeze. The television pauses. Everything around us stops including the other people in the waiting room.

Milo too, but not Demi.

"Hey, Sidewalk."

I gasp, clutching Storm to my chest to protect him from a familiar shadow figure with skeletal features.

"I'm not here for the feral raccoon, okay?"

"Don't call my son a raccoon," Creed growls.

"Tomato. Tomahto. I'm Lorcan. Hello. Hi, everyone."

"You are not here for what I think you are here for," Rhett says. "There has to be another way."

Lorcan frowns, flipping a coin in the air before catching it. "There are many people here fighting for their life. I'm not only here for her."

"You're here for Minnie?" I stand, giving Demi her son. "You can't take her. What are you? How can you take her?"

"I'm a Void. I work for Death, one of the four horse-men," he sounds bored as if he has said this one too many times. "I take the souls of the dead and take them to Death. He figures out where they go. Her soul called to me, Mickey. She's not dying. She's holding on, but it's touch and go."

"There has to be another way. Please," I sob. "I'll do anything."

"I don't bargain. You're lucky your mate fed you his blood or I would have taken you too."

"You said you weren't there for her." Rhett steps beside me, pushing me behind him.

"Hello?" His hand runs up and down his body. "I'm a Void. My place of business is Hell. I work there. I lie. I was there for her and the other guy, but you saved her."

An idea clicks. "What if he gives Minnie his blood? That would work right?"

"I don't know, Minnie. I don't know what my blood or Creed's blood would do to her."

"It saved me. That's enough."

"Maybe because you're my mate. What if it isn't the same for her? Do you want her like me?"

"I don't care as long as she lives! Lorcan, would it work?"

"We don't know. Creed and Rhett are the only ones of their kind that we know of. We have nothing to say the blood wouldn't hurt your sister."

"What about your friend, Caden?" Demi asks from her seat. "You said your witch friend is mated to a vampire."

"Oh, the Monreaux's? You know them?" Lorcan asks Caden. "Aren't they just the best? I love their house."

"Read the fucking room, Graveyard," Rhett sneers. "This isn't the time."

He rolls his eyes dramatically. "You all act like she's already dead. I'll be back in a second."

And just like that he disappears, and time unfreezes. Everyone goes back to their tasks. The nurses on the phone, the doors opening, kids crying, TV playing, and Milo pacing.

"I hate that guy," Rhett and Creed say in unison.

And then time freezes again.

"Looky." Lorcan showcases a redheaded woman with a tall, pale man with bright blue eyes and a head full of thick black hair. "I brought them."

"You stole us from my coven," the vampire, if I remember correctly, says.

"Be nice." The redhead nudges her mate. "Caden. It's so good to see you. I hate to see it is under these circumstances." She hugs him tightly.

Her mate grabs Caden's collar and tugs him away. "That's enough. Why are we here? My house will be without doors if I'm not there. That damn werewolf," he grumbles.

Lorcan points at me and my brother. "Their sister is fighting for her life. She lost a ton of blood. She's on my list," he says softly. "They want a way to save her, but Rhett–" he points to my mate "–And Creed, their blood is unpredictable. It heals their mates, but we don't know how it will be for others because they are human–turned–monster DNA experiments. Wow, what a mouthful. I am so thirsty. I'm in need of a soul. B.R.B, friends." He vanishes before popping back in. "That means be right back. Okay, glad we covered that. Tootles."

"He makes my head hurt," Rhett complains, rubbing his temples.

"I'm so sorry to hear about your sister. I'm Alexander Monreaux and this is my Beloved, Maven."

"What does it mean?" Rhett asks. "To be a mate?"

"Right. You wouldn't know. I'm sorry you were turned into this. It must be very hard for you. A mate is someone Fate designs for you. You're meant to be. Forever. The other half of your soul. Your forever. You can't live without them and if one of you dies, the other will follow. You're tethered in every way of the universe."

"Wow," I whisper, wishing I could be happy, but I can't, not until I know Minnie is okay.

"Here is the thing, Mickey." Alexander sits next to me. "If I give her my blood, she could change into a vampire depending on how much blood she needs and how close she is to death. We call them changelings. She would have to feed on my blood willingly for a certain immunity to transfer."

"I don't care. Do it. Please."

"She would have to come back with me. To my coven. She would need to learn how to be a vampire. Her life here would be over. Is that what you really want?"

"But she could just heal, right?"

"She could."

"Please," I beg of him. "Try."

"Oh man, that is so much better." Lorcan is back, stretching his arms as if he just woke up from a nap. "What did I miss?"

"I'm going to go give her my blood," Alexander states.

"And then we will take her back with us."

"Wait, we can't see her? What am I going to tell my brother?"

Lorcan snaps his fingers and time begins again.

"Bloom family?" A doctor in green scrubs announces from the double doors leading down a brightly lit hallway.

"That's us!" Milo and I jump to our feet, rushing over to the doctor.

"How is she?"

"It's touch and go. She's out of surgery. She is in critical condition. She might not make it over the next twenty-four hours."

"Oh God," I hiccup. "Can we see her?"

"Sure, but not for too long. I'll take you back."

Alexander steps in and locks gazes with the doctor. "You'll let all of us back. We're family. We're concerned and you won't notice anything if your patient goes missing. You won't remember a thing."

"Okay." The doctor smiles, dazed as if he is high.

"It's a little trick us vampires use. We call it mystifying."

"Oh, that's what that is," Rhett mumbles.

Walking down the hall is gruesome. I hate it. Everything smells too clean. The lights are too bright. Patients moan and groan from their rooms. The beeping from the machines is loud.

Minnie's room is at the end. Lorcan is already there at the door, looming like Death himself.

"She has minutes," he tells us, frowning. "I'm sorry, Mickey. She won't make it overnight."

"How do you know?" Tears are constant storms rushing down my face.

"I feel it. It's my job to know. If you want Alexander to do this, it has to be now."

Alexander pushes past everyone to stand at Minnie's bedside. "Oh, you're so young."

The coven master locks eyes with Milo. "I'm just a friend here to help. Okay?"

Milo nods, his eyes shining like glass.

"I have never sired anyone who has stayed with us. Maven, you need to be okay with it."

"If it saves her, I don't care," the redhead says. "The more in the family, the better."

Alexander removes the tube from her throat, bites his wrist, and presses it against her mouth.

"How much does she need?"

"Probably half of what I have. My mate will have to replenish me." Alexander's irises morph to the same red Rhett's does.

After a few minutes of nothing happening, Alexander licks his wound closed.

"It's working," Lorcan announces. "The tug of her soul feels further."

The machines flatline, showing that her heart has stopped.

"What is happening? Why is she dead?"

"Because she was already dying. My blood is healing her. I can sense it. She will wake up as a vampire now. It will only be a moment. It doesn't take long. I have to get her out of here and away from humans. She will be thirsty." He locks his gaze with Milo's. "Say your goodbyes. She is safe. She'll call you soon. Why don't you go and forget this entire thing happened? Go rest, Milo."

"Rest. Right."

"And burn your clothes."

"Sure." Milo walks out of the room in a trance.

I kiss Minnie's forehead and sob. "I love you. I'm sorry. I'm so sorry. You'll be okay. I'll see you soon."

"We have to go. Now." Alexander yanks Maven to his side.

Lorcan touches them, wiggles his fingers, and grins. "Tootles. Bye, Rocky."

Rhett slashes his claws at Lorcan, touching nothing but shadows and then they are gone.

I bend down, wailing my soul into the empty bed that's still warm from where my sister was just a few seconds ago.

"I'll kill him. I vow, Mickey. I fucking vow to bring you his head."

"Really?" My question is muted by the mattress.

"Really. You'll love me anyway, right?"

"I'll love you even more," I answer the truth with all my soul.

Screams echo in the distance, terrible horrifying sounds followed by rumbles.

"Fuck," Creed curses.

"What is it?" Rhett questions, rubbing my back.

"The Hell's Harvesters are here."

CHAPTER TWENTY-ONE

RHETT

I don't know who the Hell's Harvesters are but by the dread on Creed's face, I'm not looking forward to finding out.

We step out of the hospital, drained and exhausted. Mickey is pale with fear and worry, and her eyes are swol-len from crying. All I want to do is get her home so she can rest.

And then I'm going to focus on Ty.

That mother fucker has breathed his last day here on Earth taunting my mate, and he won't get away with it.

Five motorcycles made of bones come to a stop in front of the emergency entrance.

"Creed." The one in front greets.

"Abaddon," Creed growls his kindness in return.

"Let's meet at your mate's house." He glances at me, then at her. "We have a lot to discuss."

"Who are you and why would I take you to my mate's

home?" I scoff, standing protectively in front of her.

"Consider us paranormal police," he explains. "And we already know where she lives. We know everything when it comes to the paranormal. I suggest you meet us there or we will drag you."

"Do not threaten me," I warn, my voice so low, it sounds hoarse.

"Why not? What could you possibly do to demons who are much stronger and older than you?"

"Famine! Enough. We don't have time. You're looking for someone, right? Goes by the name of Ty?"

"Where is he? Take me to him. I want to kill him." Mickey steps forward, pointing her finger in the demon's face and he smiles. "I want him to suffer like how he made my sister suffer, how he made me suffer. I want his head."

"Oooooh, feisty. I like that. Are you sure you don't want to go for a demon ride?"

"Conquest," Abbadon groans.

I wrap my hand around the demon's throat, slam him against the ground, and snarl.

But then he is gone, nothing but black shadows in my hand.

A large knife made of some type of metal presses against my neck. "Try again, Beast."

Mickey slams herself against Conquest, standing in front of me to protect me. There's not much she can do. "Don't touch him. I just want Ty. I want to live my life with my mate and go home. That's it. I'm not interested in anything else. Is that okay with you?"

Conquest rumbles, his form a light haze so I can see him for what he truly looks like.

And it's terrifying.

He twirls the large knife in his hand before sheathing it. "Fine. You better be glad you're a little human."

"That's so sweet that you would do that for him. You'd risk your life?" The quieter demon sniffles.

"Oh, fuck me, Death. Come on. Again? How do you reap souls? How?" Famine shouts, starting his motorcycle. "Let's go before I strangle Death. Fucking gets all mushy over everything."

"Sorry. I just find sacrifice really beautiful, Famine. You could learn something from this human and her mate."

"Please, I'd rather experience the fucking plague again."

Death gasps. "You wouldn't! Do you know how hard that was for me? You asshole."

Abaddon rubs his temples, sighing. "Okay, children. We have a job to do. Let's do it, please."

Their motorcycles start-up and they leave, the loud screams echoing again.

"The screams are the worst of souls. That's what fuels their bikes," Creed explains. "I don't like them, but I'm warning you. Don't fuck with them. They will win. Come on, Demi. Let's get Storm home."

Caden and Holt follow Demi and Creed, leaving us alone.

The sky is dark, promising rain, and the air is cool, but there's something malevolent about it. A wicked evil is stirring. I don't care what I will have to do, but I will end it.

I snag her into my arms like I did before and rush us

home. Her tears wet my chest, her body bends with every harsh sob, and her pain only fuels me to do what is needed. I'm not going to play with my food.

I'm going to kill Ty the moment I see him. The longer he breathes, the longer he remains a threat to Mickey and her family. I won't allow that.

When we get home, the demons are already there, standing by the lake. The grass crunches under my feet and they turn their heads. I won't let them intimidate me.

I launch into the air and then step into the hole in the wall I created when we mated. I lie her on the bed where she sobs into her pillow, clutching what should be me.

Never in my life have I been jealous of a pillow yet here I am, cursing its existence.

"I'm going to go talk to the demons, okay? I'll be right back, and I'll hold you through the pain."

"I just want him dead," she wails, wiping his face against the pillow. "No torture. No nothing."

I frown. "Not even a little torture?"

She sits up, blue eyes the color of ice as they harden. "I want to talk to Death. I want to make a deal with him."

"You don't need to be a part of this. Let me handle it."

"I want to be. I deserve to be. After everything he has done to me and my family, I deserve this. I need this."

"I heard you wanted to talk."

Mickey yelps as five demons fill her bedroom.

"Sorry." Death apologizing is odd. "Didn't mean to scare you. At least it wasn't to death."

The one with the name "War" on the front of his vest groans. "You have got to let that joke go, man. It isn't funny."

"Is so," Death mumbles.

They are nothing like the demons I've imagined in my head.

"Mr. uh–" Mickey glances around. "Death?"

"Death is fine. Mister reminds me of my father. So formal, am I right?" He steps forward and makes himself at home by sitting on the edge of the bed. "How can I help you Mickey Bloom? You know, you've dodged me a lot in all your days. You have a very strong soul."

"You know me?"

His eyes brim with fire. "I know every life that can be taken, Mickey, for I am Death. I know everything that was done to you. It's impressive you survived."

"Thank you. For not taking me."

"It wasn't your time. So, what can we do for you?"

"Why are you here?"

"Lorcan told us of a new DNA experiment. You aren't as dangerous as Creed, I can sense that. He left dead bodies everywhere. Human bodies. Paranormals can't do that, Rhett. I'm assuming you mated Mickey without her consent too? That typically requires time in purgatory."

"He didn't," she blurts. "I was well aware. Can we get back to the point? Where is Ty? Where can I kill him? When? I need answers."

Death raises his eyebrows. "You can't kill him, Mickey. You aren't strong enough. Not even Rhett is strong enough."

"What? Why?" she questions before I can.

"He is one-third demon, but not your typical demon. He was born from a demon who went rogue, someone who is truly vile. Demons are notorious for being, well, demonic, but this is different. He is the grandson of Azazel, a demon born in the deepest part of Hell. That's where those demons usually stay, but he escaped. We are still searching for him now. It's why torture came so easily to him, Mickey. It's why he is so good at lying, so good at making you believe in him." He taps my mate's head. "He messed with your mind and your soul. He doesn't have a lot of demon abilities. Just a long life and a craving for violence. Demons torture the souls in Hell, the ones that deserve punishment. Ty craves it like humans need water."

"How do you know this?" Mickey's face somehow becomes more pale.

Death grabs her arm, grazing his fingers with discolored nails across the brand on her arm.

"I smell him on you. His scent is trapped in this brand."

"We smell him around the house too," Abaddon adds. "He's been here."

"I knew it," Mickey whispers in horror. "What do we do? He won't stop until he has me. Why me?"

"The small part of him that is demonic is rotting his mind. He doesn't belong here. He belongs in Hell."

"Where he will get to live? No! No, absolutely not. I will kill him if I have to."

"Then you will die," War clicks his tongue.

Mickey grabs my arm. "This changes everything, Rhett. I won't risk you."

"I won't risk you." I cup her face, leaning down to press our foreheads together. "I don't care what I have to do."

"I do." She presses her palm in the middle of my chest, giving me the same peace that I give her. "I care." Mickey pulls away, lacing our hands together so we are touching. "What's the plan?"

"He's already here," Famine announces. "He's hiding in the woods, waiting until you're alone." He smirks. "You know what's really great about Ty?"

"Nothing," I snap at the demon.

"He's mostly human." Famine snaps his fingers. "He has the black plague now. He won't be feeling too hot. It won't kill him because of the demon, but damn! He will feel like absolute hell."

"This is going to be easy. Easier than you thought. He will stumble out of the woods, begging for your help," Death explains.

"Aw, poor thing." Abaddon laughs.

"And we will act like we are going to help him," War explains, laughing so hard he's wiping tears from his face. "But then Conquest will take his blade and slide it across his neck."

"That's where I come in. I'll take his soul back to Hell but because he is mostly human, he will be tortured for all eternity, in the same ways he tortured you."

I don't know how this is funny.

Mickey gasps, staring at each and every one of them. "But what if he escapes?"

"He won't be able to. Humans can't escape Hell. He'll be trapped behind helliron forever."

"Helliron?"

Death lifts his stare from Mickey. "Bones forged in the fires of Hell, mixed with sins from souls, churned in iron.

Any human who touches it turns to ash."

I whistle under my breath.

"And he won't escape?"

"I cross my heart and hope to die," he snickers while the rest of his brothers groan. "Get it? I'm Death. I'm already dead. It's a good joke."

"It is." Mickey pats his leg, and he grins happily. "I have one more question."

"Shoot." Abaddon slides a chair from the corner, spins it around, and sits down.

"Can I have his skull?"

I whip my head to Mickey, my mouth agape like the rest of the demons looking at her.

"That's hot." Famine gets hearts in his eyes making me want to carve them out of his face. "Why?"

"I want him to see me live my best life. I want him to see me happy with my mate and kids. I wish there was a way for him to feel my happiness in Hell from the skull on my mantle."

"Wicked," Conquest moans in approval.

"We can make that happen. I can connect his skull to his prison cell, and he'll be able to feel the happiness in your home."

She smiles. "Please. Please, Mr. Dea— I mean, Death."

"Mickey!"

We all freeze when we hear Ty's voice. I hear my mate's heart pumping in wild beats, but it isn't fear I smell, it's anticipation.

"Mickey! Please. I need a doctor. I'm not... I'm not feeling well. Get your ass out here!" he roars.

"Wow. He has some audacity, doesn't he?" Abaddon

stands from the chair. "Well, let's go take a soul to Hell, boys."

Famine rubs his hands together. Death lights a cigarette. Conquest unsheathes his knife.

Conquest passes the knife to Mickey. "Is there anything else you'd like to cut off before we drag him to Hell?"

She eyes the knife that's bigger than her head, large rows of sharpened teeth are on one side while the other is smooth, sleek, and lethal.

"I can think of one more thing."

My mate has a diabolical side.

I'm loving it.

The Horsemen vanish into shadows. I snag Mickey, flying her to the ground.

"Be careful. I only just got you."

"Mickey, you stupid girl. Do you know how long I've been here? I've been waiting for you to be alone but you never are. You fucking whore."

I growl, stepping forward to rip him limb from limb. Mickey's hand on my chest stops me.

Right. Somehow, this weak pathetic man can kill me because he is part demon. I don't buy it, but I won't risk dying because then Mickey will die. I don't like it, but I'll listen.

Boils cover his face, neck, and arms. Blood and puss seep from the bumps. "I told you I would kill them if you didn't stay with me. Take me to the hospital." His teeth chatter together from shivering. Every step he takes becomes weaker. His knees bend as he drags himself through the grass. "I'll let Milo live."

He begins to wheeze. "Mickey."

"Tag." Famine snags Ty's arms back, then kicks the backs of his knees, forcing him to the ground. "You're it, you sick fuck."

Ty screams from the pain the plague brings to his body, his arms stretched back must fucking hurt.

Famine breaks one arm, sending a crack through the air, then another.

"You sound pathetic when you scream." Death appears at Ty's side, dragging his nose up Ty's cheek inhaling. "And you reek of me."

"What the fuck? Who are you? What the fuck do you want? I only want Mickey. You can go."

Conquest chuckles, gesturing for us to come forward.

"We don't take orders from you, Grandson of Azazel."

The black rings around Ty's irises burn gold in recognition. "You know of me."

With another snap of a finger from Abaddon, Ty is naked, and without warning, Mickey shouts, slicing Conquest's blade through the air. My brows rise at the same time I cover my own cock while gagging.

She's cut his dick off, and he is bleeding puddles onto the ground. Mickey's rage has only just begun. She slides the blade through his chest, then out, then back again, and the demons laugh.

Ty coughs blood, the gold in his eyes dimming.

Then she gives the final blow, by slicing his head off before he can beg for mercy.

She would have given him none.

"You would be an excellent demon, Mickey," Abaddon praises.

Mickey curtsies. "Thank you," she says through broken breaths, handing the blade back to Conquest.

Death picks up Ty's head, black flames encompassing him, burning the flesh and hair.

"I have his soul," Lorcan says, appearing from nowhere.

"And now you have his skull." Death hands the hunk of clean bone to Mickey. "It's tethered to his soul. He'll feel all your happiness."

"Thank you," Mickey whispers. "For all of this. You gave me something I never thought I'd ever get." She hisses, glaring down at her arm.

The brand is gone.

"The demon who gave it to you is dead. His mark can only last as long as he lives. You're free."

"That's how he found me? Because he marked me?"

"Yes. You would have never been free of him, Mickey. He would have killed you eventually."

I growl, holding her to my chest by wrapping my arms around her.

"Why could I kill him? I thought another demon—"

"You had my blade," Conquest explains. "Demon made. You got your revenge. Everyone wins."

"Thank you. I can finally breathe."

"Good. If you need us, just call our names and we are here." With another snap of his fingers, the motorcycles scream. "We have a soul to take to Hell."

"Lucifer is going to be so fucking happy. Azazel is going to be pissed." Famine throws his head back and laughs. "I wish I could see his face."

They drive away one by one, vanishing in and out of

their forms as they ride.

"Do you feel that?" Mickey whispers, holding the skull in her hand by looping her fingers in the eye socket.

"What?" I kiss the top of her head.

"Peace. This is what peace feels like."

"And I'll live every day to make sure peace is all you'll ever feel."

"Are you okay with me keeping his skull? I know it's weird–"

I silence her with a kiss and whisper, "I love you anyway."

EPILOGUE ONE

RHETT

Two weeks later

"Please don't be mad at me," Mickey says out of no-where.

I just put the final touches on the solarium. It's almost ready to use. I need to test it first. I'm going to throw my entire body against it as hard as I can to see if it will crack.

Or maybe I can bend Mickey over again and reenact what broke it the first time.

"Being mad at you is impossible. What's on your mind?"

"I know a lot has gone on over the last few weeks. We're finally getting our footing. We feel like a family, you know?"

I grin, my gaze falling to her stomach. "Oh, I know." We found out she was pregnant a few days ago and I've been riding the high ever since.

"Have you felt like something has been missing? You don't talk about your old life at all."

I think of Fitz and the thought of my best friend searching for me changes my mood. It's better off this way. He will let go of me one day and live his best life. I'll be a thing of the past.

"No, nothing."

"Nothing?"

I narrow my eyes at her, charging up to the bed. "What did you do?"

She puts her weird monster smut book down before knee walking closer to me. Her grin is guilty, more like a cringe as she gathers the courage to tell me. "I saw Fitz's commercial on TV looking for you. He has an entire operation called Rescue Rhett. I told him you were here. And now he's only twenty minutes away."

I remain calm. The panic slows my ability to think or to process. "I have to go. He can't see me like this, Mickey! What? Why? Why would you do this?" I rub my hands down my face, knowing my friend will hate me forever once he sees me. "Fitz has me as a human to remember. He has those memories. He will hate me, disown me, and he will always think of me like this instead. Mickey, I can't. You have to call him and tell him no."

"I can't do that. And I won't. You need him. I know you do, and I can tell he needs you. He hasn't stopped searching for you. I told him you weren't the same. Give him a chance."

"Not the same? Mickey, I didn't get a haircut. My entire being is different. I have a tail! A tail."

"Oh, I know all about that tail," she purrs, the words

sultry and sweet.

Thunder clashes inside my chest. "Mickey," I warn.

"Give him a chance. He deserves that much. Maybe he'll surprise you."

"Or maybe he'll kill me and skin me to use me as a rug."

"So dramatic."

The doorbell rings and I check the clock, grabbing it from the nightstand. "He's early. You said twenty minutes."

"He must have been closer than he thought." She jumps out of bed, slips on her slippers, and leaves me in the bedroom. "Stay there. I'll call for you."

I nod, standing in the bedroom as far away from the door as possible.

"Hi, Fitz, right? I'm Mickey."

"Mickey—" his voice echoes down the hallway. He's let himself in the house. "It's good to meet you. It is, but where is he? Is he here? Rhett? Where are you?" he shouts through the house.

"I know you're happy to see him, but before you do, you need to know that he was kidnapped by horrible doctors, tested on, and now he isn't the same. He looks very different. He is different, but he is the same Rhett. Okay?"

"I don't care if he is half teddy bear, okay? I need to know."

I decide to put him out of his misery and timidly walk down the hallway. "I'm fine, Fitz." I stay in the darkened hall where he can't see me.

"Rhett?"

Mickey sighs. "Rhett, come out."

I growl, inching forward into the light so he can see me. The real me. His eyes widen as he tilts his head back to look up at me. Fitz blinks fast when his brain is in overdrive. I wait for him to say something. Anything. Preparing myself for the disgust.

Instead, he wraps his arms around me in a tight hug. He holds me tight as he sobs. I wrap my arms around him too, my own emotions getting the best of me.

"I'm so glad you're alive. I have been so scared, man. So scared. I thought you died."

"I did," I push him away, patting his shoulder before gripping it and forcing him to look me in the eyes. "The old Rhett is gone. I'm this and there is nothing to be done about it."

"I don't care. You can tell me all about it and what you are, but you're alive. You're fucking alive!" He cheers. "I knew it. This time, I knew it. I felt it. I've brought everything I own to move here. It's what took me so long to get out here and Rhett, I passed a rundown shop on the way into town. We can fix it up. We can start over."

"You want to move here?"

"It's where you are, man. You're my brother."

"Your sister—"

"—I'll miss them, but we can visit."

"All your things?" I ask him in confusion. "Fitz, I'm part crocodile, gargoyle, vampire, ghost, and jellyfish. I'm a monster."

"That is a lot to unload without a beer, but I don't care. I am curious... when you say jellyfish..."

"Yep," Mickey pipes up, a hot flush taking over her face as she glances down. "Sorry. I got too excited."

"Wow. You have to show me that."

"I'm not showing you that."

"Dude, you have to. You have to show me all your ways and when am I ever going to see a jellyfish dick again?"

I snort and laugh until I can't breathe. When I meet Fitz's eyes, they are watering again.

"It's good to see you, Fitz."

He hugs me again. "I'll tell you everything you want to know but it won't be pretty."

"I'm all ears. I've been wanting to know for months. No matter what, I don't care what you are, you're my best friend. Nothing can change that. Not even this. I think it's pretty cool. It solidifies the fact that I know ghosts are real."

"They are so real. So, so, so real." Mickey sounds drunk thinking about me fucking her mouth while I was in ghost form last night. She loved it.

"Mickey."

She shrugs at me.

"See. I think I need to be jealous. I'm going to grab my bag and then can we catch up?" Fitz asks, hopeful and happy.

I nod at him, trying not to lose my control and sob. When he is out the door, I pick Mickey up and spin her in a circle.

"Thank you for bringing him here. Thank you."

"He accepted you without hesitation."

"That's weird, right?" I set her down, worried.

She shakes her head. "Maybe he has a mate or is open-minded. Who cares? Don't ruin this. He has been nonstop looking for you. He only cares that you're alive."

Everything in my life is coming together and to my shock, it's better now than it has ever been.

EPILOGUE TWO

MICKEY

A month later

"Are you ready?" I ask Rhett, sticking my tongue out at the skull sitting on the mantle with freshly picked snapdragons inside. "You double-checked with Fitz at the shop, right? He is okay without you tonight?"

"Yeah, he's good. He's only painting one of the walls tonight. He'll be home later."

Fitz moved in with us. I thought I'd be worried about a man in the house, but I'm not. I'm protected. Rhett would never let anything happen to me. Plus, Fitz is a good guy.

They also decided to go into business together. The shop is called "Snapdragons Garage."

I asked Rhett why he named it that and he said snapdragons was a word that made me feel safe. He wanted me to have another safe space.

Falling in love with him was the best thing I ever did.

Speaking of snapdragons. I placed a few flowers from my yard in Ty's skull that's sitting on the mantle. I decided to use him as a vase. I never thought he would be handy.

We've come so far as exes.

"Do we have to go? Can't we just stay in bed?" Rhett gripes, dragging his feet and hanging his head as he walks to me.

"You just want to knot me again."

Rhett growls, pulls himself out of his sad state, picks me up, and swings me in a circle. "Damn right I do. I can't keep my hands off you when you're showing like this." He places his hand on my slightly rounded stomach. "Makes me constantly want you, but you know what I miss?"

"What?" I circle my arms around his neck, giving him a peck.

"I miss your blood."

"You feed from me all the time, Rhett."

"Not that blood." His eyes become hues of red.

My cheeks heat with realization. "Well, next time. We will have to prepare for times like this. Maybe make you tea bags, bloody ice cubes, popsicles..."

He moans, and his cock rubs against my leg, hard and ready. "Sounds so fucking good, Beloved."

"It will be *if* you don't manage to get me pregnant again."

He mumbles under his breath. "Unfair choices. I love both." He frowns, his mood turning from cheery to sad again.

"We can worry about it later. Come on. Let's go to Demi's and when we come back, you can knot me."

The solarium opens, allowing us to fly from the

bedroom into the sky. Rhett fixed the solarium with the money he stole from the banks. We still have a large sum left over and he keeps it in his burrow. He refuses to put it in the bank.

We soar through the sky, the night sky beautiful and twinkling millions of stars.

"I wish I could grab one for you."

"Why?" I ask.

"To prove your light is so much brighter."

I smile, kissing his pec, wondering when I was ever this happy.

Never.

At least, not that I can remember.

I think about Milo and Minnie. Milo moved in with me since the house is big enough. I didn't want him to be on his own after Minnie had to leave to be with Alexander. I feel terrible for keeping the truth from him, but when Minnie is ready, then we will tell him.

"We're here."

"Sound more excited." I pinch his nipple through the shirt I forced him to wear.

He can't walk around naked all the time.

We land in Creed's backyard where he lights the grill with his dragon fire.

"Hey guys!" I greet, sliding carefully from Rhett's hold.

"Hey!" Demi waves from the table. "You got here just in time. He is about to cook the steak."

Creed tosses Storm a raw piece of meat and the little boy growls, thrashing his head back and forth as if the steak is prey.

Feral. Absolutely feral.

"What's all that noise over there?"

Demi groans and I turn around to see what the fuss is. An old man is peeking over the fence, his brows thick, wiry, and white.

"You couldn't have done this earlier?"

"Mr. Pete, it isn't late. We aren't doing anything wrong."

"Hi, Mr. Pete," Rhett greets.

"No, Rhett. No. Fuck, Mr. Pete. We don't like him," Creed sneers at the old man.

Rhett lifts his middle finger. "Oh, good. Fuck you, Mr. Pete."

"Rhett!"

"What?" He shrugs. "If Creed doesn't like him, I don't."

"Demi, you're a good girl. Why in the world."

"Okay. That's it." Creed points at Mr. Pete. "I'm going to kill you and fucking roast you. I'm sick of your shit."

"Creed. No. He's fine. Just let it go."

Creed stomps his way to the fence and captures Mr. Pete's gaze. "I don't know why the mystifying doesn't work very long on you. Probably due to old age so, you will leave us alone. Again. Forever. You see nothing here, okay?"

"Can I have a steak?"

Smoke billows from Creed's nose. He looks over his shoulder to Demi, and she nods.

"Fine," Creed bites.

The retractable leash buzzes and Creed gets yanked to the left as his son takes to the air again.

"Storm. Get down here, now! You won't get any more steak!" Demi shouts and Storm flies back and tumbles as he lands. "He'll figure out the landing."

I snicker, rubbing my own stomach.

"When are you due?" she asks.

"I have no idea. Rhett doesn't either. We're just taking it one day at a time."

"If you need anything, you know where to find me. We have to stick together."

"Thank you." I lean back against Rhett, my head on his shoulder, and enjoy the chaos of Creed cooking and his son nipping his ankles.

"Steak is ready!" Creed announces.

Demi uncovers all the sides she made. There's salad, loaded baked potatoes, green beans, egg salad, and mac and cheese.

We eat fast with no conversation. We're all too hungry.

"Where's my steak?" Mr. Pete yells from the other side of the fence.

Creed slaps a steak, grabs it with his claws, and throws it over the fence.

"Creed..." Demi sounds exhausted from his antics.

"What? He got the steak." Creed digs his claw into his own raw meat, picks it up, and gnaws at it viciously.

When we're all done, Creed and Rhett give each other a knowing look.

"What?" I wipe my mouth, placing the napkin on my plate.

"You'll see." Rhett takes my hand and leads the way to two piles of blankets and pillows.

One for us and one for Creed and Demi. Rhett helps me lie down before he does, pushing me against his side.

Demi does the same, holding Storm in her arms.

"Ready?" Creed shouts.

"Ready!" Rhett replies, cupping his hand by his mouth.

Creed blows his fire, lighting fuses that begin to spark. He runs to be with Demi, places his hand on her belly, and watches the sky.

Rhett's thumb brushes across my small bump.

A loud whistle sounds before an explosion fills the air. White fireworks spread across the stars. I gasp, watching from down below as if I'm in my own personal firework globe.

"You did this for me?"

Rhett nods, stroking the side of my stomach. "I can't bring you the stars, but I'll always create them for you."

"I love you." I cup his chiseled jaw, my eyes watering, and stare at him with all the adoration I can muster.

"Even though I'm a monster?"

I giggle, kissing him again, unable to take my lips from his. "I love you anyway."

The End.

If you kinda like me, check out my readers group on Facebook: January's Raynestormers. I'm also on discord: January Rayne's Raynestormers.

January Rayne is a paranormal fantasy romance author who lives in Buffalo, NY with her husband, son, two dogs, and two leopard geckos. Buffalo is freezing, but January loves when it snows as it gives her the perfect atmosphere to write a book for you to get lost in.

Scan here for easy access to follow me on social media:

ACKNOWLEDGEMENTS

This series definitely took on a life of its own after Honeysuckles. Honeysuckles was supposed to be a standalone and now it's a series. I got excited and said ten books, but I believe this series will end around 6 books. Thank you to everyone who has read so far and been on this wild rollercoaster ride of weirdness. I appreciate your support every step of the way. Thank you for loving my DNA experiments as much as I do.

My teams, thank you so much for always being there, spreading the word about my books, and helping me make them perfect. You help make Shallow Cove a success.

As always, Hubby, Tiffani, and Carolina, none of this would be possible without you. Shallow Cove wouldn't exist without your constant faith, belief, and your ability to yell at me to get my ass up when I'm down.

Thank you to my parents, while they don't read these books because I'm their little girl, they support me to the ends of the earth. I'm lucky.

And damn, I'm feeling just how lucky I am really am.

xoxo,

January

www.ingramcontent.com/pod-product-compliance
Lightning Source LLC
Chambersburg PA
CBHW040330020826
48978CB00013BC/997